THE
COTTAGE
ON
GLASS LAKE

ALSO BY AMY PINE

The Bloom Girls

ALSO BY AMY PINE
WRITING AS A. J. PINE

MEADOW VALLEY SERIES
Cowboy to the Rescue (novella)
My One and Only Cowboy
Make Mine a Cowboy
A Christmas Cowboy at Heart (novella)
Only a Cowboy Will Do

CROSSROADS RANCH SERIES
Second Chance Cowboy
Saved by the Cowboy (novella)
Tough Luck Cowboy
Hard Loving Cowboy

THE COTTAGE ON GLASS LAKE

AMY PINE

FOREVER
New York Boston

Forever
Hachette Book Group
1290 Avenue of the Americas, New York, NY 10104
read-forever.com
twitter.com/readforeverpub

First Edition: June 2023

Forever is an imprint of Grand Central Publishing. The Forever name and logo are trademarks of Hachette Book Group, Inc.

The publisher is not responsible for websites (or their content) that are not owned by the publisher.

The Hachette Speakers Bureau provides a wide range of authors for speaking events. To find out more, go to hachettespeakersbureau.com or email HachetteSpeakers@hbgusa.com.

Forever books may be purchased in bulk for business, educational, or promotional use. For information, please contact your local bookseller or the Hachette Book Group Special Markets Department at special.markets@ hbgusa.com.

Library of Congress Cataloging-in-Publication Data has been applied for.

ISBNs: 9781538718612 (trade paperback), 9781538718605 (ebook)

Printed in the United States of America

LSC-C

Printing 1, 2023

*To the siblings we love . . . those born to us and
the ones we get to choose*

THE
COTTAGE
ON
GLASS LAKE

CHAPTER ONE

BECCA

Dr. Becca Weiland pulled into her driveway, the pink sky on the brink of day. She put the car in park and closed her eyes, letting her head fall against the back of her seat. A smile parted her lips as she replayed in her head her favorite part of every delivery—introducing the newborn to its parents. Had it only been six years ago that she was the one on the delivery table, her life changed exponentially as she greeted her twins for the first time? She'd never seen Jeff cry before that day. But when he'd kissed her forehead, thanking her for all she'd done to bring their babies into the world, tears flowed freely from his red-rimmed eyes. Becca had never loved him more than she had in that moment, and she was certain he'd felt the same.

Maybe that had been it, a moment they wouldn't be able to top—or even sustain.

She needed to get the hell out of her head. She needed *sleep*. She needed to move her morning appointments because there was no way she was making it back into the office before noon. She needed...

Becca glanced down at the large manila envelope on the passenger seat next to her.

Ten years of marriage. Ten years, and all it would take was a few signatures, passing the documents off to her lawyer, and just like that, it would all be undone.

One Year Earlier...

Becca looked up from the stack of patient charts on her desk to see her big sister, Alissa, lingering in her office doorway.

"What are you doing here?" Becca asked, then went back to organizing her charts. "Your postpartum checkup isn't until next week, so if you're here to sweet-talk me into giving you and Matthew the thumbs-up to start having sex again, tell him to keep it in his pants for a few more days. Though you two might want to invest in a better brand of condoms next time." Becca raised her brows.

Alissa barked out a laugh. "Sex! Ha! How about a full night's sleep instead? Can you give me the thumbs-up for that?" She sighed. "Oh, who am I kidding? I *do* miss sex. And sleep. And sex..."

Becca scoffed and shook her head. "Welcome to

motherhood. *Again.*" Because this wasn't her sister's first go. She and her high school boyfriend, Matthew Bloom, had gotten pregnant as teens, married, divorced, and in the middle of it all, raised a wonderful daughter—Becca's niece, Gabi. But then the two succumbed to a night of nostalgia when Gabi graduated college and *boom*. Baby number two at forty, and now she and Matthew were back together.

"So...yeah," Alissa said hesitantly. "Permission to do the horizontal mambo is not why I'm here."

"You're so not a grown-up," Becca said with a chuckle.

"Never claimed to be one either," Alissa quipped. "But..." She strode toward Becca's desk and sat down opposite her. Despite Alissa's wild red curls falling out of the messy bun atop her head, the dark circles under her eyes, and the dried spit-up on the shoulder of her jacket, Becca had never seen her sister look more beautiful. She guessed happiness could do that to a person and wondered when the last time was that *she* looked that beautiful herself.

Alissa sat there for a long moment just staring at Becca, not saying a word.

"Okay. What is it, Liss? You're kind of freaking me out now."

Alissa winced, then blew out a shaky breath. "We tell each other everything, right? The good and the bad?"

"And the ugly," Becca added with a nervous smile, trying to make light of a situation that seemed to increasingly darken the longer her sister stared at her with those exhausted yet worried eyes.

"And no matter what, you know that I love you and I'm here for you and...you know what? I shouldn't be doing this now. It's just that the baby is napping and Matt has the day off, so it was, like, my one free window this whole week, and I didn't want to do this when *you* were at home because the kids and Jeff and—"

"Spit it out, Liss. You're freaking me out. Just rip off the damned Band-Aid and be done with it."

Alissa placed her phone on the desk and slid it across to Becca.

Becca's brows drew together. Wasn't her sister done with dating apps?

"I thought you and Matt were good," she started. "Plus, with a newborn, where would you find the time to..." But then the face of the man on the screen snapped into focus. The face she saw every day when she woke up and every night before she went to sleep. She hadn't recognized him immediately, though. Because—he was smiling. The man on the screen was *smiling*, and Becca hadn't seen that expression in quite some time.

Smiling. But not at her. Becca's husband, Jeff, was smiling back at the nameless, faceless bevy of women who were swiping right and left on a dating app. He was smiling at the possibility of someone else. Someone other than *her*.

"I'm gonna be sick," Becca said.

Alissa nodded, then stood, picked up the trash can next to Becca's desk, and handed it to her.

This wasn't how life was supposed to go. *Becca* was the

one handing the trash can to expectant mothers in the throes of morning sickness. Expectant mothers like her own sister, who not so long ago saw her world turn upside down when a one-night stand with her ex turned into a second foray into motherhood right when she thought she was an empty nester.

Becca Weiland's world did *not* turn upside down. She had a *plan*. She and Jeff both did. College sweethearts who supported each other through medical school. Law school. The perfect set of boy and girl twins and the house—their *dream* home—where they could sit on the deck with a bottle of wine after the kids went to bed and take advantage of the waking hours they still had together. On paper, Becca's life was the definition of happiness.

Only Jeff didn't smile at her anymore. And Becca couldn't remember the last time she'd smiled at him.

She heaved into the trash can, emptying the contents of her stomach as tears streamed down her cheeks.

"I know, sweetie," Alissa said, rubbing Becca's back as she heaved into the bin. "I'm so sorry. But I'm here for you, okay? No matter what happens, I'm here."

☼

So much for sleep.

After four hours of tossing and turning, Becca decided to clear her head with a run before heading into the office for her afternoon appointments.

A knock sounded on her door as she stared down at the sheaf of paper in front of her. The envelope had made it from the front seat of her minivan to her desk. She'd even *opened* the envelope and taken the papers out. But her hand shook every time she tried to pick up her pen.

Another knock.

Becca sucked in a breath through her nose and swiped at the wetness under her eyes before shoving the pile of papers into her desk drawer.

"Come in!" she called, dialing up the *I'm totally fine* in her voice.

The door opened enough for a hand to poke through the opening—a hand that held a white ribbon attached to a pink box that was unmistakably from Take the Cake, Alissa's bakery.

"Liss, you didn't have to—" But before Becca could finish her sentence, the person attached to the hand holding the box pushed through the door.

"Oh. Sadie," Becca said, her breath catching in her throat as she realized she wished it *were* her sister. Instead it was the sister of Liss's ex-husband Matt, except he was now Liss's second-chance-boyfriend and current baby daddy. Did that make Sadie and Becca in-laws once again?

The tall, slender woman beamed at Becca, her sandy waves bouncing against her shoulders as she bounded into the office and plopped into the chair opposite Becca on the other side of her desk, the bakery box now resting in her lap.

"Not Alissa," Sadie said, stating the obvious. "But I do

come bearing gifts from your sis—and myself, of course—
since I was going to be in the neighborhood. And by
neighborhood, I mean up in stirrups while Dr. Park inserted
my new IUD. Your twins are great, I'm sure, and I love, love,
love my new nephew, but procreating is *not* on my to-do list.
You know what I mean?" She huffed out a laugh. "Who am I
kidding? I don't make lists. But I *do* avoid procreation. That's
not TMI, right? You've got your hands all up in the lady parts
all day, so it's not like—"

"I got it, Sadie. And I'm all good on hearing about *your*
lady parts." Becca's eyes dipped toward the pink box and
then back up to meet Sadie's. "And if my sister intends on
me eating my feelings, then she needs to give me a heads-up
so I can put in an extra mile or two on the treadmill before
work."

Sadie sighed, then opened the box and pulled out raspberry rugelach. Becca's favorite.

"Suit yourself," the other woman said with a shrug before
popping the pastry into her mouth.

Becca gasped. "That wasn't…I mean, she wouldn't
only…There's more than one, right?"

Sadie slid the open box across the desk, and for a second
Becca shrank back, the déjà vu of Alissa doing the same with
her phone just a year ago making her stomach roil. But then
she saw the box was filled to the top with nothing but raspberry
rugelach, which meant Becca's sister had woken early enough
to bake extra since there was no way the bakery would go
without one of their top-selling items. Okay, fine. *Everything*

Alissa and Sadie created sold like crazy because the two women were geniuses in the kitchen. But the rugelach—the rolled pastry filled with homemade raspberry preserves—was all Alissa. She'd been baking it ever since their grandmother had showed her how. Well, she'd *tried* to show Becca too, but where Alissa shined, Becca was a disaster. Becca was much better at ordering in than creating something from scratch.

"Maybe just *one*," Becca said, reaching for the box. "But it's not because I'm sad about the...you know, the...I'm not eating my feelings because of the—"

"Divorce?" Sadie blurted out. "Come on, Bex. It's not a swear word."

Becca's cheeks burned, and she snatched the box toward her chest as Sadie reached for another pastry. "When *you* end a relationship that's lasted almost half your life, you can judge. And—and I can swear if I want to. I just choose *not* to. And maybe I choose not to say the *D*-word too. Also, don't call me *Bex*. Only my sister and my husb—" She cut herself off, her hand flying over her mouth.

Maybe she'd expected Jeff to fight her on it, but he hadn't. Maybe she'd expected herself to fight harder for him to stay, but she hadn't done that either. The truth was, their marriage had ended long before she'd seen Jeff's photo on the dating app, but neither of them had wanted to admit it.

Becca Weiland was many things, but above all, she was a mother, a doctor, and a wife. Who would she be now with a third of her identity missing?

"*Becca*," Sadie said, her tone gentle. "I know we aren't

exactly close, but if you haven't—you know—signed yet, I can be here for you while you do."

Becca swallowed the lump in her throat. This was it, right? The turning point in her life where either she stood on her own two feet or she didn't.

"Actually," Becca said. "Thanks for the rugelach, Sadie. But I have a patient I need to get to, so if you don't mind..."

Sadie held up her hands and grinned. "Say no more. I'll leave you to it." She stood and backed toward the door. "And maybe I've never ended a relationship that lasted half my life, but heartbreak comes in all shapes and sizes. I *can* relate. And while I get it doesn't have to be me, eventually you're going to want a single gal or two in your life to show you the ropes. I'm just saying." And with that, she shrugged and slipped out the door.

Show her the ropes? Like Becca was going to jump right back into dating. She had a summer of delivering babies and wrangling seven-year-old twins to look forward to. Dating? *Dating?* In the immortal words of Cher Horowitz, "As *if.*"

Becca threw open her drawer, pulled out the stack of papers—the ones *Jeff* had already signed—and scribbled her name in all the spots where her lawyer had stuck a bright yellow tab. She didn't need Sadie or her sister or anyone standing next to her to hold her hand. Except when she'd finished and leaned back in her chair, she looked around the office for someone to acknowledge what she'd done, but there was nobody there.

"I'm—divorced," she said to no one in particular, then

popped another pastry in her mouth. She picked up her phone to call her sister, only for it to vibrate and ring in her hand before she could initiate the call.

Alissa.

"Hi," Becca said, a slight tremor in her voice. "I did it."

"I'm here," Alissa told her. "What do you need? What can I do?"

Tell me who I am other than doctor, mother, and now—no longer—wife?

But as much as it seemed her big sister had finally figured out her own life, she wouldn't have the answer for Becca.

Becca was the only one who could do it, find out who she was without the labels that identified her to everyone else but Becca herself.

"Nothing," Becca admitted. "I love you, Liss, but you can't do anything. Whatever happens next, it has to be me."

CHAPTER TWO

SADIE

Sadie Bloom wasn't usually one to eavesdrop, but here she was, pressing her ear up against Dr. Becca Weiland's office door. What would she have done if she'd heard Becca burst into tears...or throw something breakable against a wall? It wasn't like Sadie could run in and hug her and tell her everything would be all right. First, Becca wasn't the hugging type. Second, despite the two women having been in each other's lives since they were in middle school, thanks to the complicated relationship between Sadie's brother and Becca's sister, they'd never been particularly close.

Becca was a Monica. Sadie was a Phoebe, and despite what a long-running sitcom made viewers believe, Sadie was sure those two would *never* have been friends in real life.

"You're still here?"

Sadie gasped, palm on her chest, as she spun toward the voice over her shoulder.

"I wasn't—" But before she could spit out the rest of her defense, she fell back against the office door, her other hand grappling for purchase on the door's frame.

"Sadie," Dr. Park said, stepping toward her.

But Sadie waved her off. "I'm fine," she insisted, still catching her breath. "You just surprised me." She let out a nervous laugh. "And sort of caught me in the act."

Sadie straightened, and Dr. Park took a step back, seemingly satisfied.

"Promise me you're calling your cardiologist as soon as you leave here."

"Promise," she lied. Sadie had just received a clean bill of heart health from the doctor in question six months prior. Whatever Dr. Park heard in her stethoscope was nothing more than run-of-the-mill, it's-never-not-weird-to-put-my-feet-in-stirrups palpitations.

Dr. Park nodded slowly. "Okay, then."

It was the doctor's turn to jump and run to the nearest window when the sound of a car alarm blared throughout the small corridor of exam rooms and offices.

Sadie scrambled to pull her phone from the bag slung across her torso, silencing the alarming ringtone by answering the call. What? It was funny. Plus if she overslept and Alissa called, it was the only thing that would wake her. When you ran a bakery, you had to be up before dawn most days, and Sadie had never quite taken to that little *perk* of the job.

"Sorry!" she called out to anyone who would listen. Becca's office door flew open to reveal a petite clenched-jaw, furrowed-brow brunette with a severe ponytail, who stared daggers at her as she spoke into her own cell phone.

"Yep. It was your sister-in-law," Becca said. "Or is it ex-sister-in-law? Can you and Matthew just get married again so I know what to call everyone?"

"Ooh!" Sadie said. "You're talking to Alissa? I've got my brother!" She held the phone to her ear, ignoring her shortness of breath that only seemed to increase. "Hey, Matty. What's up? I'm in Becca's office, and she's on the phone with Alissa."

Sadie's eyes met Becca's, and they both said, "They did?" at the same time, followed by, "You do? A month? But I can't."

Sadie pulled the phone away from her ear and stared quizzically at the screen even though her brother couldn't see her.

"Is your sister telling you something about a house in Glass Lake, that cute beach town in Wisconsin?"

Becca nodded, then put her own phone on speaker.

"I can't take a *month* off of work," she said. "I have patients. And—and children."

"You haven't taken a vacation since before the kids," Alissa said, her voice echoing from the phone's speaker.

"Hey, Freckles," Matthew called from Sadie's phone, also on speaker now. "I thought we agreed *my* sis could take the lake house."

"And I thought Gabi called *me* about Ethan's emergency appendectomy and having to give up the rental."

"And Ethan called *me*," Matthew said.

"Wait," Sadie interrupted. "Ethan's in the hospital? Is he okay?"

"He's fine," Matthew assured her. "In fact, *I* was his first phone call after he was out of recovery, offering *me* the lake house."

Alissa laughed. "After surgery? He's still trying to get on your good side even though it's been more than a year since you almost caught him knocking boots—consensually, I might add—with your adult daughter in her childhood tree house."

"La la la la la la la. I can't hear you!" Matthew's voice blared from Sadie's hand.

Becca groaned, and Sadie giggled.

"I thought the big brother and sister were supposed to act like grown-ups and set a good example for their younger siblings," Becca said to Sadie.

"We can hear you," Alissa and Matthew said in unison.

"I *know*," Becca said.

Sadie waved her off. "Why do any of us have to act like grown-ups?" But then she pouted. "Matty, I would love to take the house, but I can't leave Alissa and the bakery for a month."

But the things she *could* do in a month. For the first time ever, she was already formulating a list in her head.

"You can, though," Matthew continued. "I can cover early

mornings before I have to head to work, and Mom said she'd love to help. You know you got your baking genes from her."

"And *your* kids have two weeks of overnight camp, which means childcare is already half covered, Bex," Alissa added. "Plus Mom said she can split the other two weeks with Jeff, so really, it's a no-brainer. I know your partners would be happy to take your patient load, and it's only a couple of hours away. You could always drive back if you needed to do a delivery. But, honey, you just had a major life change. You need time to recharge. Do something for yourself for once." Alissa gasped. "I just thought of something. It's technically a one-bedroom, but there's a loft with a futon, so it could actually accommodate two..."

Becca snorted. "You want me to take a month off and spend it with *Sadie*?" Then she winced as the two women made eye contact. "No offense. It's just that...I mean you're so..."

Sadie raised her brows as the corners of her mouth turned up.

"Fun?" Sadie said, finishing Becca's sentence. "Not so tightly wound?"

Becca's mouth dropped open.

"This should be good," Matthew said.

"Can you put us on FaceTime?" Alissa asked. "I can't tell if you're angry. Are you angry, Bex? I actually think you and Sadie might be really good for each other if you spent this time together."

"I am *not* tightly wound," Becca said through clenched teeth.

Sadie reached for Becca's cheek with her free hand, massaging her jaw with the tips of her fingers. "Tell that to the night guard I'm sure you wear when you sleep."

Becca gasped. "I'm sorry we can't all live in the moment, only caring about ourselves. Some of us have kids and responsibilities and—"

"Oh no you don't," Sadie interrupted. "Being a mother is important, but it's not the only thing that makes you a responsible adult. Not that I enjoy admitting I *am* an adult, but just because I don't have extra humans to keep alive doesn't mean I don't have responsibilities of my own. And for the record, my first choice of who I'd want to spend a month with at a lake house wouldn't exactly be you either, but you know what? I'm *in*. I'll even take the open loft with the futon since I'm sure you'd *never* be able to handle such a lack of control over your environment."

Becca's mouth fell open, but she didn't protest.

"Liss, are you sure you can handle four weeks without me?" Sadie called toward Becca's phone.

"You haven't taken a day off since we opened, *and* you worked your ass off when I was on maternity leave. I would *love* to do this for you." There was a pause. "And for *you*, Bex. Let Matt and I do this for both of you. Plus now Matt doesn't have to think about what Gabi and Ethan would have been doing for a romantic month alone. At least not for the next few weeks while Ethan recuperates from his surgery."

Matthew groaned. "I *wasn't* thinking about what they

would be doing for a month alone, but I am *now*. Thanks for that."

"You're welcome, babe. Bex and Sadie, I'll email Becca the details so you can both see what you're in for and you can start making arrangements. The place is all yours starting Monday. Love you both!"

"Love you, sis," Matthew said. "And Becca..."

Becca rolled her eyes. "It's okay, Matthew. We're not there yet, so you don't have to say something that will be awkward for both of us."

He let out an audible breath. "Right. Okay. Good-bye then, everyone. Talk soon."

Both their phones went silent. Sadie stared at Becca, and Becca stared right back.

"Well, roomie?" Sadie said. "Fire up that email. We've got three days to pack and get the hell outta here. Should I drive, or do you want to? Either way, it's going to be karaoke the whole ride up, so you've been warned."

And then Sadie danced back into Becca's office singing the chorus to "Vacation" by The Go-Go's.

She'd make the phone call Dr. Park wanted her to make—after she returned from a month by the lake. Sadie learned early on not to take life for granted, especially when it offered you unexpected gifts. She knew there would be plenty of time for the serious stuff—a committed relationship, a family, maybe even her own diner someday. Thirty-seven was still young by her standards, so what was the rush?

Sadie wrote her own story. She decided what came next.

For the next month, she'd live. As much as she could, as best she could. And then...well...she'd figure out how the next chapter would go.

"I hate eighties music," Becca told her as the two women headed back toward the desk.

Sadie laughed. "I can see I have my work cut out for me, don't I? This is going to be fun. You do fun, right?"

Becca cleared her throat. "I do fun. On my terms."

Sadie nodded. "Now that is something I can get behind."

She pressed her palm to her chest and felt the reassurance of the steady, rhythmic beat of her heart.

This would be fun. And Sadie would be fine. That was her story, and she wasn't about to change the ending now.

CHAPTER THREE

BECCA

Becca stared at the photo of Grayson and Mackenzie on her phone's lock screen, her twins both doing their best to make their silliest faces. How were they already going into second grade? How was she going to go a month without seeing them? Okay, not a *full* month. She'd already planned to return briefly after the first two weeks to welcome the twins home from overnight camp, but still. If she wasn't *Mommy* or *Dr. Weiland*, who was she supposed to be for these next four weeks?

"I'm fun," she uttered aloud. "Whatever that means."

She heard the trunk slam and startled in the driver's seat. Fifteen seconds later, Sadie pulled open the door and hopped into the passenger seat, lowering her sunglasses and giving Becca's Honda Odyssey a once-over.

"*What?*" Becca asked, already dreading the next two-plus hours.

"I forgot that you drove a minivan," Sadie said with a shrug. "I always picture you in something a little more posh. Something that matches your clothes."

Becca glanced down at her Lululemon tank and skirt, her cheeks burning even as she protested. "This is *casual* wear. It's—it's practically workout clothes. It's not *posh*."

Sadie ripped a loose string from the bottom of her denim cutoffs and dropped it in the cup holder. Then she smoothed her palm over her plain, heather gray cotton tank. "I'm just sayin'... posh is as posh does."

Becca nodded at the house from which Sadie emerged. "Says the woman who just walked off the property of what some might call an estate."

Sadie snorted. "My parents' *estate*. But touché. My lease was up on my apartment, and my landlord raised the rent, so I'm in between homes at the moment. And there's nothing wrong with buying or wearing or even driving nice things. You're a doctor. A good one, I hear too!" She winked, and Becca groaned. "And this is still a sweet ride, Bex. You just project this image, you know? That's all."

Becca realized she was white-knuckling the steering wheel despite her *sweet ride* being in park. So she let go, crossing her arms over her chest and pivoting to face her companion—her companion whose company she was going to have to endure for the next four weeks. What the *hell* had she been thinking when she'd agreed to this?

"We *all* project an image," Becca countered. "I can't help it if mine is a little more polished than others. And I already asked you not to call me that. *Bex*. Only Alissa has that privilege."

Sadie pursed her lips. "Right. Right. I forgot. Sorry. But I need to call you *something*."

"How about my name? *Becca*."

Sadie shook her head. "We need nicknames. That's what roommates do. They come up with cute nicknames that only the other roommate can use. Kinda like what you have with your sister. Though *she* lets me call her Liss." Then Sadie gasped.

"What?" Becca asked yet again, knowing full well she did *not* want to hear what came next.

"Posh Spice! It's too perfect. Should I go with *Posh* or *Spice* or maybe even *Spicy*? What do you think?"

Becca tightened her ponytail, then put one hand back on the wheel. With the other she shifted the car into drive. She wasn't going to dignify Sadie pushing her buttons with any sort of answer. Instead, she pressed play on her phone's music app, her K-pop playlist beginning to blare through the speakers with her favorite song, BTS's "Fire."

"Hey, Posh," Sadie said, raising a brow at Becca before sliding her sunglasses back into place. "How am I supposed to sing along if I don't know Korean?"

Becca blew out a breath and finally smiled. "Exactly," she replied. "It's a two-hour-and-twenty-eight-minute ride to Glass Lake. Guess how long my playlist is?"

Sadie huffed out a laugh. "Well played, Posh. Well played indeed."

☀

By the time Becca pulled up the long driveway to the bungalow, Sadie had been sound asleep, her head resting against the window, for over an hour.

For a moment, Becca considered leaving her asleep for as long as she'd stay that way, but with temps hitting the high eighties, that would mean having to keep the car running so she could leave the air on. She wanted Sadie to remain blissfully silent, but that didn't mean she wanted her sister's boyfriend's sister to get heat stroke—or worse.

She sighed, then gently shook Sadie's shoulder, but the woman didn't move. So Becca put a little more oomph into her shaking while calling out Sadie's name.

Sadie bolted upright. "But I *like* doughnuts!" she exclaimed, then shot a glance toward Becca before letting her shoulders relax. "Wow," she said. "Even when I sleep, I dream of the bakery."

"You have a little…" Becca pointed toward the corner of Sadie's mouth that was wet with drool.

Sadie barked out a laugh and then swiped her forearm across her lips. "I was down for the count, wasn't I? Should I apologize for sleeping for half the drive or say *You're welcome*?"

Becca bit back a laugh. She had to hand it to Sadie. She *was* funny sometimes. And intuitive.

"Thank you," Becca told her sincerely. "I kind of needed the time to clear my head."

Sadie pressed her lips into a grin. "I get it. I like my space too, you know. Once we get the lay of the land, you can do your thing, and I'll do mine. Sound like a plan?"

Becca's eyes widened. She was so prepared to think of a million reasons why the two women should separate as soon as they unpacked that she hadn't anticipated Sadie wanting the same thing. She should have been happy that Sadie wanted her space as much as Becca did, but instead she felt an unfamiliar pang in her gut.

"Of course," Becca said, forcing a smile. "Sounds like a plan."

Both women got out of the van and met up at the vehicle's rear. When Becca opened the trunk, she chuckled at the identical rolling suitcases lined up side by side, both Louis Vuitton.

"Guess I'm not the only one who's posh after all, huh?" she said to Sadie, raising her brows behind her sunglasses.

Sadie snorted. "Mine's a knockoff. Got it for fifty bucks from a street vendor in New York a couple of years ago. Bet you can't tell which one is mine and which one is yours."

Becca gritted her teeth. She would *not* be made to feel guilty for being successful and buying herself nice things every now and then. She worked hard. *Damned* hard, and she was proud of the work she did.

She grabbed the right suitcase without hesitating, and Sadie gave her a playful nudge with her shoulder.

"*Right.* Mine doesn't have a luggage tag," Sadie said with a grin.

Becca pushed her glasses on top of her head and narrowed her eyes at her companion.

"You know, when you came to my office on Friday with the rugelach, you *seemed* like you actually cared about what I was going through. I thought maybe...I don't know...we might become friends. Or something." She kept her voice calm and collected as she continued, "But now I get this feeling like you just want to put me in my place. Like you're *enjoying* pushing my buttons, and if that's the case, then I'm putting an end to it right here. We can share this house, but we don't have to share each other's company." She extended her suitcase handle and gave it a tug, striding past Sadie and up toward the front door, heart racing and a knot forming in her throat.

Did she really think she and Sadie would suddenly become friends after never having done so in all the years they'd known each other?

"I think I'm going to explore the beach first," Sadie called after her. "I'll catch up with you later."

Becca heard the trunk door slam, and she let out a shaky breath as she reached the bungalow's front porch.

So much for the uneventful ride. Why was Sadie able to get under her skin with something as innocuous as luggage?

Whatever. They'd take some time to get their bearings and then maybe start fresh. Or they'd live together for a month separately but together. Becca certainly knew how to do that.

She pulled out her phone to look up the email from the renter that had the lockbox code. But when she was ready to enter the numbers, she glanced at the door handle and found no lockbox there.

"Huh," she said out loud. She glanced up and down the street, where she saw a family of four riding bikes, a young couple pushing a stroller, and an older woman walking a small dog. She did *not* see any sign of Sadie and guessed she'd held true to her words and had skulked off to the beach.

"Okay," Becca said to no one in particular, turning back to the house and placing a hand on the front door handle. "It's a bright, sunny day. There are *very* friendly-looking people walking up and down the street, which means I am totally safe, right?" She pressed down on the door's latch with her thumb, and it clicked, the door opening inward into the house.

"Not going to get murdered. Not going to get murdered. *Not* going to get murdered," she chanted to herself as she took a step inside.

"Hello?" Becca called out hesitantly. "It's—uh—Becca Weiland? The renter?"

A voice sounded from the kitchen—someone singing. Was that "Walking on Sunshine"? Whoever it was, they had a distinctly *male* voice. Even though Becca had spoken only to Andrea, the female owner of the house, the woman had mentioned that she and her husband—a couple in their late fifties—owned a few vacation rentals. So it was likely him— maybe here to welcome them in a more personable fashion. How hospitable. Maybe he'd even have a gift basket of local wares.

Except when Becca strode into the kitchen, she stopped short as soon as he saw him.

Not a fifty-something man and certainly no gift basket in sight. What *was* in sight was the stark naked body of a decidedly younger man, leaning nonchalantly against the kitchen island holding a mug of something steaming as his head bobbed to whatever played in his earbuds.

"Oh shit!" he yelled, louder than was necessary, as he backed up against the counter, lowering his mug to a more strategic placement. He winced as coffee sloshed over the side of the mug, then let out what looked like a relieved breath when the rogue liquid seemed to avoid contact with anything other than the floor.

Becca should have noticed his dark, disheveled hair, which was desperately in need of a trim but somehow still suited him. She should have remarked how his left cheek dimpled when he smiled, but his right did not. She should have been taken aback by his bright blue eyes and long, lean-muscled torso. And perhaps she *had* taken note of all these things, cataloging them somewhere in the recesses of her mind. But right now, all she could do was stare slack-jawed at the trail of dark hair that ran from his belly button to his nether region—his very impressive nether region, which wasn't completely concealed by the stranger's recent mug placement.

Becca swallowed and felt an unfamiliar tightening in her belly.

"Sorry! " the young man said, his voice deep but with a

sexy rasp. "I must be running late, or you're running early. Either way, so sorry if I freaked you out!"

He was still yelling.

Becca saw the phone on the island and reached for it, tapping the pause icon on the screen.

"Thank you, Ms. ..." he started, finally in what she explained to her twins was an indoor voice.

"Sexy?" Becca blurted out. "Wait, I didn't mean to say sexy."

The naked man grinned. "Your name is Ms. Sexy?"

Becca's cheeks felt like they were on fire. She covered her eyes with one hand and pointed at the stranger with her other.

"The mug is not working. Can you just cover that up? And—and who *are* you anyway?"

She heard nothing for a long moment.

"It's safe," he finally said.

At first, Becca cracked only one eye open, then let out a breath as she dared to open them both.

"Eh?" Mr. No Name said, pointing at the apron that hung over his neck and was tied around his waist. It was navy blue with white letters that read, *Shut Up and Eat My Meat.*

Becca coughed. "Did you bring that as a prop?"

He laughed. "No. It belongs to Andrea and Ted. But you have to admit it is quite fitting for the situation." He glanced over his shoulder, partially revealing his still-bare ass. "Okay, so not com*plete*ly fitting ..."

Becca waved her hand at him. "Just stay up against counter, okay? I'm still waiting for you to tell me who you are."

"Ah, yes. Introductions. Sorry about that…among other things." He cleared his throat. "Leo Beckett, at your service." He gave her a slight bow, careful not to reveal any body parts that weren't sufficiently covered by the apron. "I take care of the yard and some home maintenance for Andrea and Ted— and occasionally take advantage of the private beach to go for a quick dip. I—uh—just finished that quick dip. Apparently, I should have been quicker."

Becca swallowed, and the heat in her cheeks spread down her neck and a bit farther south. "And you occasionally go for a quick dip with—without a swimsuit?"

Leo flashed her a devilish grin. "I *occasionally* take advantage of the private beach. When I do, I *always* go without a swimsuit. Private beach means as long as the owners don't mind and the neighbors don't mind…" He shrugged.

Becca barked out a laugh and then threw a hand over her mouth, eyes wide.

Leo quirked a brow. "Did I say something funny?"

Becca nodded, then shook her head, then let go of her suitcase and threw both her arms in the air.

"It's just, I knew I never should have said yes to this, you know? I sign my divorce papers Friday, within minutes get talked into a month-long vacation when I haven't taken so much as a week off since my maternity leave, somehow *agree* to sharing this house with a roommate who drives me bananas—and then walk in to find a skinny-dipping house-boy with *his* banana proudly on display in my kitchen."

"*Houseboy* is a little harsh, don't you think? I'm twenty-six."

Leo glanced down to where his *banana* was hidden behind the apron and chuckled. Then he met her gaze again. "Unless you're saying I *look* like a boy?" His blue eyes gleamed with challenge.

"No!" Becca blurted out. "I mean, I wasn't looking—er—I didn't *mean* to look, but I wasn't expecting…" She braced a hand on the corner of the island, her knees buckling and her head spinning. "Is it hot in here? I feel like it's so hot in here."

Leo took a strategic step toward her and pulled out one of the stools that was hidden beneath the island's breakfast bar. "Maybe you should sit down. The air conditioner has been having a hard time keeping up in this heat, so I might need to take a look at it."

Becca nodded and carefully strode around the side of the island opposite Leo so as not to catch a glimpse of his bare backside. She let out a breath as she climbed onto the stool.

Once again, Leo moved backward toward the sink, reaching over his shoulder to grab a glass from the cabinet and carefully turning so his rear faced away from Becca as he filled the glass from the tap.

"So other than the roommate who drives you bananas, do you want to explain why that whole long list you just rattled off means you never should have said yes to a month-long vacation?"

Becca downed the water before answering. "Because," she said. "It's out of control." She wasn't sure why she was telling him—a perfect stranger who was perfectly naked and more than a perfect ten years her junior—all of this. She simply wanted to get it all out, to tell *someone* how hard it was to leave her comfortable, reliable routine.

His brows furrowed. "What is?"

"All of it." She shrugged. "It's all out of control." For some inexplicable reason, Becca felt as if she might burst into tears. Instead, she sat up straight and squared her shoulders, then cleared her throat.

"I still didn't catch your name, Ms., um, Sexy," Leo said softly.

"I'll be thirty-six in fifteen days," she said matter-of-factly, still rattling off her list of reasons why this month away was a bad idea, including the fact that she was now hot and bothered by a naked man ten years younger. She didn't think he was flirting with her. Hell, she didn't even know what flirting *was* anymore. But just for the record, she wanted it out there that while twenty-six might be considered a man, she was *not* here looking for one, whether he was naked or not.

"It's nice to meet you, *thirty-six in fifteen days*," Leo said, holding out his right hand.

She rolled her eyes and then groaned. Usually upon meeting someone new, she introduced herself as Dr. Becca Weiland, but this time she simply said, "Becca. My name—is Becca." Then she wrapped her hand firmly around his and shook.

CHAPTER FOUR

SADIE

Sadie strode around to the back of the bungalow, her jaw clenched and shoulders tense.

Enjoying pushing Becca's buttons? *Enjoying?* Maybe she just wanted to get something from the woman other than her calm, cool, bedside manner since the last thing Sadie wanted to think about in the coming weeks was doctors. Four weeks. That was all Sadie was asking... Four weeks to pretend like everything was fine. Did Dr. Becca Weiland ever emote, or was she some sort of artificial intelligence that seemed very human*like* but for the stuff that computers couldn't emulate?

Maybe she *had* come on a little strong with the teasing, but Sadie had always been the go-big-or-go-home type when it came to putting herself out there with others, a *Take me or leave me* tactic right from the get-go because what was the point in wasting time with pretense when that time could be spent living?

"Fine," she said as she kicked off her flip-flops where the grass from the bungalow's backyard met the sand. It didn't matter that she and Becca had been in each other's lives since before they could remember. They'd simply never clicked, and it wasn't like spending a month under the same roof would change that. So they'd be roommates and nothing more. Sadie could enjoy a beautiful bungalow, a private beach, and whatever the small town of Glass Lake had to offer just fine on her own.

She dug her toes into the warm sand as she made her way toward the water. The sun was already high in the sky, making her wish she'd had the forethought to apply sunscreen before storming off like a petulant child. Because now she'd have to enter the house sooner rather than later and face Becca, who would likely still be giving her the cold shoulder.

Cool water lapped over the tops of her feet, and Sadie waded in a bit farther so that the water almost covered her ankles. God, it felt good. She hadn't realized how hot she was until now. Spinning slowly, she took in the panoramic view of the small, private lake. Picturesque bungalows framed the water, some with kayaks and canoes sitting atop wooden docks, others with small fire pits built near the water. There were even a couple of paddleboats on the water right now. Nothing motorized, though. Nothing to pollute the water or disturb the neighbors. She remembered reading that in the rental contract.

Not too far down the beach from their rental, Sadie spotted a one-person tent pitched right there on the sand. She chuckled. If things *really* weren't going to work out between her and Becca, a solo campout was always an option. She sure wouldn't mind a night or two sleeping under the stars.

She could make one lap around the lake before the need for sunblock would outweigh her reticence to deal with her roommate. So she sloshed through the water—letting it keep her from overheating—as she squinted behind her sunglass lenses, the morning star winning out over her drugstore eyewear.

Sadie heard a child yelling somewhere in the distance behind her and thought nothing of it until she heard a dog's bark—closer than she wanted it to be. She turned around with only seconds to register the curly, golden-haired canine bounding toward her. The *big*, curly, golden-haired canine. Sadie froze—complete and utter paralysis. By the time she even thought to scream, paws were on her shoulders, and Sadie was stumbling backward until her knees gave way and she landed flat on her back, the wind knocked clear from her lungs.

She gasped for breath as her assailant lapped at her cheek and her nose, and even amid her panic, she feared she might soon be inadvertently French-kissing a dog, so she clamped her mouth shut, trying desperately to get enough air in through her nose and hoping the sloppy kisses didn't mean she was soon to be the animal's lunch.

"Shit. Shit. Shit. Shit. Shit," she heard, a man's voice.

The series of mild expletives were followed by, "*Daddy*, that's *five* more dollars for the swear jar."

"Penny!" the man yelled, ignoring his admonishment. "Dammit, Penny, *sit!*"

The licking ceased as the dog obeyed her command and sat—right on Sadie's chest. Despite the weight of the beast, Sadie was finally able to suck in at least one lungful of air.

"Daddy, the lady's lips are *blue*! Also, that'll be *another* dollar!"

"Penny, come *here* and sit!" the man called, and the dog bounded off Sadie's torso.

Sadie finally inhaled a full breath, then rolled to her side, coughing.

"Shit," she heard the man say again.

"And one more," the other voice replied accusingly.

"I know. I know," he said. "Just put Penny's leash on, okay, Peanut?"

"Okay. But don't think I'm going to forget what you owe."

There was a playfulness to the little girl's tone, one Sadie might have found charming or even cute if she hadn't almost *slept with the fishes*, for lack of a punnier euphemism.

"I'm really sorry," the man said.

Sadie's sunglasses were no longer on her face, and she distinctly felt that one of her contact lenses had gone missing, so all she could see when she stared up at him was his outstretched hand, the rest of his features obliterated by the sun and her wonky one-eyed vision.

"It's fine," she said unconvincingly, letting him pull her

up. A quick assessment revealed nothing amiss other than what she must look like at the moment. She was breathing. Her heart was beating. Nothing seemed broken other than her pride. "If I wasn't already terrified of dogs, your—*Penny*, is it?—would have sealed the deal."

Penny perked up at the sound of her name, wagging her tail and pulling at her leash.

Sadie scrambled a few steps back, then realized the man was still holding her hand.

"It's okay," he told her, holding his other hand up as if to show he was unarmed and meant her no harm. "She's on her leash, and Evie's got her. We should have leashed her sooner, but there wasn't anyone on the beach when we first came out. She's a good dog, a rescue. But she's still kind of new to us, so we're learning the ropes. She just gets really excited when she meets someone new. She wouldn't hurt—I mean, she only wanted to play. Are you sure you're all right?"

Sadie wriggled her hand free and backed up even farther. "I said I was fine. Just—just take her back to wherever you came from and keep her on that leash." She glanced down at her soaked tank, which was plastered to her torso, to her sand-caked shorts. She tried running a hand through her hair and grimaced. There was sand *everywhere*.

"I need to go," she said absently.

"Evie, sweetheart, can you walk Penny back to the yard so I can make sure…" He glanced back at Sadie. "I'm Max, by the way." He held out his hand, this time to shake, but

Sadie shook her head, still barely able to make out his facial features, but she could tell he was smiling.

The girl was already backing away with the dog, but Max wasn't moving.

"I just—" She glanced toward the bungalow, grateful she hadn't strayed too far. When she closed her lens-free eye, she could see her red flip-flops still sitting where the grass met the sand, and she let out a relieved breath. "Yeah. I'm gonna go now. It was nice to—well, no, actually I guess it wasn't, was it?" She let out a nervous laugh as she backed toward the rental. "How about you stay on your part of the beach, I'll stay on mine, and Penny there will stay on her leash. Everybody's happy then, right?"

She waved them off as she continued to add distance between them, careful not to take her eyes off the dog, even if everything was a little blurry.

"Good-bye, Max. Evie. Penny," she called to them with as much dignity as she could muster in her state. "Make sure your dad fills up that swear jar, okay?" she added, turning her attention to the young girl.

Evie giggled. "I *always* do."

"Um," Max replied, less mirth in *his* tone. "Yeah. Okay. My part of the beach and your part of the beach. Got it."

Only as the open space between them grew could Sadie tell how tall he was—and how not-so-monstrous her canine assailant appeared to be.

But she spun on her heel and scrambled back toward the

house, her earlier confrontation with Becca the least of her worries now.

She stepped back into her flip-flops and high-tailed it to the van to retrieve her suitcase. Only once she'd dragged her luggage through the door and slammed it behind her did she finally let out a trembling breath. Hand shaking, she ran her fingers over the small scar beneath her chin. She hadn't even needed stitches. Just a butterfly bandage to hold the skin together. Yet that incidental trip to the ER all those years ago had turned Sadie's childhood upside down, forcing her to grow up long before she should have.

But she was past all that now. Fully recovered and living her best life…and maybe acting like a bit less of a grownup now that she was one.

You're okay, she told herself. *You're okay.*

Dr. Park's exam didn't mean anything. A run-in with a dog was nothing more than coincidence.

"Oh my god. What the hell happened to you?"

Sadie squeezed her bad eye shut so she could clearly see the look of horror on Becca's face—and the man standing next to her wearing what looked like *nothing* but an apron.

Sadie plastered on her devil-may-care grin and cleared her throat.

"Got acquainted with the beach, and now I'm going to shower. But I can't wait to hear all about"—she motioned between Becca and her companion—"*this* when I come back."

Then, recalling the layout of the bungalow from the photos, she strode down the nearby hallway, suitcase in tow, until she found the bathroom. When she closed the door behind her and finally got a one-eyed look at the mess of a person staring back at her in the mirror, she wasn't sure whether to laugh or burst into tears. So she turned on the shower, letting the room fill with steam, and did a little bit of both.

☼

When Sadie finally emerged from the safety of the bathroom—towel piled on her head and wearing her favorite green cotton cami and yoga pants—she found Becca in the sunroom, which faced the beach, rocking back and forth on the love-seat-sized glider, two perspiring glasses of iced tea sitting on the glass coffee table in front of her.

"Is one of those for me, Posh?" The nickname slipped out before Sadie had a chance to think about whether or not it was a good idea to push Becca's buttons *now*, especially when Sadie herself was in no mood to get into it with the other woman. "Sorry," she added as Becca's cheeks reddened and her jaw tightened. "It slipped out."

Becca blew out a breath. "No. It's okay..." She paused for a beat and then added, "I've never actually had a nickname before, other than Bex."

"Which only Alissa gets to say," Sadie added.

Becca nodded, and picked up one of the glasses of tea.

She took a sip and then lightly chewed on the reusable silicone straw as she stared absently through the screen and out at the beach.

Sadie approached the glider with caution and, when Becca stopped rocking, took it as an invitation to sit.

"Liss was always the fun one, so people gave her fun little names, like Matthew calling her *Freckles*. He's done that since we were kids."

Sadie made herself comfortable, sitting cross-legged rather than letting her legs dangle. She grabbed the second glass and took a long, slow sip from her own straw, sighing as the refreshing liquid went down, her taste buds perking up at the hint of raspberry giving the tea a sweet yet subtle finish.

"No one's ever given you a nickname other than your sister? Not even Jeff?" Sadie asked, following Becca's lead and directing her attention toward the sand and water rather than attempting any sort of eye contact.

"Nope," the other woman said. "In fact, when he thought I was being *too* serious, he'd call me by my full name, *Re*becca. It was his way of telling me to relax."

Sadie growled softly. "If I had a nickel for every time a guy told me to relax and I daydreamed about neutering him . . . I'd have a shit ton of nickels."

Becca snorted, then shot a glance toward Sadie, hand over her mouth.

Sadie turned too, a smile spreading across her face.

"Did the too perfect, too serious, too posh *Rebecca* just

snort?" Sadie's eyes widened as her jaw dropped for dramatic effect.

Becca cleared her throat. "Sorry, I—"

Sadie cut her off by placing *her* palm over Becca's mouth. "Oh no you don't. A good, authentic laugh is *never* anything to apologize for, *especially* not with me."

Becca's features softened, and Sadie removed her hand.

"But it's…" Becca started. "It's embarrassing. I would never do that in public, and I can't believe it just came out like that. Jeff always—I mean, I was at this dinner once for his firm. It was way back when we'd first gotten married, before he'd made partner or anything like that. I'd had a couple of glasses of champagne, as had everyone else. His boss told a funny story, and I—I snorted." She shrugged. "No one else seemed to think anything of it, but I'll never forget how Jeff squeezed my knee under the table and said to the rest of the group, 'I guess *someone's* had more than her share to drink.' She worried her bottom lip between her teeth. "It was just a joke, you know, but…"

"A joke at *your* expense," Sadie said, her brows furrowed. "It's not like he'd never heard your real laugh, right?"

Becca sighed.

"Fine," she said after a beat. "You have me pegged, okay? Always did. I'm too perfect, too serious, and too posh, so much so that I stifled my own laugh around my boyfriend and later husband for *years* until a couple of flutes of bubbly and a tiny loss of inhibition let it *all* hang out." She stood then, smoothing her skirt and picking up her glass. "This was a mistake, right? Us? Bonding? I just wanted to make sure you were okay, and you look okay, so—I'm going to finish unpacking." She glanced down at the coffee table—at the ring of condensation her iced tea had left on the glass—and winced.

Sadie unwrapped the towel from her head and, finding a dry corner, wiped away the ring.

"Becca, you don't have to leave. We have a whole month together. Shouldn't we—"

"I really can't stand leaving my suitcase the way it is. Everything should be in its place, right? That's what you'd expect from perfect me?"

Her tone wasn't angry. Instead it was resigned, like she knew Sadie would only ever see her one way, so why should she fight it?

"There's more tea in the pitcher in the fridge. It's just a mix, but not bad, right? Anyway, if you want to head into town or something after you unpack—or maybe you don't unpack, whatever works best for you—don't worry about me. Okay?"

Then she brushed past Sadie without another word, without letting the two of them even try to start fresh after the rough morning they'd had just when she'd thought they were starting to make progress. She hadn't even had the chance to ask who the half-naked guy was standing next to Becca when she'd burst through the door looking like some sort of B-movie sand monster.

Sadie hadn't even been trying to push her buttons this time. She'd hoped they were connecting, hoped they might be able to get past the preconceived notions they'd had about each other all these years. Just because things had always been this way between them didn't mean things had to always be this way. You could change your story at any point in your life. Sadie had done it once before. Becca could do it too.

Sadie brushed a hand over the almost invisible scar again, swallowing as her fingers touched the slightly puckered skin beneath her chin. Then her hand slid down to her chest, to the heart that beat beneath protective layers of skin and bone. She breathed in deep and assured herself that the shortness of breath she'd felt on the beach was due to nothing more than falling flat on her back. It was time to get this party started. And if Becca wasn't ready for that, Sadie would have to take the party elsewhere.

She ran her fingers through her damp hair and sighed. Maybe she and Becca had simply known each other for too long. But one thing Sadie had learned in her early adult years was that she could charm the pants off anyone meeting her for the first time. It made for great customer service at Take the Cake and some pretty terrific endings to most—if not *all*—of her first dates, proof positive that Sadie Bloom made one hell of a first impression.

The earlier beach incident was, of course, an anomaly.

If Becca wanted Sadie to go to town, then she'd go to town and find someone's pants that needed to be charmed off while Becca organized her closet and wiped rings off coffee tables.

As she padded back to where her suitcase waited outside the downstairs bathroom, she heard K-pop blaring behind the closed bedroom door upstairs.

"Message received," Sadie mumbled to herself. "Message received."

CHAPTER FIVE

BECCA

Leo had excused himself as soon as the soaked and sand-caked Sadie had burst through the bungalow's front door and traipsed into the bathroom to clean up.

"I think that's my cue," he'd said.

Becca had still felt overheated and light-headed. "The air," she blurted out. "You were going to check—" But as if her words had conjured some sort of naked-man-banishing magic, the air conditioner kicked on, and a cool breeze began blowing from a nearby vent.

Leo grinned and shrugged. "Guess it just needed a little breather." He began backing out of the kitchen. "I'll jot my number on a sticky note and put it on the fridge. If the house needs anything, just shoot me a text. Promise I'll wear a couple more articles of clothing next time." He winked. "I'm gonna turn around now so I can see where I'm going. You can either avert your eyes or not."

That had been all the warning he'd given before he spun on his heel, revealing a toned, muscled back—and a firm, tanned ass atop his long, lean legs.

She'd wanted to avert her eyes—*should* have averted her eyes—but Becca couldn't look away. The sight of his body and of how confident he was in his own skin rooted her there, staring, eyes wide and throat dry.

Even now as she stood in front of her empty suitcase—her playlist having finally gone silent and a slamming door letting her know Sadie had taken her words to heart and gone to town—Becca wondered how to further occupy both her body and her brain, unable to erase the image of Leo's naked form from her mind.

What would it feel like to be that comfortable without any... without being covered up? Clothing was her armor. It wasn't about being fancy or posh or whatever Sadie wanted to accuse her of. It was about looking the part—perfect doctor, perfect mother, perfect wife.

She stood in front of the closed bedroom door, on the back of which was a full-length mirror, and stared.

Her dark ponytail was still pulled tight and clean. Her tank and skirt barely showed any signs of travel with only a minor wrinkle here and there. Toned, runner's legs ended where pedicured toes peeked out of strappy wedge sandals.

The woman behind the glass was pretty, polished, and put

together. She'd done everything right, hadn't she? Married her college sweetheart, established herself at a wonderful practice before having kids, and had carried her twins almost to full term, going into labor only a day before her scheduled C-section. Her whole life fell into place according to a grand plan that had gotten her where? The woman she stared at felt like a stranger.

Becca held her breath, then pulled her tank top over her head. She eased one bra strap off her shoulder, then the next, before popping open the front fastener and letting the undergarment fall to the floor, a long, slow exhale escaping from her lungs.

Becca cupped her breasts in her palms, pushing them back up to where they used to be before motherhood and age had let them sag a little lower and appear a little smaller.

She let her hands slide lower, over a stomach that was trim yet painted with the silvery pink stretch marks that never truly go away, over the horizontal scar that had ushered her into motherhood.

Her hands dipped under the elastic waist of her skirt, pushing the garment *and* her underwear to her ankles, where she kicked them off along with her wedges.

"Who the hell *are* you?" she asked, but the naked woman didn't respond.

Becca narrowed her eyes at her and asked the question again. "Who. *Are*. You? Huh? Answer me, dammit!"

Still no response, but something glinted back at her, and Becca gasped as her eyes dipped to the place between her legs where—as if the universe hadn't taunted her enough—she saw an unmistakable gray hair.

She screamed, covered her mouth, then remembered she was the only one in the house and let out a relieved breath. But her relief was short-lived the second her reflection reminded her why she'd screamed in the first place.

Becca had yet to find a single gray hair on her head. So why, *why*, of all places was she finding one *there*? And *now*? Why did Jeff get to look all gorgeous and happy on a damned dating app while she was going all *Golden Girls* between the legs? Not that there was anything wrong with going gray. Or aging. It happened to everyone. Logically she knew that and felt no shame in it. But couldn't this new development have waited until after what was supposed to be a relaxing month away?

She scrambled for her purse, pulling out her phone and quickly opening her internet app. Her thumbs worked furiously over the screen, typing in *bikini wax* faster than she'd thought humanly possible, silently praying that the sleepy beach town even offered such a service.

Happy tears sprang to her eyes when *Shelby Salon and Spa* popped up with the key words *body waxing* in the description. She tapped on the phone number, chewing on her bottom lip as she heard the first and second rings.

"Shelby Salon and Spa, how can I help you?" a perky female voice asked. Becca thought she also heard a slight Southern lilt.

"Yeah. Hi," Becca said, voice a little shaky. "You do waxing?"

"Sure do, sugar. What were you looking for? Eyebrows? Upper lip? Maybe a little off the chin?"

While Becca had never actually waxed more than her bikini line, she knew full well what she was looking for today.

"Do you do...Brazilians?" she asked, glancing down to where her neglected—in more ways than one—bits and parts silently reproached her.

"Honey, we do it *all* if that's what you're looking for...And if you've got the tolerance for it." She laughed.

Becca smiled nervously. She coached patients who squeezed humans out of there on a weekly basis. She could surely handle a wax.

"How soon can you get me in?" she asked.

"How soon can you get here?" the other woman countered.

And just as quickly as Becca disrobed, she threw her clothes back on, but not before pausing in front of the window, staring out at the small, clear-as-glass blue lake—hence its name—and wondering what it would feel like to simply wade in, free of worry or inhibition like Leo.

Like—*Sadie*. Sadie probably walked around naked without even a second thought—without caring whether or not she was sporting gray hair between her legs.

"Okay," she said to no one in particular when she found herself behind the wheel of her minivan once more. "A fresh start means I have to *start* somewhere, right?" She glanced down at her lap, squirmed in her seat at the thought of what she was about to do, and then backed out of the driveway and onto the main road.

Adrenaline coursed through Becca's veins. She felt renewed simply by having made a decision to point herself in a specific direction—even if said direction was simply a mile away to a small-town salon. But her bolstered confidence quickly deflated once she'd made it to her destination and realized there were no parking lots, only street parking. *Parallel* street parking.

"Come *on*," she whimpered as she circled the block not once, not twice, but *four* times even though there was an empty space right in front of Shelby Salon. Had it been an empty *end* space, she would have been fine. But this one looked barely big enough to fit her van.

Her heart raced, and her palms began to sweat as she slowed to a stop in front of the salon, already five minutes past her appointment time.

She pulled up next to the car in front of the open parking spot, cranked her wheel to the left, and slowly attempted to back into the space until she was completely perpendicular to the two cars on either side of her.

"Oh my god," she said before pulling out and trying again. This time she managed to get *most* of the way there, with nothing more but the nose of her van sticking out next to the bumper of the car in front of her, but no matter how many microscopic three-point turns she attempted, she could not get the rest of her van to fit.

She could feel the stares of passersby boring holes through her already fragile ego, but she didn't dare look to see just how big of an audience she'd amassed.

"Forget it," she mumbled under her breath. "I'll just—wax it or pluck that taunting, silver bugger out myself."

She turned the wheel as far as it would go to the right in an attempt to free herself from her predicament when her van jolted, her front bumper *bumping* the one attached to the other car.

Becca gasped and threw the van into park, her panicked breathing growing quicker and shallower until she began to feel light-headed for already the second time since she'd arrived in Glass Lake.

A knock sounded against her window, and Becca yelped. She turned to see a young woman with a chin-length bob and side-swept bangs smiling at her, her brown eyes glinting in the sun.

Becca let out a shaky breath and lowered her window.

"Hey, sugar," the other woman said. "You want me to park this beast for you?"

"Shelby?" Becca asked.

Shelby winked. "As I live and breathe. You must be my Brazilian."

For a second Becca considered winking back but realized she'd never be able to pull it off. She wasn't the winking type. She actually wasn't sure she'd ever winked at anyone in her life. Was that odd? Was winking a thing done by everyone but her?

"What do you say, darlin'? Want me to park it, or do you want to give my Bug another love tap?" Shelby asked, startling Becca back to the moment.

Her eyes widened as she stared at the yellow convertible VW Bug in front of her.

"I'm *so* sorry!" she said. "I'll pay for whatever the damage is." It was then that Becca finally acknowledged the throng of sunglasses-wearing and flip-flop-clad onlookers gathered in front of the Salon.

Shelby nodded over her shoulder, urging Becca out of the driver's seat.

Becca undid her seat belt with a wince and a sigh, then opened her door and slid out onto the curb next to which her van was wedged.

"If you could get me *out* of the spot, I'll just head back the way I came. I'm sure I've already missed my appointment."

Shelby waved her off. "Nonsense. We're all on beach time here." She held up a fist, brandishing a bare wrist. "See? No watch means no actual appointment time. You get here when you get here, and I fit you in before I close. Simple as that. But we have to take care of this"—she raised her brows and glanced between the van and the Volkswagen—"situation first."

"Right," Becca said. "Okay. Then . . . I guess . . . park it? And again, I'm so sorry about the—uh—love tap." She winced.

Shelby responded by hopping into the driver's seat, adjusting the mirror, and successfully parking Becca's van in mere seconds. When she hopped back out, she inspected both bumpers before tossing Becca her key fob, which she gratefully caught.

"Looks like you put plenty of love in that tap," Shelby said, "because there's not a scratch on either one." She glanced over Becca's shoulder and made a shooing motion with both her hands. "Show's over, folks," she added. "Nothing more to see here."

Becca's audience dispersed as quickly as they'd gathered. Shelby strode toward the salon's entrance, holding the door open as she waited for her still-chagrinned patron to enter.

Smoothing out nonexistent wrinkles in her skirt, Becca squared her shoulders and marched through the open door. Certainly, she'd made it through the worst of the day, right? First, Sadie's jabs and then Leo's p—*presence*—and now total and complete humiliation. If bad luck came in threes, she had to have paid her dues.

The second the door closed behind her, Becca sighed, breathing in the soothing aroma of eucalyptus and spearmint, the warmth of the salon's wood floors and exposed brick walls a welcomed respite from the stress of what she'd just endured.

"You know," she said with a nervous laugh. "I can successfully deliver a baby who is in breech position without having to do surgery, but I can't parallel park a car."

Shelby appraised her with her arms crossed. Despite the woman's simple attire—a black tank top French-tucked into a pair of slim-fitting jeans that came to a stop at a pair of red Chuck Taylors—she had an air of style and confidence that reminded Becca of her sister, Alissa. Even when Alissa was covered in flour, her wavy red hair piled on top of her head with a messy bun and her feet clad in sensible clogs, she had a sureness that Becca always envied and never seemed able to emulate.

"We all have our talents," Shelby finally said, breaking the silence. "If everyone was good at every little thing, how boring would that be?"

Becca worried her bottom lip between her teeth. "Yeah. I guess you're right. It just kinda stings when I'm bad—no, *terrible*—at something that everyone should know how to do. I'm a little bit of a perfectionist." She winced.

"Oh, honey, I can tell by those little beads of sweat on your pretty little brow that you are a *lot* of a perfectionist, but that's okay. We all have our talents, and we all have our—"

"Faults," Becca interrupted. "I know."

Shelby raised a perfectly defined brow. "I was actually going to say *quirks*."

Becca smiled. She liked quirks, and she liked how the word sounded with Shelby's accent.

"Do you mind my asking where you're from? I just love your accent. It's calming."

She grinned and blew her bangs out of her eyes. "You mean when I tell you I grew up in Chapel Hill, North Carolina, you're not going to follow it up with, 'But where are you *from*?' Because my great-grandparents might be from South Korea, but I am third-generation Korean-American, thank you very much."

"No! God, no," Becca said. "I know it's not exactly the same, but another doctor I interned with—when she found out around the holidays that I was Jewish, she said, 'Huh.

You don't *look* Jewish.' Ugh. Why can't people just shut *up* sometimes?"

Shelby crossed her arms and nodded. "Right? People can be the *worst*. But I have a good feeling about you, Dr. Becca. Now," she continued, brows raised as she lowered her gaze from Becca's eyes to the place in question when Becca had made her appointment. "Let me guess. First time?"

Becca nodded.

"New, sexy swimwear or your first gray hair? "

Becca's eyes widened and she twisted at the spot on her finger where her wedding rings used to be. "The—the second one," she admitted.

Shelby sighed.

"You're not going to try to talk me out of it, are you?" Becca asked.

"Of course not, sugar. You gotta do what makes you feel good about *you*. That's why I got into this business, you know. No one should be shamed about whatever makes them feel beautiful. I just hope it's for you and nobody else. Because if you aren't taking care of you because you love you, well then . . ." Shelby waved off the rest of whatever she was going to say and shook her head.

Becca swallowed. She had no idea whether this was for her alone, for the woman Jeff wanted her to be, or the woman she was supposed to become. All she knew was that she was being forced to start over in what felt like the middle of her life, and right now she couldn't handle any physical reminders of the fact that age was more than just a number.

"How do I know if I'm...taking care of me because I love me? What if I don't know the answer to that?" she asked, admitting more to this stranger than she'd intended. What was it about the people in this town—Leo and now Shelby—that made her say things out loud she'd barely admit to thinking before today?

"You'll figure it out," Shelby said with a smile, her lilting accent putting Becca at ease. "But I should warn you," she added with another wink and a smile. "It's gonna hurt like hell."

CHAPTER SIX

SADIE

Despite the iced tea Becca had made for the two of them, Sadie's walk had made her parched all over again. Sure, the adorable storefronts and awnings that lined Lake Street— the main thoroughfare that ran from the county road on which the bungalow sat all the way into town—offered some respite from the heat, but the first half of her journey had been through Glass Lake's residential area, which meant that by the time she'd reached the shade, you'd have never guessed she'd showered barely an hour before.

She peeled her damp cami away from her torso, airing it out. At least she'd swapped the yoga pants for her black cotton shorts. But it wouldn't have mattered if she'd been wearing nothing at all. The Midwestern sun was relentless in July, and Sadie was foolish enough to think she could walk a mile in the heat without so much as a water bottle—or proper shoes.

She glanced down at her sporty yet not entirely supportive Adidas slides. Sure, they were as comfortable as slippers. But people didn't generally walk a mile in slippers—there and back.

She needed to cool off, clear her head, and figure out what people did for fun in Glass Lake, Wisconsin.

Then, like a beacon, a shop sign called out to her: COOL BEANS CAFÉ.

Sadie chuckled at the kitschy—if slightly dated—name. Then her mouth watered at the thought of the tallest, coldest, iced coffee the place could concoct. A venti? Trenta? What came after that, a Big Gulp? Whatever it was, she wanted it, and she wanted it *now*.

A bell jangled above the door as Sadie stepped over the threshold and into Cool Beans. She was greeted with a burst of cold air and then by speakers that boasted the crooning of—was that Tom Jones?

"What's new, pussycat?" she heard, but the song hadn't gotten to the chorus yet. The question came instead from the woman behind the counter. She was around Sadie's age, maybe a few years older, with blue hair piled in a messy bun on top of her head and tortoiseshell-colored cat-eye glasses perched on her nose.

Sadie squinted at the woman's name tag as she approached, her brows rising as the letters came into focus.

Delilah.

Delilah raised her brows right back and then crossed her arms as she pursed her ruby red lips.

"You're wondering if I was named because of *The Tiger* or if I'm a fan of *The Tiger* because of my name."

"Is that what people call him?" Sadie asked, referring to the singer?

Delilah nodded.

Sadie laughed. "Then I'm guessing you get that question about your name a lot."

Delilah shrugged. "Only in the summer when the tourists come to town. The locals all know that—"

"Delilah's *not* your real name, but in the event you ever come face-to-face with Sir Thomas John Woodward OBE—that's the Most Excellent Order of the British Empire—in anything other than a groupie meet-and-greet, you're sure he'll fall head over heels for the namesake of one of his greatest hits, even though the song's about a guy who murders his cheating girlfriend."

Sadie's mouth fell open as she stared at Delilah, even though the explanation came from over Sadie's shoulder, from a voice that *wasn't* Delilah's but that of a man—a voice that shouldn't have sounded familiar because Delilah was right. Sadie *was* a tourist. Yet somehow she knew who she'd see as she pivoted on her heel to face the person in line behind her.

"Max," Sadie said, unable to hide her surprise. Now that she was wearing a fresh pair of contact lenses, she could finally make out his features—his tanned skin and stubbled jaw, the strands of silver that ran through his dark hair, and the deep blue eyes that crinkled at the corners as he offered her a nervous smile. Her aesthetic appreciation of the man before her was short-lived as she remembered how they'd met in the first place. Her eyes darted past his toward the door as she scanned the sidewalk for his canine counterpart.

He held up his hands to show her he was unarmed, just like he had at the beach.

"Penny's at home with Evie. Her uncle stopped by to use the shower and offered to take her to the park." Max's jaw tightened on what should have been an innocuous string of words. "So I'm hiding out here until they're done. Unless, of course, you're deeming the café *your* side of the beach, in which case I guess I'll have to take my business elsewhere." He glanced past her and toward the woman behind the counter. "No offense, Delilah."

"None taken, Maximus," Sadie heard the other woman say. *Maximus?* "Since I know there's no *elsewhere* for you to go."

Sadie swallowed, then cleared her throat. "I—uh—I think this can be considered neutral territory."

Max looked her up and down, and Sadie realized she must look as swampy as she felt, but Max's expression relaxed into a more confident grin rather than a look of horror or disgust.

"You really are okay, right?" he asked. "I was worried about you."

Sadie's brows furrowed, and Max chuckled.

"What?" she asked.

"Nothing," he said, and before Sadie could press him further, Delilah chimed in.

"This is the girl from the beach? The one your sweet Penny knocked over? I swear dogs don't have any clue about their size. My two German shepherds fight over who gets to sit in my lap when we watch TV, and I have to keep reminding *both* of them that *neither* of them fit!"

Sadie dropped her head into her hands, mortified.

"Does the whole town know about—the beach?" she asked, her voice muffled in her palms.

She heard Max sigh. "Small-town living," he said. "Doesn't matter if you're a local or a tourist, any and all news travels fast."

Sadie blew out a breath, dropped her hands, and squared her shoulders. She didn't waste time on emotions like embarrassment. "It's fine," she said, jutting out her chin. "Being the center of attention is sort of my thing."

Max tilted his head to the side, an amused grin on his face. Then he lifted his hand and softly pressed his index finger to the space between Sadie's brows.

"What—what are you doing?" she asked, eyes wide.

She expected him to lower his hand, but instead he massaged the small patch of skin with his finger, and Sadie's shoulders relaxed, though she hadn't realized until then that they were pulled tight, almost to her ears.

"Maybe you do like being the star of the show," he said softly. "But I think something about today was different."

She finally came to her senses and backed away, causing

him to lower his hand. She pinched the bridge of her nose and then rubbed vigorously at the patch of skin he'd been touching, not sure if she was trying to erase the memory of his touch or the worried *eleven* that belied her bravado.

"You don't know me," Sadie told him, her jaw tight. "So please don't pretend like you do."

She pivoted back toward the counter, where Delilah patiently waited with a knowing grin on her face, though what the woman thought she knew was beyond Sadie's imagination.

"Whatever your largest iced coffee is, do you have a cup slightly *bigger* than that? And one pump of vanilla syrup." She tapped her index finger against her lips and then added, "Decaf." No reason to add extra stimulation to an already stimulating first day in town.

"How long are you in Glass Lake?" Delilah asked.

Sadie felt the telltale eleven reappear between her brows and instinctively smoothed it away with her thumb. "A month...why?"

Delilah dropped to a squat, disappearing behind the counter. A moment later, she popped back up with a box, the photo on it displaying a bright blue insulated tumbler replete with its own stainless steel straw. Judging by the size of the box, the tumbler's size was somewhere between a trenta and a Big Gulp.

"Then you're going to need this," Delilah said. "We're the only coffee establishment for miles, and while I'm sure you can brew your own, mine's better. Also, this big guy keeps your hot stuff hot and your cold stuff cold for hours—maybe even days, but no one has tested the theory yet. Plus, you get an extra punch on your frequent sipper card just for buying the tumbler, which means you get your free sip sooner, and voilà! This puppy practically pays for itself."

Sadie laughed. "How can I say no after that sales pitch?" Maybe she could learn a thing or two from Delilah's convincing delivery so she could change Alissa's mind about adding Sadie's doughnuts to the bakery menu.

"It's on me," Max said from behind her. "The tumbler and the coffee."

Delilah's brows rose, and this time Sadie took a giant step to her left, spinning only halfway so she could volley between both Delilah *and* Max.

"I'm good," Sadie said, staring at the man, his dark blue eyes so serious and inscrutable. What was his motivation here? And what did it mean if she said yes? "I'm not, like, going to sue you for your dog attacking me or anything."

Max crossed his arms. "While I *am* sorry for Penny scaring you, it wasn't an attack. She saw you. She liked you. And she wanted to make sure you *knew* that she liked you. Still, we're working on her understanding her size better, and—wait. That wasn't my point. I just…" He scrubbed a hand across his jaw. "I wanted to welcome you to Glass Lake. That's all."

The bell over the café door jangled, and Sadie let out a long breath, never dreaming she'd be so relieved to see Dr. Becca Weiland. Except, despite her always put-together attire, her perfectly coiffed ponytail with no single hair out of place, Becca hobbled through the doorway, her legs bowed and her eyes wide like she'd seen some things. Some *terrible* things…

"Oh my god," Sadie said, but Becca held up a hand to keep her from continuing.

"If you promise not to ask me anything—and I mean *anything*—about where I've been, I'll buy whatever you're about to order and *all* your coffees for the rest of the month."

Sadie grinned at her roommate, then at Max.

"I thank you for your offer of hospitality," she said to him, "but I believe you've just been outbid." This was her in with Becca. She could feel it. Sure, Sadie could have one hell of a time on her own this next month. But with a cohort, an accomplice, an unexpected friend, she had a feeling it could be so much more.

She directed her attention back to Delilah. "You heard the good doctor. And because any and all news travels fast…" She raised her brows at Max after quoting his words back to him. "I trust you will hold my roommate to her word and in return keep whatever secret she's keeping from me from the rest of the town."

"Much appreciated," Becca said from over Sadie's shoulder. "And I'll have whatever she's having. To go."

A few minutes later, Sadie held a tumbler in each hand as she grinned at Becca. "You're driving me back to the house, right?"

The other woman shook her head. "*You're* driving us back

to the house. As long as you're able to get a minivan out of a particularly tight parallel parking spot."

Becca winced, and Sadie wasn't sure if it was because of her indirect admission about her parallel parking skills or whatever was making her walk like she'd just hopped off a Clydesdale.

Sadie laughed. "Lead the way, Posh," she said as she handed Becca one of the tumblers.

Her roommate groaned but didn't protest as she slowly hobbled toward the door.

"Rain check on the coffee?" Max asked with a shrug, but Sadie politely reminded him that her coffees were basically prepurchased for the remainder of her Glass Lake stay. "Then maybe an adult beverage? Or dinner? Or are we back to my side of the beach and your side of the beach?"

Sadie took a long sip from her straw, then sighed blissfully as the ice-cold liquid hit her tongue.

"I'm not suing or pressing charges or whatever," she reminded him. Or had she not yet made that clear?

Max huffed out a laugh. "And I'm not trying to buy you off. I just—wanted to see you again."

Despite the cooling effects of her beverage, Sadie's cheeks warmed. He was cute. Sure. She'd give him that. But she was nothing more than a tourist in the town where he lived with his supposed *not*–attack dog—and daughter.

Sadie was—impermanent.

It shouldn't matter, but for some reason the thought made the hairs on the back of her neck stand up.

She worried her bottom lip between her teeth before saying, "It's a small town, right? I'm sure we'll bump into each other again. Good-bye, Max. And thank you, Delilah!" she called over her shoulder.

Once in the van, Sadie raised a brow at Becca, then dipped her gaze to Becca's lap. "First Brazilian," she said. A statement rather than a question.

Becca put her sunglasses on and kept her gaze focused straight ahead. "I found a gray hair, okay? Now—you promised. Not. Another. Word."

Sadie bit back a grin as she pulled out of the parking spot with ease. Then she mimed zipping her lips as she steered them both home.

☼

That evening, the two women again shared the glider on the screened-in porch, Becca with her legs stretched out in front of her—a bag of frozen peas between her thighs—and Sadie on the other cushion, rocking the two of them slowly as she swirled the sparkling rosé in her wineglass.

"Should we order food?" Sadie asked.

Becca huffed out a laugh. "And here I thought I'd at the very least scored a personal chef for the next four weeks."

"I bake," Sadie reminded her. "You want pastry for breakfast, lunch, and dinner? I'm your girl. But *food* food? Not so much." She finished what was left in her glass, refilled it with the bottle they'd left on the coffee table—no sense putting it back in the fridge when both of them knew they were going to finish it—and then turned toward Becca, topping off her almost empty glass as well.

"You sure you don't want to talk more about...?" Sadie nodded toward Becca's pelvic region, and Becca swatted her gaze away.

"Do *you* want to talk more about why you came into the house covered in beach less than an hour after we arrived—or about the guy at the coffee shop who couldn't take his eyes off you?"

Sadie raised a brow. "Says the woman I caught with a *naked* man when I was covered in *beach*."

Becca grimaced. "Okay. How about we just put a full moratorium on everything that happened today and start fresh? I mean, we do have a month to spend together, right? We should make the best of it."

Sadie leaned back into the glider, putting her feet to work once more, lulling them into a soft rhythm. "Why, Dr. Becca Weiland...are you saying that you want us to be—*friends*?"

Becca groaned, and Sadie waited patiently for a response.

"Fine," Becca conceded. "Before we put the *full* moratorium on today's events, I will admit that I was kind of, sort of, maybe—relieved when I saw you after my panic-induced spontaneity to get, um, waxed where I've never been waxed before. Especially when you got me out of that parking spot. And when you suggested the frozen peas and wine and didn't ask me any other questions—"

"Until now," Sadie interrupted. "I'm not the best at following the rules," she added with a wink.

"Let me finish," Becca chided, but a smile played on her lips. "I'm trying to admit that I might have been wrong about you—not just today but for all the years that we've known each other. I mean, I thought I knew my husband, and look how that turned out for me. So... fresh start?"

Sadie held up her glass. "Fresh start. On one condition..."

Becca's eyes widened, and Sadie laughed.

"It's not a big ask," Sadie assured her. "But if we're going to enjoy ourselves—like really do it up right—then I need you to turn off your mom brain, your doctor brain, and basically all the brains that might put the brakes on some good, clean fun." She waggled her brows. "And maybe a little bit of trouble." She held up her glass. "What do you say? To Becca and Sadie, a whole lotta fun and a little bit of trouble?"

Becca shook her head, and Sadie's stomach sank. Had she misread the situation?

Becca cleared her throat and raised her own glass. "To Sadie and... Posh." Her cheeks grew pink, and Sadie gasped. "I *told* you... I never had a nickname. And while I do not agree with your assessment of me, I know nicknames are actually terms of endearment and I kind of like it as a reminder of who I was before today. It's not like I'm expecting some monumental life change at the end of four weeks, but I want—something, you know? Is that weird?"

Sadie shook her head. "Not weird at all."

But before they were able to complete their toast, they heard a scream—actually something more like a whoop or holler—coming from the beach.

Though the setting sun caused a glare off the water, Sadie didn't need her contacts to be sure that what she saw through the screen was the backside of a very naked man.

Becca tossed the bag of peas to the floor and sprang up from the glider. In a matter of seconds, *both* women stood at the screen, mouths agape as they watched the man jog into the water and then dive under its surface.

Becca swallowed. "I know the ad for the rental said something about a picturesque view, but it really didn't do *this* view the justice it deserves."

Sadie laughed.

"That's your guy from this morning, isn't it?" she asked.

Becca nodded slowly. "Wait. No," she sputtered. "Not *my* guy. But it's *the* guy. I didn't mean—he's not—" But no other words came out.

"Someone has a crush," Sadie teased, then nudged Becca's shoulder with her own. "Get it, girl!"

Becca's gaze shot to Sadie. "I do *not* have a…I didn't come here to…" Her hand flew over her mouth. "He's twenty-*six*. I'll be *thirty*-six in a matter of weeks. And I'm a mom—a divorced mom. With twins. I have no business…" She trailed off.

"Sure," Sadie said. "You are *all* those things. And you're also a hot AF woman who can still Get. It. So own your hotness and crush on that baby man out there because, *damn*, woman."

Becca snorted, then covered her mouth with her hand.

"Snort away, my friend!" Once again, Sadie held up her glass. "To Sadie and *Posh*—getting into maybe a bit more trouble than expected, appreciating the view, and remembering that age is only a number and any woman—no matter what stage in her life—can still be hot as fuck and worthy of crushing on a beautiful specimen of a man who isn't afraid to share that beauty with the viewing public."

They clinked their glasses and downed the bubbly pink liquid.

Now for Sadie to find a little trouble of her own.

CHAPTER SEVEN

BECCA

Becca warily opened one eye, squinting at her phone on its charging cord next to the bed.

1:17 PM.

PM?

She bolted upright, then regretted the sudden movement as a throbbing in her head like nothing she'd experienced before made her stomach roil and her heart race.

She licked her lips, but her tongue felt dry as a tumbleweed. That was when she noticed the can of Coke next to her phone—and a Post-it on which sat two pills and a short message that said: TAKE THESE AND DRINK THE COKE. I PROMISE IT'LL BE YOUR HANGOVER MIRACLE.

Becca was certain that anything she tried to ingest would come right back up, but considering her stomach was already on the verge of revolt, she decided to give Sadie's remedy a shot.

Shot? Shots? *Shots!* There were shots last night. After the wine. After seeing Leo in his—after seeing him *swimming*.

Oh god. How drunk had she gotten last night? How much of a fool had she made of herself in front of Sadie?

It was only Becca's second day of vacation. She couldn't turn off her people-please-o-meter that easily.

Her stomach lurched, and she tossed the two pills in her mouth, then opened the can of Coke—downing it as if she'd just found a desert oasis and not once thinking about the sugar or calorie content.

When the can was empty, she set it back down on the nightstand with a shaky hand and then let loose a burp that mortified her even though no one else was in the room. Her cheeks flamed, and her hand flew over her mouth. But—the urge to pray to the porcelain god was suddenly gone.

She glanced at the empty can of soda with awe but swore she would *never* drink like that again.

She scratched the back of her head, then felt the urge to scratch another itch a bit lower down. Like—between her legs.

"You may experience a bit of itching or irritation tomorrow or the next day," Shelby had warned her before handing over a tube of aloe gel. "*Don't* scratch. Put some of this on, and then give the area a few minutes to breathe before putting your panties back on."

Becca reached over the side of the bed, her head still

throbbing a bit, and found her purse. She rummaged in it for the aloe and let out a sigh of relief when she found it. She lay back down, pulling up the thin cotton of her nightgown and shimmying out of her underwear. The cool air felt good on her irritated skin, and when she applied the gel, her whole body relaxed, melting into the mattress.

As she pulled her hand away, her finger slipped over a sensitive spot that hadn't been touched in longer than she could remember, and she let out a surprised "*Oh.*"

Becca had talked a good game about her sex life to her sister, but the truth was, she'd never... She hadn't ever tried...

Oh god. She couldn't even *think* the word, let alone do it. Could she?

She squeezed a bit more of the gel onto the tip of her finger, pulled the blanket up over her waist, and slid her hand below.

This time when she made contact, she let loose a soft moan. How was it that she was as familiar with the female body as she was yet had never explored her own?

At first, her touch was tentative, playing it safe. But when she gave herself permission to slip inside, all bets were off.

"Oh my god," she said out loud as she dipped and caressed, letting herself learn and feel and—she gasped—*enjoy.*

When she brought herself to climax, she buried her face in her pillow so as not to cry out for Sadie and all the neighbors to hear. As her heart slowed and her breathing returned to normal, she swiped a finger under her eye to find that she was crying.

When had the tears started? And why?

Maybe it was having the courage to try something new. Maybe it was that Jeff had never made her feel like *that* before. Or maybe it was learning that at least in this one little corner of her life, she could take care of herself.

Becca wasn't sure what had just happened to her, but she knew without a doubt that something inside her had been set free. Something more than an orgasm, that was.

Her tears quickly turned to laughter as she finally rose from the bed, ready to greet what was left of the day.

"Take that," she said to no one in particular.

Then she caught a glimpse of herself in the full-length mirror, and her elation quickly turned to horror as she took in the nest on her head that had been her neatly coiffed ponytail, the raccoon-like streaks of mascara under her eyes, and some sort of green stain—was that guacamole?—over her left breast on her nightgown.

She found the ponytail holder dangling from a lock of hair and attempted to tame the nest into a messy bun that didn't look so—messy. She licked her thumb and began scrubbing at the green stain but only managed to make it wetter and bigger.

Wait. Who was Becca trying to please? The only person here was her, and she'd already pleased herself quite well. So what if she wasn't the picture of perfection?

"You just had your first orgasm in *months*. Maybe even closer to a year," she said out loud, which meant *nothing*—not even the woman in the mirror—could bring her down.

✦

"Okay, what's with the goofy grin?" Sadie asked when Becca finally made it down to the kitchen for something other than Coca-Cola and ibuprofen. "My hangover concoction works, but it's not *that* good."

Becca pressed her lips together, trying *not* to smile, but she simply couldn't stop.

Sadie was cleaning the kitchen island, which looked like it had seen better days, judging by the opened pizza box with a half-eaten pizza that looked like it had been out all night, toppled-over shot glasses, the empty bottle of rosé, and a not-quite-empty bottle of sour apple schnapps.

Becca shuddered as she remembered the sweet taste of the cheap liquor, the warmth that spread through her chest as she downed what she guessed was more than a couple of shots.

"I know," Sadie said. "Gross, right? But it was all we could find in the cabinet. The owners said we were welcome to whatever nonperishables were left by them or previous renters, but I have to admit—never took you for a schnapps girl."

Despite the Coke, the pills, and brushing her teeth twice, Becca's mouth still felt like it was filled with sand, so she made a beeline for the fridge, retrieving the pitcher of iced tea. She bypassed using a glass and instead drank straight from the rim of the pitcher itself, for the moment not caring about the loud gulps coming from her throat.

When she'd drained the pitcher of its contents, she set it down on the island and swiped her forearm across the dripping tea mustache she'd just created.

Sadie stopped what she was doing and crossed her arms, giving Becca the once-over.

"That was impressive, Posh. Almost as impressive as your shot-downing skills."

Becca shuddered again. "Can you please never say the words *shot* or *schnapps* again? Like, *ever*?"

Sadie narrowed her eyes, still sizing her up. "Something's different about you. I can't put my finger on it, though. I mean, other than you getting rip-roaring drunk for what I'm guessing was your first time in a *long* time yesterday... If I wasn't sure that you passed out alone in your room, I'd say you got lucky last night."

Becca's whole body lit up from within as she remembered what it felt like to give herself both pleasure and release.

Sadie gasped. "Your hair is down!"

Becca ran a finger through her still-damp hair. "I just showered," she said defensively. "I don't usually put it up until it's dry." The truth was, she usually combed her leave-in conditioner through her hair and then immediately pulled it into her signature do, being able to make the ponytail tighter when it was wet.

Sadie tapped a finger against her lips then nodded at Becca's attire.

"Yeah, but you're just wearing a T-shirt and cotton shorts and"—she dramatically gasped again—"rubber flip-flops I *know* cost like three bucks at Old Navy because I have a *ton* of them."

Becca sighed. "I wasn't sure how clean the showers would be here, so they were intended to be my shower shoes, but I don't know. I think they're kind of cute." She glanced down at the bright yellow shoes, admiring how nice her pedicured toes looked in them.

Sadie laughed. "Oh my god, did you think we were staying in a college dorm using a communal shower? You're not going to get athlete's foot in a vacation rental."

"I know," Becca admitted with a groan. "I think we've already established that I'm sometimes a little too quick to judge, but there's nothing wrong with being prepared for *what-if?* But the shower was actually very clean and very nice and—"

Sadie grabbed a piece of pizza from the open box and tore off a bite.

Becca tried not to dry-heave.

Then Sadie pointed at her with the partially eaten piece. "You *did* get lucky, didn't you? You're all relaxed and casual, and I know for a fact you do your ponytails wet. So *spill*, Posh."

Becca felt heat creep from her abdomen all the way up her neck and to her cheeks. She had *zero* poker face, so what was the point in trying to hide. Plus, she kind of *wanted* to tell *someone*. Why not Sadie?

"Okay," she relented. "Fine. I—I might have . . . I mean no

one else was with me so I...I pleasured myself!" she finally blurted out, then squeezed her eyes shut. "Twice. Once in the bed and once in the shower, and oh my god, Sadie...I never knew I was capable of that."

She thought of all the times Alissa had gone on about her favorite battery-powered devices and how in her head she'd actually pitied her sister for not having a partner to take care of her needs like Becca had.

But as much as she'd thought she loved Jeff, he'd never made her feel like she had upstairs in a stranger's bed—and again in a stranger's surprisingly clean shower.

Sadie still hadn't responded, so Becca slowly opened one eye and then the other. Sadie began to slow clap, a huge approving grin spread across her face.

Becca rolled her eyes, but inside she was running circles through the house, screaming for joy like her twins did whenever they had space enough to run.

"Dr. Weiland," Sadie began in a mildly accusing tone. "Are you insinuating that while you are up to your elbows in vaginas day in and day out, you've *never* plunged into your own?"

She waggled her brows, and Becca covered her wide-open mouth with her palm.

"I've never...I mean, I'm not—comfortable in my own skin. I'm not some twenty-six-year-old beautiful man swimming naked on a private beach or—or—or *you*." Sadie's eyes softened when Becca said this. "Your confidence is intimidating. You remind me of my sister, and I've always envied her ability to just be *her*. I guess maybe that's why it's always been hard for me to like you." She shook out her shoulders. "Wow. This whole masturbation thing is apparently my truth serum."

Sadie grabbed the two shot glasses off the counter, and Becca help up a hand in protest. "Oh god. No more shots. You promised."

Sadie carried the shot glasses to the sink, rinsed them out, and then filled them each with water from the tap.

"Here," she said, handing one to Becca. "It's a metaphor. I just want to toast the woman who's finally getting to know herself—and to maybe admit that I admire her too."

Becca's heart squeezed as Sadie held up her metaphorical shot.

"To masturbation," Sadie said. "The truth serum we all need!"

Becca snorted but did not cover her mouth and instead held up her glass as well. "To masturbation!"

Two words she never imagined she'd say in the company of a woman she never thought she'd like.

Two surprises she never imagined finding in a sleepy beach town where she never intended to be.

CHAPTER EIGHT

SADIE

The lights in the house flickered as the storm raged outside later that night.

"Do you think we'll lose power?" Sadie called over her shoulder. "Because if we finally agree on something to watch only to get thrown into a blackout, I'm really going to be annoyed."

"Um…" Becca called back from the kitchen. "We may have bigger things to worry about than just the power."

Sadie spun on her knees, leaning over the back of the couch, her eyes widening as she saw Becca *standing* on the kitchen island, pressing her fingers to a wet spot on the kitchen ceiling.

"We have a *leak*?" Sadie asked. "But this is a two-story!"

"Yes to the former, and not exactly to the latter. The bedroom and loft are above the living room, but the kitchen is right under the roof." Water dripped from under Becca's fingers. "We should call the owners, right?"

Sadie checked the nonexistent watch on her wrist. "It's pretty late, isn't it? I mean, we ate at least two hours ago. Or was it three?"

Becca crossed her arms and glared at Sadie. "How do you *not* wear a watch?" But before she could scold Sadie more, the drip turned into more of a dribble.

Sadie scrambled off the couch and grabbed the pot from the stove they'd used to make dinner. And by *they*, she meant spiralizing zucchini herself and experimenting with different herbs and spices to create her own tomato sauce. She might have acted a bit precious about *having* to cook for the two of them, but the truth was, she kind of loved it—figuring out the sauce with no direction and using nothing more than her palette to test and retest until she thought she had it right. The proof was in Becca's reaction after her first bite.

"Oh. My. God," Becca had said with a full mouth of zucchini noodles. Then she moaned.

"Are you sure you're not taking care of business under the table there?" Sadie had teased as the two women sat opposite each other at the table in the dining area portion of the open great room.

Becca had snorted—and also hadn't turned crimson with embarrassment. Progress.

"It's *almost* that good," Becca told her. "But seriously, Sadie. You say you only bake and then you create something like this on the first try? I call BS."

"You mean bullshit?" Sadie prodded, brows raised. "Come on, Posh. Lemme hear it. Just once. Say something naughty."

Then Becca's cheeks *had* gone a shade of pink.

Sadie had decided to let her off the hook. After all, the woman had only just learned the art of self-pleasure earlier that day. There was plenty of time left to loosen all of her tight spots.

Except now, as the good doctor stood atop the island, Sadie could see all the muscles in her body tense as she watched what was getting closer to a steady stream of water.

Sadie threw the pot onto the growing puddle on the island, and the two of them listened to the drips clank against the metal in rapid succession.

"Okay. We need to call someone," Becca said, lowering herself to her knees and then hopping off the island.

Sadie glanced at her bare wrist again. "Okay, but don't Andrea and Ted live like ninety minutes away? And I don't know a whole lot about roofs, but I don't think you're supposed to fix them in the middle of a thunderstorm. What about your naked houseboy? He's local, right? We can call him in the morning when the storm lets up." She glanced at the water still dripping into the pot. "I guess that means we have to take shifts keeping an eye on the leak, right?"

Becca's eyes brightened, and she grinned. "I'll be right back!" She spun on her heel and strode out of the room, leaving Sadie scratching her head as to why her perfectly polished and organized roommate would be *excited* about keeping an eye on a roof leak.

Only when she returned less than a minute later did Sadie fully understand.

Becca held up a small dry-erase board, complete with marker and eraser.

"It's magnetic," she said. "So we can put it on the fridge. We can list the shifts…" She glanced at the pot. "I'm thinking maybe every two hours it will need to be dumped? That's also a good chunk of time to sleep. When I was a resident, I went days without sleeping more than that each night, so it's totally doable. And if the rain lets up, we might be able to stretch the shifts a little longer!"

The woman was positively giddy as she slapped the board onto the refrigerator door and began listing two-hour increments, placing Becca's name, then Sadie's, by every other one.

"I'm not even sure where to begin," Sadie started. "How about with *why* you brought a dry-erase board on *vacation.*"

Sadie strode to the sink, pressing her palms to the counter as she stared out at the lake, its choppy waves visible with every burst of lightning.

"We're *living* here for four weeks," Becca said, continuing with her chart. "Organizational issues are bound to come up. I mean, here we are barely through day two, and I've already found the perfect use for it. You're welcome, by the way."

Thunder crashed again, making both women jump. Then Sadie gasped.

"Holy shit!"

This got Becca's attention. She spun to face Sadie.

"What happened? Did the house get hit? Are we on fire?

I located all the extinguishers in the house when I first got here, so if it's small, I think we can handle it."

Okay, who *was* this woman? Sadie was pretty sure that if she told Becca that it was an explosion rather than fire, she'd escort Sadie to the bomb shelter she built after she unpacked the day before.

"We're not *hit*," Sadie said. "But that tent is still out there. Whoever is in it cannot be in great shape right now. I mean, if our *house* is leaking, what does that say for the person trying to sleep under a dome of nylon?"

"What tent?" Becca asked, sidling up to Sadie at the window.

Sadie sighed. She'd made it two days without having to talk about Max or his dog or thinking for several brief seconds that she was going to *die*. But it would be hard to bring up the tent without bringing up the rest.

"When we got here yesterday...when you and I weren't..." She groaned. "I didn't want to face you, so I headed around back to check out the beach. A little ways off from our yard, I saw this tent, and because I was looking *that* way..." She pointed to the right of the window. "I didn't see the *dog* coming from the other direction. It knocked me down, and that's why I came into the house looking like I did. Also, the owner of the dog is the guy from the coffee shop, and that's all I'm going to say. Back to the moratorium."

Becca opened her mouth to respond, but the sky lit up once more.

"See?" Sadie said. "Right there!"

Right—it looked like—where the lightning hit.

Sadie might have thought Becca was a bit off her rocker suggesting the house might be on fire, but she guessed the tent occupant was not sitting at the ready with a bevy of fire extinguishers.

"We need to go make sure they're okay!" Becca said, reaching under the sink and grabbing a Maglite and a first-aid kit.

"Yeah," Sadie said. "Sure. But one quick question... How did you know those things were down there?"

Becca bit her bottom lip and gave Sadie a nervous smile.

"You—brought them from home. Of course. I'll try to find an umbrella, and you can lead the way."

"Front hall closet, top shelf. There's a regular-sized and golf-sized, both with rubber coating on the top metal point thingy so it doesn't conduct electricity," Becca said, then shrugged.

Sadie shook her head and laughed.

"You are one of a kind, Dr. Weiland."

But the truth was, amid a violent storm, a leaking house, and bringing up the scare she'd had yesterday on the beach, Sadie felt safer than she had in longer than she could remember.

BECCA

Sadie held the umbrella over both women as Becca guided them to the tent with the flashlight. Who in their right mind would camp on a night like this? It was a private beach, after all, so whoever was in that tent surely had a house into which they could retreat. Yet Becca could see flashlight movement inside, indicating whoever was in there was determined to rough it, which was fine. But she had to at least make sure they were okay.

Becca recalled her first year of residency in obstetrics. Barely a month into her position at the hospital, she was finishing rounds for her attending physician when she came across a woman in early labor who was experiencing excessive bleeding, putting both her and her baby in distress. She'd had undiagnosed placenta previa, and Becca told her the baby had to be delivered immediately via C-section.

But the mother had refused.

"I don't want to be cut open!" she'd insisted. "I don't want to be cut open!"

She'd paged Dr. Han, her attending, and met her outside the room.

"The patient is refusing the surgery," Becca told her. "If she doesn't consent, there's nothing we can do, right?"

The other doctor didn't waste even a second to give Becca a response. Instead, she strode through the patient's door, and ninety seconds later, the patient was being wheeled to the operating room.

Becca had stood there in the OR, frozen as she watched Dr. Han calmly perform the surgery, deftly saving both the mother and her new son.

"What did you say to convince her?" Becca asked after she and Dr. Han had both scrubbed out.

Dr. Han lowered her surgical mask and crossed her arms.

"It doesn't matter *what* I said. What works for one patient won't work for the next. What matters is that I said what needed to be said, that I didn't give up—no matter how stubborn the patient might have been—on what *I* knew would save both that mother and her child. The second you give up on preserving life—even if you think your hands are tied—that's the second you stop being a doctor, Ms. Weiland. I suggest you make a decision right here and now where you stand on the issue."

She'd left Becca standing there, speechless, as *Ms. Weiland* echoed in her head.

Ms. Not Dr.

For a brief second she'd considered giving up not just on her patients but on medicine altogether. What if her hesitation had cost that patient her life? Her child's life? She'd gotten lucky that night. But if she wanted to be a doctor, she couldn't rely on luck again. She couldn't give up on herself or her career, no matter how scared she was. Not when she'd come that far.

If it meant begging a patient to go through with a life-saving procedure, she'd do it. If it meant sleeping in the on-call room even after her shift had ended just to make sure a patient made it through the night, so be it. And if it meant that even when she was technically out of the office for four entire weeks, she checked up on stubborn neighbors who willingly put their lives in danger during a summer storm, then that was what she would do.

Maybe Becca Weiland was still figuring out who she was now that *Mrs.* no longer preceded her name. But she realized now she'd always be a doctor—and a damned good one too.

"What do we do?" Sadie yelled over the whipping wind and rain once they'd made it to the tent. "Knock?"

Becca had already dropped the first-aid kit onto the grass and was fumbling with the zipper at the tent's entrance. But her hands were soaked and her movements clumsy.

"Are you okay in there?" she called out but could barely hear her own voice.

When no one responded, she yanked frantically on the zipper again. The tent's occupant must have done the same because this time it flew open with unexpected force, causing Becca to pitch forward and the person inside to fall back.

Suddenly she was straddling Leo Beckett—who was fully clothed, thank god—and the guy had the nerve to smile at her.

"It's nice to see you, *Thirty-six-in-fifteen-days*," he said. "But you're kind of letting the storm in."

For a second, Becca lost the ability to form coherent speech, but then her eyes caught the gash on his right cheek, and her reaction to his flirting melted away as she went into full-fledged doctor mode.

"You're bleeding!" she said, crawling off him.

"Am I?" he asked, brows furrowed. "Must have happened when I stepped out to anchor a stake that kept coming loose. Lots of debris flying around out there."

He raised a hand toward his cheek, but Becca swatted it away. "Don't touch it! It needs to be cleaned. You might even need stitches."

"Everyone okay in there?" Sadie called from where she squatted under the umbrella just outside the tent. "Oh! Naked guy!" she added. "So that's what you look like with clothes!"

Leo laughed, but Becca was already rummaging through the first-aid kit. There was barely room to move, though, in what was clearly a *one*-man tent, and even if she found the antiseptic and gloves—there they were—being able to see and properly irrigate the wound would be next to impossible in this space.

"We're going to need to go inside your house to take care of this," she told him. "I need better light and space, and a trip to the ER might be in order if—"

"This *is* my house," Leo said, obeying the doctor's orders and lowering his hand.

Becca's eyes widened as she took in the space that included Leo, a large backpack, sleeping bag, and lantern. That was it.

She shook her head. "Not tonight it isn't. You're coming with us."

His smile faltered, and a muscle ticked in his jaw. "I'm

fine, Becca. Just leave me an antiseptic wipe or something and a Band-Aid, and get back to *your* house. I can take care of myself."

Say what needs to be said. Don't give up, no matter how stubborn the patient is.

"Yeah, well, I'm a doctor, and that cut needs more than a Band-Aid. Plus there's a leak in the kitchen ceiling. I was going to text you anyway after I checked on this crazy neighbor of mine who was sleeping in a tent during a storm, so you might as well come and take a look. If the house needs *anything*, just shoot you a text, right?"

Leo sighed. "There's really a leak?"

Becca narrowed her eyes. "No. I'm lying about a leak just so I can lure you back to my vacation rental and have my way with you. I mean—as far as fixing your wound. Not...You know. I wasn't saying…"

Oh god. What happened to her unflappable doctor mode? He was turning her into a stammering teenager when all she really wanted to do was help him, not *have her way with him* like she had her way with herself in both the bed and the shower.

His devil-may-care smile returned. "Okay," he relented. "I'll take a look at the leak and let you take a look at what I'm sure is a silly little scratch on my cheek. But then I'm coming back to *my* place, okay?"

A clap of thunder shook the ground beneath them as lightning lit up the sky.

Becca gasped and slammed the kit shut. "Deal!"

A minute later, the three of them were running through the wet sand and grass back to the bungalow. Once inside, they were all dripping wet, the golf umbrella no match for the growing storm.

CHAPTER NINE

LEO

"Y ou're drenched," Becca told him, and Leo laughed.

"Yeah, well, so are the two of you. So much for rescuing me from the storm, huh?"

He tried to keep it light, but when he laughed, his smile quickly turned to a wince. Maybe he hadn't noticed the cut yet when Becca and Sadie showed up, but now that he wasn't trying to keep his tent from blowing into the lake and had a second to think, the sting had finally set in.

Becca's eyes darkened. "See?" she said. "Not just a s-s-scratch." Her teeth chattered.

"*You* need to change," he said.

"*You* need to let me dress that wound," she countered.

"You two are *adorable* when you flirt," Sadie added, staring at the two of them with her arms crossed.

Even though her lips were turning purple from the cold,

Leo bit back a smile as the skin on Becca's neck turned pink, the flush running all the way up to her cheeks.

"We weren't…" Becca said. "I mean how can you say…?"

"It's just good bedside manner," he told Sadie. Then he turned his attention back to Becca. *Dr.* Becca. "Don't worry, Doc. I know the difference." He nodded toward the front door. "Andrea and Ted keep some spare clothes in the entryway closet just in case—well, probably for situations like this. I'll just grab something and change in the bathroom. Then you can have your way with me." He winked at her and strode away as her mouth fell open, not waiting for her to respond.

Once in the bathroom with one of Ted's Hawaiian shirts and a pair of board shorts—seriously, *that* was what the guy left in case of emergency?—Leo let out a long breath, bracing his hands on the counter.

Of *course* the beautiful, sexy woman he'd met while wearing his birthday suit was a doctor. He had nothing against successful women. On the contrary, it only made Becca more attractive. But women—okay, one *particular* woman— seemed to have something against a guy who put passion before paycheck. Granted, spending the summer living in a tent on the beach wasn't for everyone, but then again, Leo Beckett wasn't for everyone, and that was fine by him.

He glanced up at himself in the mirror, his dark hair soaked and the gash on his cheek looking angrier than he'd anticipated.

"Shit," he hissed. He knew someone who'd take this as an

opportunity to give him an earful for how irresponsibly he lived his life when he was doing just fine. He made a living. He supported himself. Wasn't that all that mattered? Why did everyone seem to have an opinion about everyone else when they clearly had their own shit to deal with?

He sighed, then peeled off his soaked clothes, and exchanged them for Ted's tourist trap of an outfit. The shorts were a little big, but the drawstring took care of that. And the shirt? He squinted at his reflection. Yep. Those hula dancers were definitely topless.

He chuckled, guessing this was all par for the course.

When he made his way back to the living room, Becca was already there, but Sadie hadn't yet returned.

He padded quietly into the room, admiring for a few seconds as Becca lined up her medical supplies on the coffee table. Her dark wet hair looked as if she'd combed through it, but it wasn't pulled into the taut ponytail she'd worn the day before.

Her shoulders shook, and she paused what she was doing to rub her hands up and down her forearms even though they were covered in a hoodie that read I AM GROOT.

She was beautiful, but the tiny bit of whimsy in showing off a fandom made her downright adorable. Watching her concentrate was also extremely endearing, especially when he realized she was doing it for him.

Fine, she was a doctor preparing to care for a patient who just happened to *be* him, but Leo wasn't one to dwell on technicalities.

"So do you need my license and insurance card?" he asked, and she gasped as her head shot up, and her relaxed posture switched to ramrod straight. "Sorry. Didn't mean to scare you."

"How long have you been standing there?" she asked, absently patting down her still-soaked hair.

"Just a few seconds," he lied. "I have both, though. License and insurance—just in case you thought a guy living on the beach would be without." His jaw tightened as he realized his attempt at playful had instead gone the way of defensive.

"I wasn't thinking anything, actually," Becca said. "Where you choose to live is your business, not mine." He heard no judgment in her matter-of-fact tone.

He did hear water rushing overhead and glanced up at the ceiling.

"Not the storm," Becca said, answering his unasked question. "Just Sadie using the upstairs shower."

So it was just the two of them for the time being. The thought sent an unexpected tingle up his spine, buoying him forward until he was sitting next to her on the couch.

"Does that mean you're ready to have your way with me, Doc?"

Becca cleared her throat. "No license or insurance necessary," she replied, her words clipped. "As long as you understand that I'm simply a neighbor doing a favor for *another* neighbor and that I—in no official capacity—am treating you in any physician-patient sort of way. If you want a professional medical opinion—one where license and insurance are required—then I'm happy to take you to the ER." She paused for a beat. "But you should really treat the wound sooner rather than later so it's less likely to scar."

He leaned forward, his lips a breath away from her ear. She smelled like rain and summer with a hint of citrus, and he wondered if she'd been wearing the scent before she'd gone outside or if she'd put it on when she'd changed.

"Are you afraid I won't be pretty anymore if I'm scarred?" he whispered.

She shivered, but he didn't think she was cold anymore.

What was he doing? She'd already made it clear she thought he was a boy—a *houseboy* at that—so why was he flirting when she clearly wasn't interested?

She swallowed.

"We're all scarred in one way or another," she said, a slight tremor in her voice. "It's the beauty beneath that matters, right?"

Wait...what? She was supposed to come back with some clinical, doctor-like response to put him in his place, but instead this felt—real. *Vulnerable.* Which made him retreat.

Leo backed away and took a deep breath through his nose, trying to erase the scent of her with whatever else was in the air, but it was as if she filled the entire space despite the two-story ceiling or still-opened door to the screened-in porch.

"We should probably get this over with so I can check out that leak and get back to my—get back home," he said coolly.

"Right," Becca said. "Of course." In her gloved hand, she held up a syringe with what looked like a curved spout—or else one messed up looking needle.

"What the hell is that?" Leo asked, flinching backward.

Becca laughed. "Saline solution. I need to irrigate the wound so I can see how deep it is and to make sure it doesn't get infected. It'll sting a little because of the salt, but trust me when I say that it's better than what I'll have to do if infection sets in. *Then* we get into debridement, which includes scraping out the dead and infected tissue, and I might also have to—"

"Okay!" Leo interrupted, then cleared his throat, bringing his voice back to its normal, *deeper* register. "I mean, okay. I was just asking. I'm not afraid of needles or anything. I just usually like to buy a girl dinner first before we get to syringes and irrigation."

Becca narrowed her eyes, then flicked the curved tip of the syringe. "See? Just plastic. But you might want to close your eye since the wound is so close. Unless your vision needs clearing up as well?"

"Nope," he said, closing his eyes. He could see her just fine. Her wet hair, her dewy skin, those soft lips. And that look in her eyes reminding him that she saw him as nothing more than a houseboy.

"Also, just in case you have a latex allergy, these are nitrile gloves," she said, a second before he felt the cool touch of her nitrile-covered fingers on his skin.

He winced when the solution first hit the wound.

"Sorry," she said softly. "It's been a while since I've done ER triage. I might be a little rusty."

"It's fine," he said. "Just didn't know it was coming. Maybe a warning next time. You know … should you have to do triage on me again."

She was lightly blotting the dripping solution with what felt like gauze.

"Do you have a habit of getting yourself into situations that require triage?" she asked.

For a second he thought of telling her about the myriad trips his parents—and often his older brother—took with him to the ER throughout his childhood. He could have mentioned the time when he was four and tried to jump from his bed to his brother's—because the floor, of course, was hot lava—and miscalculated the distance only to face-plant on his brother's metal bed frame, cutting his lip open and needing four stitches. Then there was the time his brother and dad got into one of their usual arguments, his brother speeding off in their dad's car while six-year-old Leo chased after him on his bike, only to wipe out in a pothole, resulting in a broken arm and fractured rib. Hell, he could have thrown in that really shitty night last year when he'd gotten into his first—and hopefully last—drunken bar brawl, which ended with a concussion, a broken nose, and him almost losing one of his first clients for his new business— Deputy Derek Dempsey, his arresting officer.

Yep. Leo Beckett's life was chock-full of situations requiring triage, but the doctor sitting in front of him didn't need his résumé. She just needed to treat him and send him on his way.

"Nah," he lied. "I pretty much walk the straight and narrow. Storm just got out of hand tonight."

He felt her pinch his skin together. Then a few seconds later, she let go, and this time he felt a pulling sensation.

"All done," she said. "The cut was deep but nice and symmetrical. The glue should start peeling off in a few days, but maybe take a day off from the—um—skinny-dipping, just to keep it dry for the first twenty-four hours."

He blinked his eye open and raised his brows.

"Should I worry about what kind of glue you just used?"

Becca huffed out a laugh. "It's *surgical* glue."

"And you just carry that with you wherever you go?"

She shrugged. "We're here for a month, so I came prepared. You're welcome, by the way. For the *non*professional treatment that would have cost you a few hundred bucks if you'd have gone to the ER."

She peeled off one glove, turning it inside out. Then he watched as she did the same with the other glove, wrapping the first one inside the second. Everything else already sat sealed in a medical waste bag on the coffee table.

"You are just full of surprises, aren't you, Doc?" he asked.

She shook her head. "Actually...I'm not. I am the least surprising person you will ever meet. I do everything by the book. I do exactly what's expected of me. And I'm super predictable. It's probably why my husband—*ex*-husband—took to swiping left and right instead of turning his attention to the woman sleeping next to him in his bed."

She gasped and threw a hand over her mouth.

Leo gently wrapped his fingers around her wrist and pulled her hand away.

"Becca... It's *okay*."

"No," she said, an added vigor to her head shaking this time. "It's *not*. I don't even know you, and I keep spewing all this word vomit every time I see you."

Leo chuckled. "I guess it's better than any other sort of vomit, right? And if I'm being honest, I kind of like it... The words you spew. Not the other stuff." He let out a nervous laugh and shook his own head. Apparently he had zero game around her, but it didn't change that she somehow felt compelled to confide in him or that he enjoyed it. He'd never had that kind of relationship with a woman before—or anyone, if he was being honest. Leo Beckett was the type of guy who liked to *do* more than *say*. Hence the broken nose and overnight stay in jail a year back. Maybe he wasn't the best at expressing what was on *his* mind, but he sure as hell liked hearing what was on hers.

"How's our patient?" he heard from over his shoulder. "Aside from wearing that obscene shirt, I'm guessing he's doing a little bit better than our ceiling." Sadie laughed, and Leo suddenly remembered he'd been sitting here, letting Becca take care of him, all while wearing a shirt full of topless women.

Becca pressed her lips into a smile. "Saved by the room-mate," she said under her breath, but Leo still heard.

"I should check on the leak anyway," he said, standing up and brushing off his board shorts. "Thank you, Doc," he added. "You're not rusty at all."

He moved toward the kitchen, where Sadie stood behind the center island, her eyes volleying from the steady stream falling from above to the half-filled pot below.

He'd been expecting drips, but this was a small fountain.

"Shit," he hissed. "This—is not great. I'm going to have to call a contractor in the morning. I could go up on the roof now and see if I can figure out a temporary fix, but without enough light and the storm seeming in no mood to let up anytime soon..."

Sadie waved him off. "We knew there'd be nothing you could do at night. And I'm sure there's no way the doc's going to let you up on the roof anyway..."

He glanced back at Becca, who was still in her triage spot on the couch.

"Used an emergency to lure me into your home even though you knew there was nothing I could do, did you?"

Becca stood and squared her shoulders, striding toward the kitchen. "Maybe if you weren't being so stubborn and insisting on staying in that ridiculous tent..."

Leo cleared his throat. "Right. Well, since there's nothing else for me to do here, I should be getting back to my ridiculous tent."

"Wait!" Sadie said, grabbing his shoulder. "You should just crash here tonight."

"What?" he said, just as Becca said the same thing.

Sadie shrugged. "We have a perfectly dry couch. And since you *are* technically in charge of maintaining the house, we can split the shifts in three as far as who's watching the leak. Feels like a win-win-*win* to me."

Leo sighed. He *was* responsible for maintaining the house. And Becca *had* just saved him a nice chunk of change in avoiding a trip to the ER.

"Yeah. Okay," he said. "I'll stay and help out, but I'll sleep outside on the porch." It was close enough to sleeping outside in his ridiculous tent.

"Whatever floats your boat!" Sadie said with a grin, then yawned. "I'm beat. Okay if I sleep the first shift?"

Becca nodded, but she was staring at *him*.

"You should sleep, too, after what you probably went through out there tonight. Storm's been raging for hours."

Leo let out a long breath, exhaustion finally setting in. While he didn't want to admit she was right, he really could use an hour or two of uninterrupted sleep without the side of his tent whipping in the wind as he tried to anchor it back down.

"Okay," he relented. "But I'll take the next shift." He pulled his phone out of his pocket. "Still has some juice left. I'll set an alarm for...two hours?"

"Make it three," Becca said. "I'm not really that tired."

Not too long after that, Leo set himself up with a make-shift bed on the porch floor, the sound of the rain lulling him to sleep. He woke with a start sometime after that. He wasn't sure if it had been minutes or hours—or if what had woken him had been the storm or something he couldn't remember from a dream.

He propped himself up on his elbow and checked his phone. He still had just over an hour to go, but before he could roll over and fall back asleep, a flicker of light caught his eye, and he pushed himself to sitting. He saw the flash-light beam as a figure headed up the stairs, and then—as a bolt of lightning briefly lit up the house—he caught a glimpse of the doctor's *naked* form as she padded back up to her room.

Predictable, his *ass*. This woman was, indeed, full of surprises.

What wasn't surprising at all? There was no way in hell Leo Beckett was falling back asleep tonight.

CHAPTER TEN

SADIE

Sadie strode down from the loft just after sunrise to check the kitchen leak. The storm had tapered off over an hour before, so she'd emptied the pot into the sink, set it back under the increasingly slowing drip, and then allowed herself to go back to sleep, setting her alarm to go off just before the end of her shift. Only she hadn't needed the alarm to wake her, not when she could hear what sounded like someone hammering inside her brain.

"What the actual...?" A string of superlatives rattled off in her head as she flew out of bed.

Lucky for her, the loft was over the living room, which was practically the same room as the kitchen, and *someone*—she guessed it was their injured overnight guest—was already up on the kitchen roof taking care of business. With a hammer. At six o'clock in the morning.

She glanced back up to where Becca's bedroom door was still closed, no discernable movement coming from the room, which was much better guarded from outside noise. *Not* that Sadie was complaining. She'd happily taken the loft, after all. But come *on*. The storm was over. Did Leo have to get started so early?

She shuffled into the kitchen, her eyes still groggy with sleep. The storm had woken her on and off throughout the night so that she'd only truly fallen into a deep sleep once it had let up. And that was barely two hours ago.

She scratched absently at her neck, her finger catching on the tag of her tank top—which she'd apparently thrown on inside out *and* backward before heading downstairs. She adjusted her glasses on the bridge of her nose—she needed coffee before putting in her contacts—and glanced down at the cotton shorts she'd pulled on as well, silently commending herself for the second garment being not only right side out but also the tag in the back, where it was supposed to be.

She yawned and grabbed the travel mug from where it sat rinsed beside the sink. She could hop in Becca's van and head to Cool Beans for some of Delilah's coffee, but that would mean fixing her tank and putting on a bra as well as considering what to do with what she was sure was a crazy nest of bedhead. She patted her head with her palm, nodding to herself in confirmation that whatever was going on with her hair was so *not* appropriate for public viewing.

Another yawn stopped her mid-thought, after which she rummaged through the cabinet and then the refrigerator until she found a packet of ground coffee from, of course, *Cool Beans.* Looked like everyone supported local around here, and Sadie grinned at the thought. While she didn't love the idea of living somewhere where everyone knew everyone's business—hello, she grew up in a Jewish family in a predominantly Jewish suburb—there was something to be said about the feeling of comradery or connectedness she'd felt at the coffee shop the other day.

Until Max had walked in. Why did that man keep turning up when she was at her worst, either paralyzed with fear or sweaty and out of breath after a mile-long walk in the wrong shoes with zero hydration?

Well, he'd missed her drenched from the storm last night, so ha! One point for Sadie Bloom—not that anyone was keeping score.

She filled the coffee maker and set it to brewing, only snarling a couple more times at the pounding of the hammer above before her much-needed elixir was ready for consumption.

There was no vanilla syrup—something she *would* remedy when she was presentable enough to head to town—so she opted for sugar instead, sighing with pleasure as she finally took her first sip.

THWACK! THWACK! THWACK! THWACK!

Sadie's sigh morphed into a groan. It was time to check on

Leo and thank him for fixing the leak but also ask him *why* for the love of god he had to do it at the butt crack of dawn.

She slid into a pair of flip-flops that were at the back door, then stepped out onto the covered porch. Leo's bedding supplies were neatly folded and set atop the glider. Well, at least the guy could clean up after himself.

While the clear sky above made it seem almost impossible there had been such a violent storm last night, Sadie's foot squishing into the muddy grass was a wonderful reminder. She yelped as she slid, righted herself, then slid again—her coffee sloshing over the top of her mug as she came to a stop halfway to the splits. Why hadn't she put the lid on?

That was when the hammering on the roof ceased, and Sadie's eyes met *not* Leo's but—of *course*—Max's.

He squinted at her, hammer raised in his frozen hand.

"Leo called about the leak, said you needed it fixed ASAP, so I came right over. It was either now or wait until after my official jobs today, and I didn't want to take a chance of another storm making things worse."

Sadie wanted to say something in response, but she was afraid that even a single word would throw her off balance and send her face-first—or ass-first—into the mud. The jury was still out on which way her center of gravity leaned.

"Are you okay down there?" He used his hand to shield his eyes from the sun.

"Yes?" she finally called back, and when the word didn't send her careening to the swamp below her feet, she took it as a sign that the universe was on *her* side today.

Slowly she inched her feet back together, salvaging as much coffee as she could in the process and somehow *not* letting whatever spilled land on her tank.

Her tank. Oh god, her *backward*, inside-out tank, which was doing nothing to hide her braless breasts beneath.

Her 1980s thick-as-Coke-bottle glasses.

Her *hair*.

She took a step back toward the house, and as she slipped once more—barely catching herself before the worst could happen—her coffee-holding hand flew into the air, tossing the entirety of its contents onto the grass behind her.

"*Seriously?*" she said aloud. "You!" she added, pointing up at the man on the roof. "You are like the angel of doom or something!"

But instead of looking wounded, Max had the audacity to laugh.

"Then I guess you don't care that I have an iced coffee with one pump of vanilla waiting for you in my truck? It's *not* an attempt to buy you off, by the way, for the dog situation *or* for maybe waking you up this morning. It's just coffee, okay? That's what people do around here. They buy each other a cup of coffee. Not that you have to buy *me* one. I did that for myself. Brought one for your friend, too, so it's not like this is—I mean I'm not coming on to you or anything."

Butterflies danced in Sadie's stomach, which she chalked up to the heart-stopping fear she had of attempting another step. It had nothing to do with the man's mildly adorable awkwardness.

"Meet me at the front door in *five* minutes," she said, sliding one foot to the side and then the other. She'd moonwalk her way back into the house if she had to, as long as she stayed upright. "*With* the coffee," she added, then let out a relieved breath when her fingers met the door handle of the screened-in porch.

Sadie kicked off her muddy flip-flops, then hightailed it into the house and through the first-floor bathroom door.

She let out a squeak when she caught sight of herself in the bathroom mirror.

Of *course* he wasn't coming on to her. She looked like she'd slept inside a wind tunnel. The backward shirt she could fix—and *did*—and she had just enough time to run up to the loft and throw on a bra before she heard a soft knock on the door.

"Shit!"

She pulled off her glasses and squinted, deciding that sight was better than taking a tumble down the stairs, and pushed them back on.

She finger-combed her hair as she took the stairs two at a time, all the while asking herself *why* she even cared what Max thought of her, then reasoned that she wouldn't want anyone she barely knew seeing her fresh out of bed after being rudely awakened by a hammer at sunrise.

She took a steadying breath, hand on the front doorknob, and then finally pulled it open—but only a crack.

"Show me the coffee," she said coolly.

He laughed, and she spotted a dimple in his left cheek she hadn't noticed before. Then he held up a drink carrier that contained two iced coffees, just like he'd promised.

"No dog?" Sadie added, her heart rate increasing just at the mention of the furry beast.

"No dog," he confirmed.

When she finally opened the door all the way, she startled to find Becca standing next to Max, slowly jogging in place, an iced coffee in her hand as she stared at her watch.

"Aaaand, five miles. Done!" She held up her coffee and grinned at Max. "Thanks for this. Just need to run in and grab my water bottle first." Then she turned her attention to Sadie. "I'll get out of your hair and into the shower so you two can catch up." She winced and leaned forward, whispering in Sadie's hair, "Speaking of hair, honey, take this."

Becca's hand was on Sadie's, a hair tie slipping off Becca's fingers and onto Sadie's wrist before her roommate jogged past her and into the house.

"Okay," she said, ushering Max inside. "So my roommate runs five miles before dawn. That's not intimidating or anything."

As soon as Max's back was to her, Sadie scrambled to pull her hair into something other than the nest it was, wrapping Becca's hair tie around what she hoped was the type of ponytail that looked *intentionally* messy but also somehow chic.

Chic? Since when did Sadie care about chic?

"Do you run?" Max asked, pivoting to face her as she backed into the door, pushing it shut.

"Only if someone's chasing me." She let out a nervous laugh, then cringed at what was clearly a dad joke even though Sadie was *not* the dad in the room.

He humored her with a chuckle. "I actually prefer paddle-boarding. It's a good workout and a great way to watch the sun rise."

Sadie shook her head. "My job requires me to be up at the crack of dawn, but you and she do it by *choice*? What's wrong with you two?"

Becca was jogging up the stairs now, coffee in one hand and her water bottle in the other.

"There's nothing like starting your day before everyone else does," she called over her shoulder. "It's like being let in on a secret, you know?" She kept moving, not waiting for Sadie to respond, until she was through her bedroom door, kicking it shut behind her.

"I'll take these to the kitchen unless you want to drink your coffee right here," Max said, nodding toward the drink carrier in his hand. "No judgment, though, if you're a take-your-morning-coffee-at-the-front-door kind of girl."

"So one of those is for *you*," Sadie said. "Because Becca already has her coffee and there are two more."

"Impressive math skills," Max said, biting back a grin. Then he pivoted away from her and strode toward the kitchen.

"I guess I assumed you already drank yours before pounding away at my roof!" she called after him. Sadie rolled her eyes at herself and groaned softly. What was *wrong* with her? She didn't get all wound up around guys. Guys got wound up around *her*. At least, those were the kinds of guys she went for—the ones where mutual physical attraction was all they really had in common. Simple, easy, and straight to the point.

"You coming?" Max asked after setting the drink carrier on the island.

"Oh my god," she squeaked to herself. "I mean, yeah!" she called back. "Coming!"

She strode into the kitchen with as much grace and dignity as she could muster, considering she still wasn't sure she was fully awake and had no idea what she looked like now that she'd put Becca's hair tie to use. Was it better or worse than what Max and Becca saw when Sadie had first opened the door? Who knew?

"Guess this is my rain check, huh?" Max asked, pulling one of the coffees from the carrier and handing it to her.

Sadie sighed, accepting the much-needed offering.

"Thank you," she said, then took a long, slow sip. "It was really—um—thoughtful of you to bring Becca and me coffee. How early does Delilah open anyway?"

He shrugged. "It was the least I could do when I was pretty sure I'd wake you both. I didn't realize your roommate—Becca—would already be out. And Delilah doesn't open until six, but I have a key. She lets me pop in and grab some cold brew when I need it."

"Oh," Sadie replied, a sinking feeling in her stomach of which she did not approve, but apparently, her physiology was not connected to her brain. "So you and Delilah..." She trailed off, remembering how the other woman had playfully called him *Maximus*.

Max laughed, his T-shirt pulling taught over his lean torso as he did—*not* that Sadie was looking.

"No. Just friends. The only man for Delilah is Tom Jones, something I'll never understand. Otherwise she's been with Shelby for...I don't know...five years now, I think? I'm just Delilah's contractor—and friend, I guess. One of the perks of installing the locks—among other things like laying the tile—means I get a key and access to the cold brew whenever I want."

"Shelby?" Sadie asked, trying not to think of him on his hands and knees laying tile.

"Oh. Right. Sorry. You're new in town. Shelby owns the salon and spa that's just a couple doors down from the café."

He ran a hand through his dark hair. The ends were damp with sweat, curling up above his ears. Something about it made him seem boyish, innocent, and not this man with a kid and a dog and responsibility—everything Sadie shied away from.

Everything in her told her to run, but she was in *her* vacation rental. The other option was to kick Max out, or at least back onto the roof, but she couldn't bring herself to do it.

"So everyone's pretty much connected to everyone around here, huh? I'm guessing that means Evie's mom..." Ugh, why couldn't she finish a question?

He shook his head, his smile faltering. "No. She lives

in Madison. I fought hard to prevent her moving so far away—with Evie. But she's the custodial parent, so…" He cleared his throat. "Anyway, I usually only get her every other weekend, but my ex agreed to letting me have her for half the summer if I put in writing that I'd build my work schedule as best I can around the time she was with me. I mean, a guy's gotta work, and I have plenty of friends to help out when I can't be with Evie, but…" He gave her something between a smile and a wince. "That's the real reason I had to do this so early. So I could squeeze it in before Evie wakes up."

Sadie's eyes widened. "You got up before dawn to fix our roof so you wouldn't miss any time with your daughter? Wow. I feel like an asshole now for all the names I called you for waking me up."

Max's brows furrowed. "You didn't call me any names."

He took a sip from his cup, and Sadie laughed. "Trust me. The thoughts that were going through my head when I sprang out of bed to the melodic sound of your hammering could have filled your swear jar for the next week."

He laughed mid-sip, struggling, it seemed, to keep the coffee that had already entered his mouth from exiting just as quickly.

"Sorry!" she said, grabbing a napkin from the holder on the center of the island and handing it to him. Though truth be told, she wasn't sorry at all, not when this tiny little incident filled her with warmth and made her forget for a moment that she was exhausted, looked like a mess, and only minutes before had been braless with her shirt on backward as she almost pitched face-first into the mud.

Sadie had worked hard through the years to earn the label *life of the party*. Making other people laugh, making them *want* to be around her because she was the fun one—it had become so ingrained in her MO. Lately, though—even before her appointment with Dr. Park—it had started to feel forced, so much so that she'd forgotten what it felt like when it happened naturally. But the dribble of coffee Max wiped from his upper lip was the shred of evidence that it could still happen even when she wasn't trying.

"Okay," he finally said. "I should get back up there and finish. You two should be good to go if another storm hits. But, um..." He scratched the back of his neck. "Since we finally got our coffee date out of the way, how about you let me take you to dinner? Tell me a night that works for you, and I'm sure Evie won't mind a movie night with Shelby and Delilah. Plus it gives those two a reason to watch Pixar movies without shame."

Sadie pressed her hand to her chest and gasped. "There is *no* shame in watching Pixar movies—and maybe shedding a tear or two—whether there is a child present or not. Also...this wasn't a *date*," Sadie insisted, then regretted the condescension in her tone. "I mean, a date requires one person asking, the other saying yes. I'm just saying there's a protocol for these things, and us drinking coffee right now does not follow said protocol."

"Fair." Max cleared his throat. "But what about the part where I *did* ask? Friday? Dinner?"

"Why?" she asked, not meaning to sound defensive. "Why do you want to take me on a date? I'm a stranger. A *tourist*. I'll be gone before you know it."

He dipped his head, glancing at his own feet before meeting her gaze again.

"I'm...not exactly sure," he admitted. "But it might have something to do with me not being able to get your look of exasperation out of my head since the beach incident yesterday."

Her eyes widened, and her mouth fell open.

"That's the one!" Max grinned.

His blue eyes seemed so earnest, and the dimple in his cheek was way cuter than it had any right to be. But that was all the more reason for her response.

"No," she said flatly.

He laughed, but when she didn't laugh with him, his smile faltered. "No? Just like that? No making up an excuse like it's girls' night or hair washing night or whatever people say to get out of dates these days?" He shook his head ruefully. "Shit. I didn't realize how out of practice I was until all of that just came out of my mouth."

Sadie's heart tugged at his unapologetic sincerity, but she held her ground. She was here for only a month, and despite Glass Lake not being that far from Chicago, Sadie didn't know what she was going home to other than a doctor's appointment she didn't want to make. "Have you not dated since—since your divorce?"

"Is it that obvious?"

She nodded, then placed her palm on his hand, where it rested on the island.

"I'm temporary, Max. There's no point in getting mixed up with me because I'll be gone before you know it. And then what? You already have a long-distance relationship with your daughter. You don't need any complications beyond that."

"It's just dinner, Sadie," he said, but she shook her head.

"That's just it," she replied. "For me it would be *just* dinner. But somehow I get the feeling that's not exactly how you roll."

He sighed. "I'm that obvious, huh?" He offered her a smile.

"Yeah," she admitted. "You are."

He downed the rest of his iced coffee, then slammed the empty cup on the island.

"Well then, let me fill you in on another little secret about me—one that's a little less obvious." He leaned toward her, and Sadie could smell the coffee on his breath, the scent of rain-soaked grass on his skin.

She swallowed.

"I'm not a quitter. The way I see it, I've got just under four weeks left to ask you again, and maybe again after that. I'll respect your no, every time you say it. But I'm going to take my chances that one of these days—before the clock runs out—you might just say yes."

He backed away, an unexpectedly confident grin on his face.

Sadie felt as if all the oxygen had been sucked out of the room because she suddenly couldn't breathe. And despite the impossibility of a them, she hoped desperately that he was the cause of the tightness in her lungs.

"Unless," Max added, "you tell me right now that you'll keep turning me down, right up until your last day in town. I won't bother you again if that's the case."

"I…you…I mean we…" Sadie tried to form a coherent sentence, but nothing else would come out.

"Okay then," Max said. "I guess we're in agreement. It's a no for today, but there's always tomorrow, right?"

He stepped back from the island and shoved his hands into the front pockets of his jeans, which made his T-shirt rise up enough for her to catch a glimpse of the tanned skin underneath.

"Good-bye, Sadie," he said before spinning toward the living room and striding toward the back door.

When he was finally outside and she could hear him on the roof again, she sucked in a much-needed breath, air flowing freely into her lungs once more. Then she bit back a grin as she wondered what surprises tomorrow would bring.

CHAPTER ELEVEN

MAX

Max barely stepped on the gas as he guided his truck back home. It was still early, which meant Evie hopefully hadn't woken up yet.

He shook out his left hand at the stop sign, mumbling a swear word he was glad his daughter couldn't hear. Meant one more dollar remaining in his pocket instead of filling up the jar. The first two knuckles were already starting to bruise, the ones that had borne the brunt of his hammer a time or two—utility gloves be damned—as he'd finished patching the leak after his coffee date with Sadie.

Except it wasn't a date, and she'd said *no* to an actual date, which meant he was back at square one. What was he doing anyway? Max didn't know how to date. He and Caitlin had been together since sophomore year of college. Before her, there had been some random hook-ups his first year and prior to that was high school. Who counted high school as actual dating?

He was a thirty-eight-year-old man with *no* experience and just about the same amount of trust.

"I put a picture of you on the dating app where Shelby and I connected," Delilah had told him a few months back. "And you are *killing* it with the matches, Maximus." Not his name but the one she'd used on the app. Only now, she wouldn't call him by anything else.

"Isn't that app for men seeking men or women seeking women?" he'd asked.

Delilah laughed. "It's for *people* seeking *people*. But if you want to get technical...Okay, you are probably the only cis-het person on the app but a *very* popular one. I just think it's important you know that you are a tall drink of water, and there are a *lot* of thirsty singles out there. Maybe it's time you at least *try* dating."

So he'd tried. But in their little Midwestern vacation town, there weren't many new people to meet. He wasn't opposed to traveling beyond the town line, but he was already traveling back and forth to Madison every other weekend during the non-summer months. His parenting life was complicated enough. When it came to his personal life, he just wanted simple, which was easier said than done.

Except now he couldn't get Sadie off his mind. In fact, he hadn't stopped thinking about her since they'd "met" on the beach—and then again at Delilah's. And again this morning on her roof as he watched her almost do the splits in the mud to avoid wiping out.

When his phone woke him before dawn—and he saw Leo's number—he prepared himself for the worst. "Are you hurt, in jail, or both?" was how he'd answered the phone. There was a long pause before Leo responded.

"Andrea and Ted's rental has a roof leak," Leo had said coolly. "I told the tenants I'd call a contractor when the rain let up, so I'm calling a contractor."

"Oh," was all Max had said at first. "But I have Evie," he added.

"I can hang at your place while you take care of the leak. I could use another hour or two of sleep under a leak-free roof myself, and you do have that comfy-as-hell couch."

Max sighed as he rubbed his eyes with his thumb and forefinger. "Yeah," he'd said. "Okay. If it's not too big of a job, I should be able to finish before Evie wakes up. The back door is open."

And with that, Leo had ended the call.

When Max had finally made his way downstairs, the kid was already asleep on what *was* his comfy-as-hell couch, a blanket covering almost his entire face and Penny spooning him like she hadn't just been in Max's bed only minutes before.

"Traitor," he'd mumbled under his breath, but he'd also been relieved that he didn't have to deal with Leo's antics this early in the morning.

Now, as he pondered whether or not he needed to ice his bruised hand when he got home, he pulled out his phone and brought up Leo's number.

"Hurt, in jail, or both?" Leo answered, the words coming out as a yawn.

"Funny," Max replied, admitting only to himself that it *had* been a shitty way to answer Leo's call a couple hours before. He couldn't help it, though. Old habits die hard, especially ones that took years to build. "I'm about a minute away, so if you want to avoid having to talk face-to-face..."

He wasn't sure who was avoiding who anymore, only that they'd both gotten really good at it.

"I'm already out the door," Leo said. "Evie's still down for the count. Checked on her before putting on my shoes."

Max sighed. "Thank you—for staying with Evie and for taking good care of the rental. You're doing a good job over there."

This time Leo audibly sighed. "I don't need a gold star from you, Max. I know I'm good at my job. It would be refreshing every once in a while, though, if you didn't sound so surprised. Tell Evie I said hi."

Again, just like there had been no *hello*, there was never any formal *good-bye*. By the time Max walked through the front door, he knew Leo was halfway back to that ramshackle tent or wherever he went during the day.

Penny barely picked her head up from the couch, where she stared mournfully at the indentation that used to be Leo.

"Seriously?" he asked, and Penny let out a sigh.

He kicked off one work boot, then stumbled when he tried to do the other, catching himself against the wall with his bruised hand.

"Shit!" he hissed.

"That's a dollar!" he heard from over his shoulder, and he turned to see his daughter rubbing her eyes as she shuffled out of her bedroom doorway and down the hall toward the ranch house's front entrance.

One boot on, one off, and his hand still throbbing, he scooped his little girl into his arms, spinning her as she squealed with delight. His thoughts about Sadie and his worry about Leo melted away, and all was right with the world the second he heard his daughter laugh.

"Did I ever tell you you're my favorite person in the whole wide world," he said, lowering Evie to her feet and kneeling so they were eye to eye.

She pressed her palms to his cheeks, her bright green eyes—her *mother's* eyes—intent on his.

"You need to get a life, Dad."

He choked on any response he might have had to such a statement coming from his ten-year-old's mouth.

"I'm *serious*," she said. "I'm okay being your favorite person, but what about—like—some friends? Or a girlfriend? Mom has a boyfriend." She shrugged as if this were a conversation he and his daughter had every day, and Max felt the wind knocked clear from his lungs.

"Mom has a—a boyfriend?" Why did he care? He didn't, did he? He'd been resistant to the divorce, but after a while, he realized it had been because he hadn't known anything other than him and Caitlin for all of his adult life. Maybe they *had* gotten married only because they'd been together as long as they had, but because of Evie, they were family—and for a time the type of family Max had always wanted but never had. Somewhere in the back of his mind, had he hoped they'd reconcile? For Evie's sake, he might have. He'd have given her the stability she needed, even if the price was a piece of his own happiness.

"Have you—*met* him?" Max finally worked up the nerve to ask.

Evie nodded like it was no big deal. "His name's Jake. He has *two* dogs. And a daughter named Sara. She's eight, so I'm kind of like a big sister."

Max scoffed. "Is Penny not enough for you?" But he was stuck on the *big sister* part. How quickly she took to it. How much it seemed to fill her up that she could possibly be expanding her family with this—this Jake and his two dogs and a daughter. Weren't *he* and Penny enough for her?

She giggled, her brown curls bouncing against her shoulders. "I love my Penny and I love *you*," she said, as if reading his mind. "But I want you to be happy like Mama's happy."

He kissed the tip of her nose, then pressed his forehead to hers. "*You* make me happy, Peanut. You and Penny. That's all I need."

For almost a year he'd believed those words to be true. Now, though, he wasn't so sure.

"What should we do today?" he asked, deciding it was

time to take the focus off his nonexistent life outside of work and fatherhood. "It's going to be another scorcher of a day."

Evie tapped her chin as if she was deep in thought.

"A scorcher, huh? Then there should definitely be some ice cream somewhere on our agenda."

Max laughed. "Agenda? Where do you get your vocabulary?"

"A trip to the bookstore for some air-conditioning as well," Evie added, as if to answer his question. "And of course, some time on the lake. We could paddleboard across to Uncle—"

"Hey," he interrupted—his voice gentle but his meaning firm. "When you're with me, you're supposed to be with *me*. That was the deal I made with your mom."

Evie sighed. "If the three of us hung out together instead of you only letting him in the house when I need looking after... Which I don't, by the way. You know I'm responsible enough to stay home alone while you run to town for a cup of coffee or something like that."

Max opened his mouth to protest, but his daughter held up a finger, silencing him before he could get a word out.

"I'm just saying... Family is important. And he's not just my family but yours too."

Max scrubbed a hand across his jaw and stood, unable to look his daughter in the eye anymore because she was right, but she also didn't know their history. She didn't get what it was like for him as a kid not much older than her to see someone else get the life—the *family*—that was supposed to be his. Then he looked at the spot on his left hand where a wedding ring used to be and realized she probably *did* get it, more than he'd ever wanted her to.

"Paddleboarding is a great idea," he finally said. "How about I let you lead the way, and wherever we end up, we end up, okay?" Maybe he couldn't give her a firm yes, but a non-committal answer? That much he could manage.

She held out her right hand, and Max gripped it with his.

"Deal," she said, giving him a firm shake. "Now let's go make some blueberry pancakes."

He laughed. "I'll wash the blueberries and—"

"I'll mix the batter," she added, finishing his thought. "We don't want a repeat of last time."

She let go of his hand and marched toward the kitchen.

"Hey," he called after her. "It's not *that* uncommon to mix up the salt and sugar."

"Admit it, Dad," she called back. "You're helpless without me."

His heart squeezed. He could read a blueprint like no one's business and fix a leaking roof almost entirely before dawn, but his daughter was right. Without *her*, none of it mattered. Maybe he was a disaster when it came to all other relationships in his life, but at least he had Evie, which meant that in the long list of things he'd done wrong, he'd gotten one perfectly right.

CHAPTER TWELVE

BECCA

Despite the pleasant coexistence they'd had for the last few days, Becca still wasn't sure where she and Sadie stood as far as, well—were they friends? There had been some mild teasing after Becca had treated Leo and after Max had shown up on the roof the following morning, but for the rest of the week they seemed to be roommates who happened to hang out only when they were in the same place—mainly the living room or the back porch. But it was Friday. People *did* stuff on Fridays, right? Like *social* stuff? Becca was single now and childless for the time being, so she should take advantage of the situation.

She unplugged her phone from where it charged on the nightstand and scrolled through the pictures the camp had sent of the twins again. Mackenzie smiled from the bow of a canoe, her counselor behind her in the stern. Her six-year-old was rowing a *canoe*. And there was Grayson rounding third base as he hit a triple for his cabin. They were having so much fun, living their best lives without her, which was—great. Truly, it was. But if they didn't need her...

She checked her in-box for the third time since she'd woken up, startling when she saw a new reply from Dr. Park, one of the other partners.

> I've installed an app that lets me see how many times you open an email I sent you. You're a fantastic obstetrician, Becca, but we are fine without you. At least for three more weeks. Enjoy yourself. Go do something you love, and then email me about it on Monday (not over the weekend).
>
> Best,
> June

So everyone—her children and her colleagues—was living their best lives without her.

Becca wanted to live *her* best life, but how? She didn't even know what that meant. Did it mean having fun? Being fun?

Am I fun?

Ugh. Who had to ask themselves such a question? Maybe someone whose roommate found a way to always be out when Becca was in. Or someone whose husband found it more enjoyable to swipe right and left rather than address the situation at home.

Alissa thought she was fun, didn't she? She brought up her sister's number from her contact list, her thumb hovering over the call button when the phone rang.

Becca flinched with her whole body, almost throwing her phone at the wall, but then stopped herself just in time, answering the call.

"Liss!" she said. "Oh my god. I was just about to call you when the phone rang. It's like I conjured you or something!"

"Why are you calling me when you're on vacation?" Alissa asked, accusation in her tone. She could hear her nephew, Elliott, saying *Mama* in the background, except instead of stopping at two syllables, it was a constant *Mamamamamama*.

Becca laughed. "You've got yourself a talker there, huh? And you called *me*, by the way."

"Right. But you just said you were *about* to call me when you have a sister-in-law living in the same house who you could be talking to right now."

Becca glanced around her room, looking for a hidden camera or possibly a hidden sister because how did Alissa know she *hadn't* been talking to Sadie up until their phone call?

"Matt just got off with Sadie, and she said the two of you are getting along but that your schedules haven't quite meshed. Yet. Bex... why the hell are you even *on* a schedule? You're on vacation. Activate vacation mode and start enjoying yourself!"

"*How?*" Becca asked, throwing her phone-free hand in the

air. "Other than my honeymoon, I don't think I've ever taken a vacation. And even then Jeff had to do a deposition over the phone, and I was on call for any after-hours telehealth patients."

Alissa sighed. "You did that telehealth thing by *choice*. I know you. You don't know how to unplug from your life. It's time to have fun, Bex."

Ugh. There was the trigger word. "What if I don't know how to have fun?" she asked. "What if I'm not fun?"

"Do you know where I am right now?" Alissa asked. "I'm strawberry picking with my son and my baby daddy. Mom and Gigi took the bakery for the day, and I am not calling to check on them because I know how to find my work-life balance and enjoy myself. You don't need me to tell you if you're fun or how to have it. Just do something you love, Bex. For you."

She loved story time with the twins, when they'd all cram into one bed, Becca sitting between them as she read *The Day the Crayons Quit* for the hundredth time, each of them giggling at the different voices she did for the crayons. She loved movie nights when they made popcorn and she let them stay up past bedtime just so they'd fall asleep, a head resting on each of her shoulders. And she loved yoga Saturdays with Alissa, her body feeling strong and her heart feeling the connection with someone she loved.

But what did Becca Weiland love for herself alone?

"I don't know what I love, Liss, unless it involves what someone else loves."

Her sister laughed. "You love running, green smoothies, my rugelach...especially after a particularly long run, and an Athleta sale. I'm sure you're knocking some of those out in Wisconsin. I mean, no one makes rugelach like me, but we can't have everything we want anytime we—"

"No," Becca interrupted, her hand flying over her mouth as soon as the sole word escaped.

"No?" Alissa asked. "What do you mean? No, my rugelach is not the best? Because if that's how you feel, you could have said something before now!"

Becca laughed. "Wow. Your connection to your pastries is intense. But that wasn't what I meant."

"Oh," her sister replied with what sounded like a sniffle. "Well, what did you mean?"

Becca sighed. "That whole list you rattled off? It's not true. I don't love running."

Her sister gasped dramatically.

"I mean it," Becca continued. "I do it as a means to an end. To keep this body that my husband seemingly loved and to look how I was expected to look on his arm at dinner parties or events for his firm."

"Yikes," Alissa said.

Becca nodded even though her sister couldn't see her. "Right? How messed up is that? And the green smoothies? God, I know I act like they're delicious and that I give you hell for ordering something more akin to a McFlurry when we go to the juice bar, but Liss. Green smoothies taste like grass."

"More like ass," her sister added with a laugh.

"My front lawn and ass!" Becca continued, and the two women burst into peals of laughter.

Several seconds passed before Becca finally admitted, "Okay, that was fun."

Maybe she was calling herself out, but Becca had thought she was doing all those things for all the right reasons. She thought she'd been living her life as genuinely and truthfully as possible. It took hearing Alissa say it out loud for her to realize that maybe she was doing what she did for someone else, for a marriage that was about as genuine as the way she'd been living.

Alissa sighed. "Oh, Bex. You needed this trip more than I knew. I'm so glad Ethan's appendix burst."

"Alissa!" Becca gasped.

"He's fine. I love Ethan. He loves my daughter. It's all good. I wish him no harm. You know what I meant."

Becca smiled. "Yeah, okay. So maybe I do need this time, but I still have no idea what I'm doing or who I am by myself. But you do, which begs the question of why you are calling me when you're supposed to be enjoying your day with your baby and baby daddy."

"Right!" Alissa cried. "Mom and Gigi. Working together at the bakery. For an *entire* day? If Matthew's mom and our mom can find common ground after all these years, I bet you and Sadie can transcend the label of *in-law* and maybe even be friends. Also, she's really good at the fun thing."

Becca sighed. "Yeah, well, Gigi probably slipped Mom an

edible to bring her down a notch. Actually, maybe that's what *I* need."

"Right! You would *never.* Plus, it's illegal in Wisconsin, so I guess you're saved by the law." Alissa laughed. "Just go find Sadie and plan a day together. Find your fun. "

Becca groaned. "Why do I feel like I'm about to go ask someone out on a first date? She could turn me down, you know."

Oh god. That was it. If Sadie said *no,* it meant that Becca truly didn't remember how to be fun. Or worse. What if she never actually was?

"You're spiraling, aren't you? I didn't mean to make you spiral. You're *fun,* Bex." But Alissa's voice was getting drowned out by another *Mamamamamama.* "Okay, Elliott's telling me it's time to hang up and eat more strawberries. So go find that roommate of yours and ask her out on a friend date. You got this! Love you, byeeee!"

Alissa ended the call, and Becca had no choice. Either she hid in her room until Sadie maybe left the house again, or she put on her big girl panties and did as her sister said.

She took the stairs down to the first floor slower than she normally would. Her closest friend—and really the *only* person who knew the real Becca—was Alissa. Her sister. That was sad, right? And not sad as in made you misty but sad as in made you pity the woman whose BFF was a blood relative.

Hey, Sadie. I was going to head to town and check out some of the shops. Wanna come?

Hey, Sadie. We should rent a canoe. Do you know how to canoe because one of us should?

Hey, Sadie. Wanna put the U in fun by YOU spending the day with ME?

Oh. My. God. She was literally the worst at platonic pickup lines. How would she ever get back into the dating world?

The second her foot left the last step and hit the first floor, she didn't have to pick anyone up, because Sadie sprang up from the couch, nodding as she typed on her phone while simultaneously making her way toward Becca.

"Come on!" she said, shoving the phone into a tiny cross-body bag. "That was Delilah, the coffee shop owner. She said that Glass Lake Street Fest starts today and runs through the weekend, and if we head to town now, we can still score a parking spot—and a free scone if we pop into Cool Beans first."

Becca let out a long breath, trying to hide the relief from her face.

"Sounds like fun," Becca said. "I'll get my keys."

She bit back a smile as she ran upstairs for her purse.

She had a date. A *friend* date. And she was going to show Street Fest just how fun she could be.

☼

They found a parking spot on a local side street since the main road was closed off. While Sadie offered to park the van, Becca insisted she could do it—even if it meant circling the block a few times until she found an end space into which she could easily back the van.

As planned, their first stop was Cool Beans, where Becca splurged, letting Delilah fill her tumbler with an iced caramel macchiato.

"You made it with almond milk, right?" she asked as Delilah screwed the top back onto the tumbler and handed it over the counter to Becca. Tom Jones's "It's Not Unusual" blared through the speakers while Delilah hummed along.

Delilah grabbed a square carton off the counter that was next to the espresso machine, holding it up for Becca to see. "It's even the unsweetened kind, sweetheart. The caramel and whipped cream, though? You can't substitute those when the originals are perfection."

Becca smiled. She'd forgotten to say no whip. But maybe fun Becca got a little crazy every now and then . . . with a dollop of whipped cream.

"You know what? Put an extra drizzle of caramel on there," Becca added, heart racing as she waited for someone to ask if she was sure she wanted to sacrifice looking like the picture of perfection for Delilah's decidedly different definition.

But no one said a thing, and she now realized the voice in her head that would say such ugly words wasn't her own but one belonging to a man who didn't find her perfect after all.

Sadie nudged Becca's shoulder with her own. "Atta girl," she whispered.

Becca bit back a triumphant grin.

Sadie tapped her chin with her index finger, then handed her tumbler to Delilah with a grin.

"I'll have the frozen peppermint mocha with extra whip. Oooh! Actually, can you put some whip at the bottom of the mug, then the frappe or whatever you call it, and then more whip?"

Delilah winked at her. "Now *that's* my kind of girl!"

Becca rolled her eyes, thankful that her sunglasses were still on. But really, the gesture was at herself. She'd never had that easy, breezy way about her like Sadie did. And she certainly couldn't be easy or breezy about an indulgence like a frozen peppermint mocha with extra whip. Just the thought sent her reeling back to that moment in their bedroom—hers and Jeff's—three months after the twins were born. She'd been standing with her robe open, playing with the flap of belly skin that hung over her C-section scar, a smile playing at her lips and happy tears welling in her eyes when her husband came up behind her, wrapping his arms around her torso.

"Your doctor said it's okay to start running again, right? Just add another mile or two to your route, and you'll be back to the old Becca before you know it."

She remembered her tears spilling over—no longer happy—and Jeff kissing them away, telling her everything would be okay as he assumed she was mourning the pre-pregnancy body *he'd* seemed to be mourning. How could he have known that, only seconds before, she'd been marveling at her changed form, at what her body had accomplished by bringing her two beautiful babies into the world. *Their* beautiful babies.

So she'd done as he suggested, adding another two miles to her morning routine, taking it from three miles to five. She'd said good-bye to any and all pregnancy indulgences even while Jeff's midsection grew softer as his own requisite "dad bod" set in. Funny thing was, it hadn't bothered her. She'd even found his doughier center endearing—a sign of him slowing down and focusing more on her and the twins. When he'd joined a new gym in the city that had given his firm a corporate discount, she hadn't batted an eye when he'd started leaving earlier to work out and shower *there* before heading to the office. She'd thought nothing of him making a second stop at the gym on the way home or of his increasingly toned physique over the past couple of years. They both had competitive personalities, and when Becca had come in second in her age group in her very first half marathon, Jeff had stepped up to the plate.

Or so she thought.

Had he done any of it for her? Or had the goal always been finding validation *outside* the marriage? She'd probably never know. Yet even now, a year after finding out the truth, she was still measuring her self-worth against the backdrop of a marriage that had likely been flawed from the start.

She still couldn't believe she'd walked naked from her room to the kitchen the other night to check the leak during the storm. Despite the cover of darkness, the thought of someone seeing her—of judging what they saw—had made her tiptoe faster than she'd thought possible, biting her tongue as she stubbed the hell out of her toe on her way back upstairs.

"Here you go!" Delilah said, handing a tumbler overflowing with whipped cream to Sadie. "Frozen peppermint mocha sandwiched between two generous helpings of whip. Enjoy!"

Sadie swiped a dollop of whipped cream onto her finger and plopped it into her mouth with a satisfied sigh. "Hea-*ven*," she said around the mouthful before swallowing.

"You know what?" Becca said, unscrewing the top from her tumbler and handing it back to Delilah. "Extra whip for me too."

Fun started here. Now. With no voice in Becca's head other than her own.

Enjoy, it said. *Live. For you.*

"That's what I'm talking about!" Sadie remarked. "And this is just the beginning! We are going to eat our way through Street Fest until we can't eat any more. And then—we'll *still* eat more!"

Becca smiled nervously. "Baby steps," she told her, and Sadie glanced up at her with whipped cream on the tip of her nose. Becca laughed.

"What?" Sadie asked, feigning ignorance and brushing at her cheek. "Do I have something on my face?" She screwed the lid back onto her tumbler.

Becca bit back a snort, *not*, however, out of embarrassment but in an attempt to play along.

"Nope," she said. "The coast is completely clear."

Sadie let out a relieved sigh. "I would hate to walk out there and greet the Glass Lake public without looking perfectly Instagrammable. Hashtag no filter!"

Becca's smile faltered. "Are you planning on posting pics of us on social media?" She glanced down at her plain gray ribbed tank, her pull-on shorts, and running shoes—they were going to be walking a lot, after all.

"Pic or it didn't happen, right?" Delilah said from across the counter as she handed Becca a tumbler that was now so overflowing with whipped cream that Becca had to lick the circumference of the travel mug as if it were a melting ice cream cone.

Sadie sighed. "I'd never post anything without giving you full veto power first, but come *on*, Posh. You need to show the viewing public that you are flirty, thirty-something, thriving, and living your best goddamn life."

Ah yes, the snort. Here it was. "I don't *have* a viewing public. I don't even think I've logged into Facebook in over a year."

She had poked around Instagram, though. Not by actually creating an account, but Jeff's profile was public. And he posted pictures of him and the kids. Was it wrong of her to be curious about what else he might post? Of *who* else he might post? It wasn't even that she missed *him* but the idea of him that she'd built up in her head—the story she'd told herself about their idyllic life until her sister made one final swipe on a dating app to find that Becca's story had been a fantastical piece of fiction.

Sadie put her arm around Becca, backed her toward the counter, and pulled her phone out of her pocket. She held it up high, saying something about angles, and then made sure there was enough room between them for Delilah to pop her head into the selfie without looking like she was photobombing them.

"Say *whipped cream*, everyone!" Sadie said.

And they all yelled, "Whipped creeeeaaaam!"

Even Becca, a weight lifting off her chest as she grinned a little too wide and yelled the word *cream* a little too loud. Maybe none of this—attempting to let go a little—felt entirely natural. But right here, right now, in the middle of a selfie with two women she barely knew—despite one of them having been in her life since middle school—Becca realized why she'd never seen the signs, why she hadn't known her marriage was crumbling even when Jeff did.

Becca Weiland had become such an expert at faking happiness, she'd forgotten how the real thing felt. But she was fairly certain that, at this very moment, she was having fun.

CHAPTER THIRTEEN

SADIE

So far Sadie had scored an adorable tie-dye sundress from a local designer, a straw sunhat from a local artisan who—when she wasn't dealing with curious customers—was weaving a new hat by hand and using nothing *else*.

"Why do I suddenly feel so inadequate?" she asked Becca with a laugh as the other woman pulled her toward a stand where a husband-and-wife team who ran a local brewery were handing out beer-battered cheese curds along with taster-sized cups of their brews. "I mean I can whip up a perfect meringue for a batch of macarons, but that woman made *this*, with her *hands*. And she said it takes at least a full day—if not more—to make one hat. *One* hat!"

Becca stopped, pinning Sadie in place with her stare.

"We've been here almost a week, and you have not made macarons for us?"

Sadie's brows furrowed. "I know we had our little moment on the porch our first day, but this is the first, like, friend date we've been on since we got here. I didn't even know you liked macarons."

Becca backhanded her on the shoulder. "I was totally about to ask you out when you asked *me*! I was so nervous that I even practiced what I was going to say!"

"You're different today, aren't you?" Sadie laughed. "Or is this just what you're like on inordinate amounts of sugar?" Whatever it was, Becca seemed more alive than all the years she'd known her. It was contagious—her aliveness. Sadie's pulse raced, and she felt dizzy with excitement. Becca shook her head, grinning. "Not the sugar. All me, but I don't know this me. So I'm not sure what to do with her."

Sadie shrugged. "It's your vacation, which means you can't do it wrong as long as you do *you*."

Becca's eyes lit up. "Yes! More *me* doing *me*! Right?" She spun toward the brewers' booth, marched straight up to the table, and grabbed two sample cups of beer. She handed one to Sadie, and then downed her own before Sadie's lips had even touched the rim of her cup.

"God, beer is *good*," Becca said. "I forgot how good it is. Like—I *really* like it. I'm not just saying I do, you know? I—Becca Weiland—*like* beer."

Sadie downed her own cup, wincing as the tart yet hoppy notes assaulted her taste buds.

"What is this?" she asked, and a man with salt-and-pepper hair and matching beard smiled from behind the table.

"That's our blackberry sour," he said. "We just tapped it today."

Sadie's tongue was still processing the experience as Becca threw back *two* more sample cups.

"I don't suppose you have any frozen margaritas hiding back there, do you?" Sadie asked.

The man laughed. "Sorry," he said. "Just the sour, but if you come back later tonight, we'll be tapping our saison, which is much milder."

Sadie nodded, opened her mouth to answer, but the sky opened up first. There was barely enough time to react between hearing the crash of thunder and then feeling the first drops of rain. While most of the booths were covered with tents, Sadie and Becca were *not*.

"Shit!" Sadie yelled as the initial drizzle turned into a steady downfall. "Come on!" She grabbed Becca's hand. What the hell, Mother Nature? Did Glass Lake have a hurricane season she wasn't aware of?

"But—cheese curds!" Becca said. "And—and the sour!" She downed another sample cup, and then another. Sadie wanted to remind the woman of her recent schnapps encounter, but the crowded but mellow street scene had just turned into pure chaos, so between Sadie and Becca, Sadie had to take charge.

"Come on, ya lush," she teased as she grabbed Becca by the wrist and made a beeline for the only place she knew well enough to run to during a storm—back to Cool Beans Café.

As soon as the two women made it through the door,

another crash of thunder shook the air, and the power in the coffee shop went out.

"Shit!" Sadie heard from behind the counter, but it wasn't Delilah's voice. It was a man's.

"That's another dollar, mister," she heard after that, this time coming from a child.

"Shit," Sadie murmured to herself.

"Why are we all saying *shit*?" Becca asked with a decidedly buzzed giggle.

Despite the sky darkening with the storm, Sadie could still see Max as he rose behind the counter from where he'd been doing whatever it was he'd been doing on the floor, his eyes locking on hers.

"We have to stop meeting like this," he said with a grin. "Though, if I'm being honest, I don't really want to stop."

"He's *cute*," Becca said, not-so-subtly elbowing Sadie in the ribs.

Max's smile bloomed even wider, and Sadie shivered, realizing she and Becca were soaked to the bone. So just in case anyone was keeping score, these were the circumstances under which Sadie Bloom had *met* the man who was still smiling at her:

1. On her back in wet sand, a beast of a dog about to make her her lunch.
2. Sweating like she'd just crossed the Sahara after she'd made the mistake of walking to town in the oppressive Midwestern summer heat.

3. At the butt crack of dawn in her nest of a hairdo, her tank on backward over her braless breasts, and her thick-as-Coke-bottle glasses perched on her nose.

4. And—now, looking like a drowned rat.

"She should put a dollar in the jar too, Dad," Evie said, popping up next to Max. "Maybe if you invite her over—"

"No-ho-ho-ho," Sadie interrupted, her protestation turning into a Santa laugh. "I mean, we have to get back to the rental and make sure we still have power."

Becca squeaked as her phone chirped in her hand. She glanced down at it and then beamed as she brandished it at Sadie.

"I just got a text from our cute houseboy. You know, the naked one whose face I glued back together? He stopped by to check on the leak and wanted to let us know the kitchen is dry and the power is still on and that, if we don't mind, he's going to chill on the porch until the storm blows over."

"Wait, what?" Max said, his face growing serious. "Houseboy whose face you had to glue back together?"

"Shit!" Delilah called from the back room before emerging from behind the counter.

"That's a dollar, Auntie D," Evie said, holding out her palm.

Delilah waved her off. "Go finish off the whipped cream. Power's out here and our whole side of the lake. That means you too, Max. And I had all those burgers and dogs in the fridge for the Fourth on Monday." She pressed her lips into a sad smile. "I was going to invite you ladies, actually. I mean, you're still invited, but the food's going to go bad if we don't get power back before morning."

Becca gasped. "You should come to our place. Tonight. Like—right now. You can store the food in our fridge, or maybe we can have a little indoor barbecue tonight! I'll invite cute houseboy too!"

Sadie looked at Becca in horror as the other woman began firing off a text, likely to Leo. Then Sadie glanced at Delilah, whose worry morphed into a sigh of relief.

"Really?" Delilah asked. "Shelby and I would be so grateful. Max and Evie too?"

"Sure!" Becca cried, motioning for them all to join as if she was going to pack them into the van right now. "It'll be like—like Shabbat dinner!"

Sadie groaned. "Since when do you host Shabbat dinner?" She turned her attention to Max and Delilah. "It's—a weekly Jewish holiday thing that I know Becca never observes, so—"

"So maybe I do *now*," Becca said, crossing her arms over her chest. "We can just call it Friday night dinner. And— and you're all invited tonight and the following three Fridays until Sadie and I head back to Chicago."

Sadie's mouth hung open. Who *was* the woman next to her, and what the hell had she done with her careful, reserved roommate who would never throw such caution to the wind—and commit Sadie to *four* Friday nights with Max?

Max cleared his throat—speak of the devilishly handsome

man who hadn't left the room. "Um. Yeah. An indoor barbecue sounds nice. I know Evie would like that a lot. Right
Eves?" The young girl nodded with a grin.

"Okay," Sadie said. "But—give us thirty minutes to
straighten up. We—uh—we weren't expecting guests."

And before she knew it, Sadie was piling her tipsy roommate into the passenger side of the van and then hopping
behind the wheel so she could hightail it back to the house
and make herself a little less drowned rat looking.

Because like it or not, Sadie was having dinner with Max.

☼

"You were supposed to keep me from drinking like that
again!" Becca said, trying to warm a chilled can of Coca-Cola
by rolling it between her palms. "Will this really not work if
it's cold?"

Sadie rushed around the living room folding throws, picking up discarded socks, and fluffing pillows. Since when did
Sadie Bloom *fluff* pillows?

"I didn't know that was *my* job!" Sadie exclaimed, throwing her hands in the air—one holding a throw pillow and the
other an ankle sock. "You could have given me a heads-up
after the schnapps incident."

Becca scrunched up her nose and cracked open the can of
soda. "You're grumpy when you clean."

Sadie clenched her jaw but reminded herself that while
she didn't know she'd have to be Becca's alcohol chaperone,

she was the one who encouraged her new roommate to let go a little. Wasn't she doing what Sadie asked? Also, getting angry at someone who had a good buzz going wasn't going to take away that buzz, so what was the point in getting angry? And *third*—oh god, was she making lists now?—*third*, they had guests arriving in fifteen minutes, and while the living room was looking more presentable, Becca and Sadie were still in their wet clothes.

"Hey...wasn't our naked houseboy supposed to be on the porch?" Becca asked, following her question with a hiccup and then a belch. "I haven't seen another text from him since I told him about the barbecue and that *your* cutie, Max, was coming with his daughter as well as Delilah and Shelby so that it was in no way me asking him out on a date."

Sadie glanced behind her at the empty porch, her brows furrowed. Where *had* Leo gone? The storm was still in full swing, and she knew his tent could not be doing well.

She finished with the pillows, rolled the socks together, and threw them at Becca.

"Go take these upstairs and put on some dry clothes. I'll do the same. And from here on out, you are allowed only water or iced tea, got it?"

Despite her loose, happy state, Becca caught the socks, proving her reflexes were still intact, which hopefully meant she was getting closer to sober than not.

Becca downed the rest of her soda and wiped her forearm across her mouth. "I'm sorry I invited everyone over without asking you first," she said. "I just—I'm trying to not be so *me*, you know? The old me. Okay, not old because I'm not old. The previous me." She swatted at the air. "You know what I mean. Does that sound stupid?"

Sadie sighed and shook her head. "No. It doesn't sound stupid. That's what this month is supposed to be, right? Figuring our shit out?"

Becca nodded slowly. "What do you have to figure out? You have a great life, and *you* know what you want. Don't you?"

Sadie cleared her throat. "Sure do, Posh," she said flatly, but Becca didn't seem to notice. "Great job, no mortgage, no one tying me down until I'm good and ready because I have all the time in the world for that. It's definitely everything I planned."

At least, she thought she had all the time in the world. Now she wouldn't know for sure until she went back to Chicago and followed up on one stupid, tiny, meaningless irregular heartbeat.

What if her false sense of invincibility meant she'd squandered the years she'd already had? What if she never got to open her own diner or grow old with someone special? What if she never got to grow old at all?

Sadie sucked in a sharp breath.

"What?" Becca asked, making her way toward the stairs.

She let out a bitter laugh, wiping the dampness from the corner of her eye. "Nothing," she lied. "Just my inner monologue getting *way* ahead of me when this group dinner thing is *so* not a date."

Becca gasped. "You *do* like Max! Like—*like* him, like him. Do you want to kiss him? You should totally kiss him tonight."

"Oh my god," Sadie said. "Is this what it would have been like if we were actually *friends* in middle school?"

Becca's smile faltered. "I don't know. But we're friends now, aren't we?"

Sadie paused for a beat, realizing that there was no way she would have wanted to embark on this evening's activities without Becca. Maybe when it was over, she'd even tell her about her appointment with Dr. Park. But for now, Sadie refused to worry about anything she couldn't control and decided to focus on something she could.

"Yeah," she told Becca. "Friends. But we are friends who need, like, the quickest and best makeover montage in rom-com history."

CHAPTER FOURTEEN

BECCA

Becca smoothed out the olive green maxi dress—*after* mistaking one of the short sleeves for the head hole—and then slipped her feet into the yellow flip-flops that were definitely *not* needed as shower shoes.

She laughed. *Nothing* this week had been what she'd expected. Not the house, not her roommate, not her waxed nether region, and certainly not the naked walk she'd done *through* the house the other night. She still didn't know much more about herself than she did five days ago, but she couldn't expect to figure out the rest of her life during business hours.

She sighed. Her hair was still damp, but she kind of liked how the lake air gave it a little more wave than it had at home, so she left it down. Come to think of it, she hadn't pulled it into her signature ponytail since the aforementioned birthday suit walk the other night.

"Huh," she said out loud.

She brushed her teeth, then used her hands to rinse her mouth and then down the equivalent of an eight-ounce glass of water. She was already feeling less intoxicated than when they'd first arrived home, and she decided to stick with Sadie's order of only water or iced tea from here on out. That ought to keep her from saying *cute houseboy* out loud again.

She groaned. Whether or not she said it, she still thought it. The only problem was that Leo wasn't actually *cute*. He was—sexy. And maybe a little crazy for calling that tent home, but who was Becca to judge anyone else's life when she wasn't sure how the hell to move forward with her own? Besides, she and Sadie were here for only three more weeks. What was the point in even *thinking* about Leo being sexy when she had only just learned how much fun it was to be sexy with herself?

Maybe it was because sometimes it was nice to have someone else do the work—if they did it well. She had been with one man. *One* man. Which meant she'd had no means to compare, no possibility of knowing if the way it was between her and Jeff was simply the way it was or if *it*—could be better.

Jeff wasn't the only one to blame. It took two to tango or horizontal mambo or whatever you called it. But the truth was, Jeff had simply realized it *could* be better. Not just the *it* but the *them*. Had he gone about remedying that situation in the worst possible way, which in turn made him easily agree to all of her divorce terms? Sure. But that didn't change the fact that she had chosen to live in ignorant complacency because she didn't think there was any other option.

The doorbell rang.

"Oh!" she said, taking a jump back and then laughing. She was about to host her first Shabbat dinner. Okay, so maybe she'd never done it before, and maybe the spread wouldn't be entirely kosher. Did they sell Hebrew National hot dogs in Wisconsin? She couldn't worry about that now. But what if she could find some candles? What if she could make tonight the first step toward some sort of significant change in her life? She might not be the best cook, which in turn would make her even worse at being a dinner party host. But she had Sadie for the next few weeks, and together they might be able to start a tradition, no matter how short-lived it would be.

She opened her bedroom door and almost ran over Sadie, who was running from the loft to the top of the stairs as well.

"Sorry!" Becca said, just as Sadie blocked her from mowing her down by holding up two candlesticks, replete with candles.

"Look what I found in that armoire thingy on the wall! They look like Shabbat candles, right? I mean I'm pretty sure *any* candles can be Shabbat candles. I'm guessing the reason why they even exist in the rental has more to do with summer storms and power outages, but not too shabby for our first Friday dinner, am I right?"

Becca's heart swelled, though she didn't entirely understand why. It just felt like—a sign. She shook her head and chuckled.

"What did I say? I *know* they aren't the real thing, but you said Shabbat dinner, and this will make it feel like Shabbat dinner."

"No," Becca replied, hoping to placate Sadie with a smile. "I was laughing at me, not you. I just—I believe in science, you know? And there's nothing scientific about me suggesting this dinner and *you* happening to find candles."

Sadie bumped her hip against Becca's and grinned. "Maybe you're starting to realize that when you put something out into the universe that you really want, the universe might actually hear you. Now let's go see if the universe can hear your thoughts about our cute houseboy."

Becca's mouth fell open, but Sadie didn't wait for her to respond. She spun on her heel, her towel-dried sandy hair swishing against her bare shoulders as she sauntered down the stairs in a casual but sexy black tube dress.

Maybe they were both tossing out requests to the universe tonight. Because with every step Becca took down the stairs, she silently hoped it was Leo on the other side of the door while she was pretty certain Sadie was praying it was Max.

So it was no surprise that they both deflated a bit when they opened the door to find Shelby and Delilah standing together under a giant Green Bay Packers umbrella.

"My father would be so proud," Becca said from over

Sadie's shoulder. "He's one of those Chicagoans who turned into a Packers fan."

Shelby cleared her throat as she stepped over the threshold and wiped her red Chucks on the welcome mat, a grocery tote in each of her hands. "*D's* the Packers fan," she said with her lilting accent. "*I* couldn't care less about football, base-ball, basketball, tennis ball..." She laughed. "I guess that last one's just *tennis*. Let's just say I'm not a fan of *balls* in any way, shape, or form." She laughed at her own joke, as did the other three women.

"Right there with you," Delilah said. "You know, unless The Tiger comes knocking on my door."

Shelby rolled her eyes as Delilah closed her umbrella and set it against the wall next to the door.

"Yeah, yeah. My girl gets a free pass," Shelby said. "It's not even that he has *balls*. But that *tiger* is past eighty."

Delilah scoffed. "And Helen Mirren is seventy-seven."

All four women sighed.

"I *do* love Helen Mirren," Becca said. "The woman can do Queen Elizabeth, Catherine the Great—"

"And drive the *hell* out of a car in *F9*," Sadie added.

"There it is," Shelby said. "Okay, I stand corrected. You can like your seasoned crooner if it means I get Helen Mirren."

"Deal," Delilah said, and Shelby set one of her bags down so the two women could shake on it.

"Come on in," Sadie told them, leading the two women out of the entryway and toward the kitchen, with Becca trailing behind. "I cleared out room in the fridge. I figured we'd wait until everyone got here to decide who wants what before we start cooking."

"Oh, Max is here," Delilah called over her shoulder as she and Shelby started unloading the perishables into the fridge. "Evie's waiting in the car while he wrangles his brother from the tent."

Becca stopped short, and Sadie—several steps ahead—did the same.

Becca gave herself a beat, then started moving again until she was in the kitchen with everyone else.

"Could you repeat that last bit again?" Becca asked, her pulse quickening.

Delilah straightened and pivoted to face Becca and the still-silent Sadie.

"Max's brother, Leo, lives in the tent on the beach. I thought you both knew that. He maintains the property for Ted and Andrea and a couple other homeowners on the lake. Have you ladies not met Leo yet?"

Becca swallowed. Oh, they'd *met* Leo. Seen him in the buff. Treated his injury. Maybe had an impure thought or two about the guy. Okay, those last two were all Becca...she hoped.

"Max never said..." Sadie started.

"And Leo never said..." Becca added.

Shelby finished what she was doing, closed the fridge, and brushed off her hands before joining the fray.

"Yeah, they're estranged," Shelby said. "Which is pretty

funny when you think about the fact that they live in the same town and kind of sort of work together sometimes. Plus, Evie *loves* Leo, so she won't put up with not seeing him when she's here, which is the only reason why Max is coaxing him out of the tent right now. But the two boys—and I say *boys* because that is what they act like when it comes to their relationship—well, I guess that's their story to tell. Anyway, tonight should be interesting."

Sadie spun slowly to face Becca, a strained yet puzzled expression on her face that Becca was sure mirrored her own. Neither one of them said a thing, but Becca imagined their silent conversation in her head.

They're brothers!

This is bananas.

What are the odds that you would be attracted to—and that I would be attracted to—

We can't mess with family when all either of us could have is a vacation fling.

Wait. Did Becca want a vacation fling with *the cute house-boy*? She'd never—*flung*—before. Would she even know how? Would *he* even want to? Did it even matter that she was asking herself these questions because clearly she and Sadie had *just* wordlessly established that both men were now off-limits?

Hadn't they?

The porch door slid open in time with a crash of thunder, and all four women yelped as a waterlogged Max squelched over the threshold.

"Where's Leo?" Becca asked before anyone else could.

Max's jaw tightened, and his hair dripped onto his shoulders. "Still in that damned *tent*. He didn't even have the decency to unzip it to talk to me."

"Did you ask him *nicely* to come out?" Delilah asked, clear accusation in her tone.

Max unzipped his rain jacket, which had at least protected his torso, but his jeans were positively soaked.

"D...now isn't the time...I need to get Evie out of the car, and I'm *sure* I'll be getting an earful from her."

"I'll get her!" Sadie said. "I mean, you need to dry off. There are plenty of towels under the sink in the downstairs bathroom."

Max's shoulders relaxed, and his gaze softened. "Are you sure? That would be—I mean, *thank* you, Sadie."

"You can use the Packers umbrella!" Delilah called as Sadie turned for the door. "It's an umbrella built for two!"

Max kicked off his sand-and-mud-caked work boots and headed—with a little less squelching—toward the bathroom.

"We can't just leave Leo out there," Becca said, especially when she knew now he was only there—and not taking shelter on their porch—because Max was here.

She grabbed her phone from her pocket—because *thank you*, maxi dress with pockets—and fired off a text to Leo.

Becca: **Please come in. I don't want you to get hurt again.**

Three dots appeared immediately.

> *Leo:* **You worried about me, Doc?**

Becca groaned and realized that Delilah and Shelby were watching her more intently than she wanted to admit.

> *Becca:* **Yes. I'm a doctor. Doctors worry about their patients.**
>
> *Leo:* **So that's the extent of our relationship? Doctor/Patient?**

She sighed.

> *Becca:* **Just get inside. Please. I promise Max will behave. But maybe you should have told me he was your brother before I invited you both to dinner.**
>
> *Leo:* **Maybe you should have told me you knew my brother.**
>
> *Becca:* **I didn't know he was your brother. OMG. This is the dumbest argument. Please come inside and stop acting like a child.**

She regretted the text as soon as she sent it. But there was no taking it back. Shit, she wanted to take it back.

Three dots appeared, then disappeared, then appeared again.

Becca started typing an apology, but Leo's text popped up before she could finish.

Leo: **You sound just like him.**

"What's he sayin'?" Shelby asked in a loud whisper. Becca's throat burned.

Becca: **I was out of line. I'm sorry. Please come inside. For me. Not as your doctor, but for me.**

Ten seconds passed without a response, then thirty. No three dots either. So she finally looked up.

"Things are really bad with them, huh?" she asked, and Delilah and Shelby both nodded.

The front door flew open, ushering in Sadie and Evie. Delilah and Shelby rushed over to greet the little girl Becca knew must be the star of the show whenever Max had her in tow.

Becca, however, made her way out onto the screened-in porch. Watching. Waiting. *Hoping.*

Then she saw it, the bouncing light headed her way. A flashlight.

She pulled open the porch's outer door just in time for Leo to run in, one hand holding the flashlight and the other making sure the hood of his rain jacket didn't fall off his head.

"Oh, thank god," she said, and without thinking, threw her arms around his neck and kissed him square on the lips.

"Holy shit," she heard from Sadie over her shoulder.

Becca jumped back and covered her mouth.

"Holy shit indeed," Delilah said with chuckle.

"Ho-ly *shit*," Max echoed, having popped up behind Becca's audience.

Leo looked at her with his devilish, one-dimpled grin, and her heart felt like it stuttered before it began pulsing again.

"*Holy* shit," she whispered, realization in her tone. "Holy *freaking* shit."

"That'll be five bucks, folks," Evie said, holding out her palm. "Though I wholeheartedly agree with every single word you all just said."

CHAPTER FIFTEEN

SADIE

Leo had surprised them all by showing up with a large tote bag hanging from his shoulder that contained a portable electric grill. No one had *noticed* the tote because they'd been too focused on Becca and Leo locking lips the second he made it through the door. And then, after everyone who'd dropped a *holy shit* willingly gave Evie a dollar—because *anything* to change the subject at that point—they'd gotten busy in the kitchen.

Without realizing it, Sadie had taken on the role as head chef, barking orders—lovingly, of course—to Shelby and Delilah as they seasoned the burgers, Max and Evie as they scrounged through the fridge deciding whether or not to add goat cheese or blue cheese to the salad. Of course, Sadie told them to use goat. She'd put Becca on table-setting duty and had stationed Leo at the grill since it belonged to him, and he seemed to know it well.

Sadie's makeshift restaurant was a well-oiled machine, with a tally of zero injuries when all was said and done and only *one* hot dog casualty—a *kosher* dog, by the way—that had gotten a little too charred when Leo seemed to get lost in thought staring at Becca as she set the table and situated the makeshift Shabbat candles.

"Can that thing catch on fire?" Sadie asked. "Because you are testing the limits of the dog *and* the grill."

"Shit! Sorry." That had snapped the man out of his haze, but it cost them the dog.

"Uncle *Leo*," Evie called from the other end of the island.

"Add it to my tab, Small Fry," he responded with a wink, but Sadie noticed that Max hadn't looked up from where he was expertly—yet tensely—slicing an apple into thin half-moons to add to the salad.

Things were coming together. Sadie had even been able to sneak off to an empty side of the counter, where she used a can of pumpkin puree she'd happened to find to whip up the batter that would be her baked pumpkin doughnuts. Maybe Sadie had given Becca a hard time about her whiteboard and over-the-top first-aid kit, but Sadie herself was a different kind of prepared. She might not be able to glue someone back together after suffering a nasty gash to the cheek, but if you needed a stainless-steel doughnut pan, Sadie Bloom had you covered.

Just before the last burger was flipped and the last dog

charred, Sadie snuck up behind Becca as the other woman straightened napkins that didn't need straightening and repositioned plates that didn't need repositioning.

"Are you physically unable to enter the kitchen?" Sadie whispered over Becca's shoulder, and Becca jumped. "Is it like a vampire thing where you need to be invited in?"

"I'm busy doing what you *told* me to do," Becca whispered back through clenched teeth without turning around.

Sadie grinned. As much as she wanted this friendship between them to keep moving forward, the good doctor certainly deserved some button pushing after what they'd all witnessed between her and Leo. Didn't Becca get it? There was nothing wrong with shooting her shot. No one was judging. Sadie, for one, wanted to cheer her on. But Becca had to cheer herself on first.

"So you're really going to pretend like you didn't lay one on the naked houseboy?" Sadie asked.

Push.

Becca finally spun on her heel, forcing Sadie to take a step back.

"He wasn't *naked* when I—when I...you *know*," Becca whisper-shouted as she glanced wildly over Sadie's shoulder into the kitchen, where everyone else was still hard at work.

Sadie bit back a grin, but she wasn't fooling her roommate. Becca narrowed her eyes, fixing Sadie in place with her stare.

"Yikes," Sadie said. "You look exactly like Evelyn when you do that."

Becca's mouth fell open. "Did you just accuse me of being like my mother?"

Push. Push.

"I don't know. Does your mother kiss men she barely knows after inviting them over for dinner?" Sadie threw her hand over her mouth to keep from bursting out laughing as Becca simply stared at her in horror.

Becca was so close to finally choosing herself. If Sadie had to be the one to give her a little nudge, well then, she would nudge away.

"Come *on*," Sadie told her. "*Someone* has to acknowledge what happened and admit it was badass. You are a badass, Becca Weiland, and you need to own it. "

Becca's shoulders fell, and she let out a breath. "I don't *know*," she whispered. "I just *wanted* to, and I think—god, I *hope*—he wanted it too."

And there it was, the reason Sadie pushed. She wanted Becca to see that *she* wanted Leo. And there was nothing wrong with that.

"Order up!" Evie called from the kitchen, playing the role of Sadie's line cook to perfection.

"I'm proud of you, Posh," Sadie added under her breath, and then she pivoted back toward the kitchen to bark her orders—*lovingly*, again, of course—to her makeshift staff.

Now, as everyone took their seats, the dining room table was covered with platters of hot dogs, hamburgers, grilled corn on the cob, arugula salad, a couple bottles of red, a bottle of white, and a six-pack of Spotted Cow beer. The room was filled with mouthwatering aromas of an early Fourth of July—and tension as thick as the frozen custard they were selling at the street fest.

"So," Delilah started, popping the cork from one of the bottles of red and filling Shelby's glass before filling her own. "Tell us more about this Shabbat dinner thing you mentioned earlier, Becca."

"Oh!" Becca responded, looking both relieved that Delilah hadn't asked her something *else* but also a little freaked out to be put on the spot.

"In Judaism it signifies the day of rest," Leo interjected, and Sadie raised her brows, impressed not only that he knew the holiday but that he used it as an opportunity to come to his lady love's rescue. "You know the whole deal—God's creations took six days, and on the seventh he rested. So—we remember and we recline. That was what my mom used to always say when I was a kid and I'd forget why we lit candles and said prayers. I appreciated it less in high school, but now I kind of miss it." He shrugged.

Becca kicked her shin under the table. "Ouch!" Sadie growled under her breath, and she guessed her expressed amusement hadn't been as subtle as she'd hoped.

"You're Jewish?" Becca asked.

"Our *father* is," Max said before Leo could respond. "But Leo's mother isn't."

Leo sighed. "She converted. You *know* this. I was raised Jewish just like you were."

Max shook his head and laughed, but Sadie could tell it

wasn't a real smile. "So you're all grown up now, living in a damned *tent*? And what's with the healing gash on your cheek? Get into another bar brawl or is there an even better story this time?"

Leo's jaw tightened, and his cheeks flushed, but he didn't engage. He simply raised his glass of water in a not-so-sincere gesture of cheers and took a long, slow sip.

Evie looked up at her dad, then *Max* grunted an "Ouch" under *his* breath, and Sadie was pretty sure that Becca and the young girl were employing similar tactics.

"Max?" Sadie asked. "Can I talk to you really quickly on the front porch? I just remembered that the light's out, and I can't seem to reach it to replace the bulb."

"Now?" Max said, staring at her from across the table with a furrowed brow. "In the rain?"

Sadie slid her chair back. "It's a covered porch, and it's only a drizzle now. Plus I don't want anyone tripping or falling on their way out if they can't see. Come on. It'll be really quick. The food won't even have a chance to get cold."

"Um—okay," he agreed, then followed her to the front door and out onto the porch, which was perfectly well lit. "I don't—the light's fine. Why did you—?"

Sadie backhanded him on the shoulder. "What are you *doing* in there?" she chastised.

"What do you mean?" he asked, either playing dumb or blatantly unaware of his behavior.

"How old are you, Max Beckett?"

He shoved his hands into the front pockets of his jeans, his navy blue polo rising up for a second to give Sadie a peek at the tanned skin underneath. The man needed to shop for some longer shirts.

"Thirty-eight, but why do I feel like this is a trick question?"

Sadie shook her head—clearing it of any impure thoughts for the moment—and crossed her arms over her chest. "Because you just acted more like *eight* in there, embarrassing your brother in front of the whole table."

"*Half* brother," he corrected.

Sadie groaned. "You're doing it again. Family is family, Max. And whatever is going on between you and Leo, I get that it likely has to do with divorce *and* that it's none of my business. But you are setting a *really* shitty example for your daughter in there, who—if I'm not mistaken—is a child of divorce herself and *might*, someday, have to deal with a stepsibling or half-sibling situation herself. Now, I've only met Evie a couple times, but she seems like a pretty sharp kid. But let me tell you something, mister. You're never too young to turn jaded, and I'd hate to see that happen to that sweet girl in there."

Max opened his mouth to respond, hesitated, then asked, "Are you done?"

Sadie gave him one definitive nod of her head. "Yes, and thank you for coming to my TED Talk."

Max chuckled, and it took everything in her power not to smile back at his one-dimpled grin.

"Do you have kids?" he asked. "Because you sure as hell just put me in my place like no one has before—other than Evie, of course."

Sadie recoiled in horror. "*God*, no. It's a full-time job just taking care of *me*. I'm not going to add someone else to that list."

His expression softened, and she wondered if he saw through her humor-filled deflection or if that was just what happened when a parent talked about the subject of children.

"I'm sorry," he said, scrubbing a hand across his jaw, "for ruining your dinner. Things with me and Leo are just— complicated. But you're right. I was behaving like an asshole when really I should be trying to impress this beautiful woman I can't stop thinking about."

Sadie's mouth fell open. "You did *not* just try to use flattery to get out of the doghouse, did you?" This time she used her humor to hopefully mask the heat in her cheeks that was slowly spreading to other parts of her body.

"Will you answer one question for me?" Max inquired, taking the tiniest step closer to her.

She swallowed and wished for one or both of her contacts to fall out so she couldn't see that dimple, those deep blue eyes, or the stubble on his jaw.

"What?" she asked, rolling her eyes, defiance in her jutted-out chin as she hoped he couldn't tell he was getting to her.

"Did you wear that dress for me?"

She threw open the front door, desperate for the air-conditioning and for a room full of witnesses to keep her from taking a page from Becca and letting her body take the lead.

"I wore it for *me*," Sadie told him, raising a brow. "And so you could watch me walk away *while* it was on." And with that, she did her best sashay through the door, skidding only once on the slick tile before righting herself again. She didn't dare look over her shoulder before she made it back to the table, crossing her fingers that, despite her continued lack of poise whenever she was around this man, he took the time to appreciate the view.

But Sadie stopped short before sitting down, and a few seconds later she felt Max approach behind her, then do the same thing. She'd been worried either that everyone would be awkwardly waiting for them, which would then require some explanation or a continued lie about the outside light everyone probably knew was working just fine, *or* that dinner would be in full swing and their returned presence would interrupt the first bout of normalcy they'd had so far. But instead, they arrived to find Evie holding Leo's wrist as they lit the candles together, then waved their hands over the flames to welcome in the day of rest. Sadie and Max stared on as Leo continued by teaching Evie the Shabbat blessing, reciting one part and then waiting for her to repeat. Evie stood next to her uncle so that she was almost the same height as he was while sitting.

Sadie swallowed a knot in her throat. She'd never envisioned herself as a mother, but it wasn't because she didn't want children. She'd simply put off thinking about it because what was the rush when she was enjoying life one day at a time? Wasn't that what so many people strived to do, be present in their lives? So Sadie did it. She'd survived a childhood health scare and decided to grab life by the horns and enjoy the ride. Had she pushed her luck too far to think she could be present these next few weeks and enjoy her time with a certain man, his dimple, and his adorable daughter?

※

"What do you think, Dad?" Evie asked, pulling Sadie from her thoughts and back to the moment to find Max standing frozen beside her. "Can we start doing the candles on Fridays? I get to light them because *I'm* the woman of the house."

Sadie elbowed him gently in the ribs, and he coughed.

"You did a great job, Peanut. We—um—we can get some candles if you want. You'll have to teach *me* the blessing, though. It's been a while."

"We could all learn," Shelby said, swirling the wine in her glass before taking a sip. "I mean I know it's not *our* holiday, but I love the idea of celebrating the end of the week by taking time for ourselves—for family." She cupped her hand on Delilah's cheek. "And since you're the only family I've got in these parts, sugar, I think we can crash the party with these folks, don't you?"

Delilah laughed, then kissed Shelby's palm.

"Well, that settles it," Sadie said. "Becca and I are here for three more weeks, which means three more Fridays, and we expect all of you here before sundown each Friday night."

Becca craned her neck to glance at Sadie, a mixture of hope and fear swirling in her eyes. "We do?"

Sadie gave a definitive nod of her head, then hooked her arm through Max's, pulling him toward the table.

"We *do*," Sadie replied, repeating Becca's words. She ignored the dance of butterflies in her belly when her skin met Max's—as he walked with her rather than pulling away.

When they were all once again seated around the table, Sadie filled her own wineglass—then Becca's too. She held hers up. "To found families and new traditions—even if it's only for a short time."

Shelby and Delilah raised their glasses. Becca did the same, and Evie followed suit with her water. Only Max and Leo hesitated, both staring at the bottles of Spotted Cow in front of their plates.

Sadie cleared her throat. "Come on, boys. I'm not asking you to kiss and make up or anything. It's just dinner. You can make it through *four* dinners together for the sake of family, can't you?"

She raised her brows, waiting for one of the men to make the first move, but it looked like they were both playing chicken with each other. So—Sadie took a page from two of the other women at the table and reached her foot across to tap Max on the knee.

He huffed out a breath and shook his head, but he raised his bottle of beer. "Yeah. Okay," he relented. "Evie and I are in."

Leo gave his brother a sly grin, then raised his own bottle. "I knew you couldn't resist my devilish charm and boyish good looks. Must remind you of someone you knew before he was a jaded old man."

Max opened his mouth to offer a retort, but Sadie cut him off before the evening devolved into disaster and her toast went out the window.

"Cheers, everyone!" she called out, clinking her glass against Becca's, Evie's, and then Max's beer bottle. "Once we drink on it, this contract is binding, so—no takebacks!"

"*L'Chaim!*" Delilah said. "That means *To Life*, right?"

Sadie nodded in approval, and they all repeated Delilah's words and drank.

CHAPTER SIXTEEN

BECCA

E vie dozed on the couch, her head on Shelby's lap and her feet propped on Delilah's knees as if she were a seat belt in the shape of a ten-year-old girl. Max sat on Shelby's right, Sadie on Delilah's left, but Leo had perched himself on the floor, his beer bottle on the coffee table as he reclined on his elbows.

Becca watched it all from where she stood next to the dining room table, having just cleared the dessert plates, which showed no trace of Sadie's amazing pumpkin doughnuts. Becca had eaten two herself and had silently lamented there hadn't been enough to go around for thirds.

She filled her wineglass with iced tea for the second time since the wine bottles had been emptied. She felt satiated, only a little buzzed, and—happy?

Tonight, all these strangers who suddenly felt like

family….This could very well be defined as fun. Becca had found *fun*.

She rubbed her hand over her midsection, swearing that after only one day of letting go, she felt softer—freer. Becca was a doctor. Logically she knew her relationship with food wasn't a healthy one. The topic came up more often than not in her bimonthly visits with her therapist. But up until now she hadn't been able to admit that her relationship with her husband—her ex-husband—wasn't healthy either. Jeff wanted perfect, so Becca wanted to be perfect. But there was no such thing. There was just Becca.

Running or not running.

Enjoying whipped cream or depriving herself of it.

Admitting that she'd been wanting to kiss Leo all damned week or denying what seemed to be painfully obvious to everyone but herself. She sighed as she took in the sight before her, forgetting for the time being that it was only temporary. She missed Mackenzie and Grayson like crazy, but in this very moment—despite the evening getting off to both an awkward and a rocky start—Becca's heart felt strangely full.

"You gonna join us or what?" Sadie called over her shoulder. "Or are you just going to stare like you're Edward watching Bella sleep?"

Becca laughed. Five days ago, she couldn't get away from Sadie and her ribbing fast enough—unable to be in the presence of someone who both called her out and made her so damned envious. But now she welcomed it all with open arms because for the first time in months—maybe years—Becca felt like she could be herself, and it would be enough. Sure, she wasn't exactly certain what *being* herself meant, but there was a safety in Sadie's presence she wasn't anticipating.

"I think I'm going to sit on the porch for a few," she finally said. "Listen to the rain on the water."

Sadie waved her off, and Becca let her eyes linger for one brief moment on Leo, whose head was tilted back, his eyes softly shut.

☼

Becca breathed in the familiar scent of rain and sighed as she lowered herself into the glider and set her drink on the table. The temperature had dropped since the storm, so she crossed her arms over her chest for warmth. She rocked back and forth, eyes closed, as the steady rainfall lulled her not to sleep but into a state of calm she hadn't experienced since arriving in the sleepy resort town.

Maybe that was why she didn't hear the porch door open again or feel the weight shift on the glider. It was only when she stopped using her toes to rock herself back and forth that she realized she was still moving.

Her eyes blinked open to find Leo sitting next to her, his eyes fixed on the beach they couldn't quite see but knew was there.

Becca shivered, the chill setting deeper into her bones,

and without saying a word, Leo put an arm around her, pulling her to his side.

She froze for a second but then leaned into his warmth, not sure what he was doing, why he was here, or what it all meant. But she didn't want to think right now. She just wanted to *be*.

"I wanted it too, you know," he finally said as he kept them rocking at a slow, soothing pace. "I wanted to kiss you the other night, when you patched me up. Hell, I had the strangest urge to kiss you when you found me in the kitchen the day you arrived, but it seemed a little inappropriate for too many reasons to count."

Becca bit her bottom lip and smiled, thankful he couldn't see the heat creeping up her neck and into her cheeks.

"Do you mean because you were naked and ten years younger than me?"

He chuckled. "I *meant* because you were a stranger, a tenant, and yes—maybe the naked thing. But when are you going to get past that age thing?"

She blew out a breath, exposing the one thing she'd been holding on to all evening that had the potential to make this night blow up in her face. "You called your brother a jaded old man at dinner, and he can't be that much older than me."

Leo stopped rocking, and she straightened to meet his gaze, expecting some humor-laden remark to lighten the mood, but instead Leo's dimple—his ever-present grin—was nowhere to be found.

"Becca…" He sighed. "Don't you ever just want to get a rise out of someone for the simple sake of getting them to react to you? To give a shit?"

Becca thought about all the ways she'd tried to get her sister's attention growing up, how the five years between them felt like fifty once Alissa was a teen and Becca was still in elementary school. Then came Gabi, and—well—Becca never stood a chance after that.

Yeah. She knew full well what Leo meant.

When she didn't vocalize her response, Leo continued, "Age is *just* a number. It doesn't mean shit to me, not when you're—well—*you*."

She swallowed a knot in her throat. Had Jeff *ever* talked to her like that? She knew she'd been in love with her husband at some point, but she couldn't remember the falling, couldn't remember her heart betraying logic, which she felt like it was doing right now.

But this wasn't *love*. She'd known Leo for a matter of days. And what did she really know other than he was a feast for the eyes and she wanted to feel his lips on hers again?

"You owe your niece two bucks," she said, not knowing how to respond. "Two shits equals two dollars."

Leo tilted his head back and laughed.

Logic told her to ignore his exposed neck, but something else propelled her closer, urging her to press her lips to his skin.

So she did.

He smelled like soap and salt and the outdoors, and he

tasted—hell, she didn't know like what, only that she wanted more.

He stopped laughing, and she pulled away, realizing she'd once again done what *she* wanted without asking—despite what he'd just said about wanting to kiss her—if he wanted it too. Right now. In this moment.

He answered her racing thoughts by threading his fingers into her hair and cradling her head in his palm. Then he leaned down and pressed his lips to hers. Softly. Tentatively.

"What if someone sees?" she whispered against him.

"I. Don't. Give. A. Shit," he whispered back.

"That's three," she squeaked before he silenced her mouth with his own.

Finally, Becca Weiland stopped thinking and simply let herself *be*.

Leo pulled her legs over his so she was almost sitting on his lap. He nipped at her bottom lip, tasted her with his tongue, and paid special attention to her chin, the line of her jaw, and then her neck. She hummed with pleasure and smiled against his skin as he let her explore as well. It never went beyond kissing, yet it felt like the most intimate connection she'd had with a man since—since—did kissing Jeff ever feel like this? It had to have, right? In the beginning? She couldn't remember. Whatever this was with Leo, it was nothing more than infatuation. A crush. He probably had some sort of older woman fetish, but right now, she didn't care. Not when he tasted so good. Not when his skin on hers made her light up from within. Not when—

A crash of thunder jolted them apart, and the lights inside the house flickered once, twice, and then *poof.* The power was out.

"Oh no!" Becca cried. "Does this place have a basement? Is there a sump pump? Does it have a battery backup? We flooded back home after Jeff promised me he'd replace the battery for the sump and then forgot and—"

She stopped herself before she went off on Leo for something *he* hadn't done and for a mistake that Jeff had made years ago. They'd gotten into a huge fight while bailing water. But the makeup sex had been better than any physical contact they'd had in months. This wasn't then. *They*—Becca and Leo—weren't *them*, a married couple so complacent in their routine that they thrived on conflict because it woke them up—made them feel alive. She and Leo weren't fighting. They weren't *anything* as far as labels went. But she felt alive nonetheless.

"Wait for it," Leo said softly, then pulled out his phone, tapping gently on the screen.

Inside, phone flashlights were lit and moving around as the rest of the guests sprang up from the couch, trying to figure out what to do.

"And three, two, one," Leo said, the lights flickering back on as he finished his countdown.

Over her shoulder, Becca watched everyone else freeze where they stood. Even Evie was awake and rubbing her eyes, squinting at the once again well-lit room.

"Are you a wizard?" Becca whispered.

Leo laughed. "Come on," he said, threading his fingers through hers and pulling her up from the glider.

Becca stood, glanced down at their hands, then back up at Leo.

"Is this okay?" he asked, brows raised.

She bit her lip and nodded, letting him lead her through the door and back into the house.

"Every house on the lake is dark," Max said, scratching the back of his neck as he stared past Becca and Leo. "So how do we have power again?"

Sadie gave Becca a knowing grin, and Becca simply shrugged.

Leo let go of Becca's hand and crossed his arms over his chest.

"Ted and Andrea had me install a backup generator after that snowstorm knocked over a power line last winter and the rental lost power and heat for twenty-four hours," he said. "I'm surprised you didn't do the same for your place."

Delilah scoffed. "Or *our* place."

Max rolled his eyes. "A whole house generator can run you anywhere between three and ten *grand*. It's not something you just *do*. And since when do *you* know how to do things like install generators?" Max nodded at Leo but didn't wait for him to answer before turning his attention back to Delilah and Shelby. "I *did* install a battery backup for your sump pump *and* emergency generators at the salon and coffee shop, in case neither of you remember. But do I get credit for that?"

Evie yawned, then brushed a big brown curl out of her eyes. "Is it really about the credit, Dad, or about doing something nice for your friends?"

"Yeah," Sadie said. "Do you want to teach your daughter to be self*ish* or self*less*?"

Evie sidled up next to Sadie. "Yeah," she echoed, hooking her arm through Sadie's. "What *she* said!"

Sadie's eyes grew wide, and Shelby burst into a fit of laughter.

Max threw his arms in the air. "I guess I'm the bad guy here, huh?" he grumbled. "Wait!" he exclaimed, pulling his phone out of his pocket. "This might be...YES!" He glanced out at the lake, seemingly to confirm something. "Power's back on over on our side, which means it's time to get *you* to bed, Peanut." He scooped Evie into his arms, and the young girl squealed with laughter.

"Time to get *you* to bed, darlin'," Shelby said, bumping her hip against Delilah's.

Becca watched Sadie's expression fall at the realization that the party was officially over, which meant Max was leaving. Then Becca realized the same would be true for Leo, who'd be heading back to his tent, right? There was no reason for him to stay. Except...it *was* still raining.

Everyone clustered at the front door at the same time, Evie's second wind quickly devolving into an overtired ten-year-old whose head lolled on her father's shoulder.

"Thank you," he said to Becca and Sadie, with no free hand to shake and no means for him and Sadie to attempt anything remotely resembling what had happened between Becca and Leo outside. Just an awkward smile from one to the other and a look of longing in Sadie's eyes that Becca would recognize even if she'd been standing on the other end of the room.

"We're doing this again next Friday, right?" Shelby asked. "It's a thing now, whether there is power or not. I mean, we don't want to impose..."

"Yes we do," Delilah added, grabbing her Packers umbrella from where it rested against the wall next to the door. "I love getting out of the house and having somewhere to go, even if it's just down the street. Plus, until Max gives our *home* a generator, your rental is about the safest place to be during storm season."

"*I* could install a generator for you two," Leo said, "if Max is too busy. I might even be able to do it for a quarter of the labor cost that he charges." Leo leaned in close but whisper-shouted so Max, who already had one foot out the door, was sure to hear: "I know his rates, and I don't think he's giving you the friends and family discount."

"Damnit, Leo, I *swear*..." Max grumbled through clenched teeth.

"One dollar, Dad," Evie warned, her eyes closed but her ears apparently still wide awake.

"All right. All right," Delilah said, gently pushing Max and Evie out the door. "We made it through *most* of the night without you two starting another pissing contest." But while she and Shelby were still on the porch, Delilah glanced back over her shoulder and mouthed *I'll call you* to Leo, her hand pantomiming a telephone.

Finally, everyone was out the door, setting off into the drizzle and after—into their cars.

Sadie pushed the door shut, then spun around to face Becca and Leo.

"I'm—uh—gonna go outside and just check on the generator before I head out. I'll show you the app and how to turn it off and on if you need it," Leo told them.

"Wait!" Becca said, then threw open the front hall closet so she could hand him one of the umbrellas.

He flashed his one-dimpled grin and thanked her before heading out the back door.

Becca sighed, and Sadie let out a soft whimper.

"You got kissed, and what do I have to show for wearing a strapless bra all night? Not that I expected anything because—well—the man is a *father* and I'm *me*."

Becca raised her brows. "You like him. And you already have daughter approval, which is a major accomplishment without you even trying. I don't understand why you're not going for it. Seems to go against your effortlessly cool persona."

Sadie scoffed, but she was smiling. "You think I'm effortlessly cool?"

"I'm not dignifying that with a response. And you're evading the question, which I guess doesn't matter because we can't—I mean, they are brothers and obviously have a *lot* between them that would get even more muddied if we got involved. Wouldn't it?"

Sadie blew out a breath. "Okay. Yes. I like Max. But he went through a painful divorce, and he only gets Evie part-time. I would definitely muddy that. But you...you're getting your groove back, my friend. And I am certain Leo Beckett would be more than happy to groove with you for a few weeks."

Becca spun on her heel and backed up next to her roommate so they were both leaning against the front door, shoulder to shoulder.

After a long moment, Sadie was the one to break the silence.

"What have you done for yourself?" Sadie asked. Then she chuckled. "I mean, I know what you did for yourself at Shelby's salon—and the morning after that. But what have you *really* done for you?"

Sadie was right.

Becca had cried. She'd taken on extra shifts at the office just to prolong going home on the nights the kids weren't there. She'd upped the mileage on her morning runs, and she'd added a self-help podcast or two to her running playlist to fill the gaps between visits with her therapist. But what item on that list had brought her any sort of joy in the past year? It had all been reactive—first to the realization that her marriage was over, then to the anger and betrayal of Jeff moving out, the months of mediation before either of them sought out lawyers, to finally—the divorce. She had done what she'd needed to survive the past year, but up until her hangover earlier this week—and the resulting self-pleasure session that had pretty much altered her worldview—Becca Weiland had never once considered doing something just because she wanted to until Leo.

"Fine," she said, the word coming out breathy and light. "Kissing our cute naked houseboy brought me joy. Except he sort of kisses much more like a cute naked house *man*."

She squeezed her eyes shut as Sadie squealed with delight.

"Did I miss something good?" she heard Leo ask and hoped to god he truly hadn't heard.

Becca's eyes flew open, and she and Sadie both stood up straight.

"Just that Becca can't possibly let you go back to your tent while it's still raining. At least not until we finish what's left of the wine and play a little—I don't know, Never Have I Ever?"

Becca's mouth parted into a perfect O, but Leo grinned.

"I'm in," he said.

"Excellent," Sadie began, heading toward the dining room table and the rest of the wine. Then she called over her shoulder, "Never have I ever hoped my roommate would be pleasured by a younger man." She threw a hand over her mouth. "Oops! I guess I have to drink!"

CHAPTER SEVENTEEN

SADIE

When Sadie woke up the next morning, she put on her glasses, kissed the empty can of cola next to her bed, and thanked the ibuprofen for getting her through the night, but she still needed a greasy breakfast and a morning caffeine kick.

Becca's door was still shut, which meant she'd already gone on her run and had gone back to bed *or* hadn't followed through on *her* pre-hangover routine. Whichever it was, Sadie did her best to keep quiet as she pulled her hair up, wiped the drool from the side of her cheek, and shuffled toward the stairs.

She'd slept hard last night. And had the *weirdest* dream. Okay, so it wasn't weird as in she was driving the Navy Pier Ferris wheel down Michigan Avenue chasing a giraffe that had escaped from Lincoln Park Zoo—a dream she *did* have last winter when she had a monster sinus infection and maybe hit the liquid NyQuil a bit too hard. This dream was weird in how it felt so real, like she was clawing at a memory rather than something her brain contrived while she was unconscious.

Max was there. He was drinking a cup of decaf and sitting outside Evie's bedroom door until the last leg of the storm had subsided. They were talking about what Evie would do with the money she collected in the swear jar at the end of the summer, and Sadie had told him—something important. But she couldn't remember what it was—only that she'd been afraid to tell him but *had* to tell him.

She stopped halfway down the stairs, squeezing her eyes shut, trying to visualize the scene. Why was it that the conversation felt real yet she couldn't actually *picture* Max sitting outside a bedroom door? It wasn't as if she knew what his house looked like, but wouldn't her brain have made something up like him sitting on a knotted pine floor, his back against a door he'd painted teal or purple or whatever Evie's favorite color might be? Instead, her brain conjured the image of—words. Words on a screen. Three dots pulsing as the person on the other end of the line typed a response to one of Sadie's items on the aforementioned list.

Her list?

What list?

Oh. My. God.

The *list*!

And...the pulsing dots were real. The conversation was

real. She hadn't dreamt about talking to Max. She'd actually talked to him—well, texted him—last night before she fell asleep.

Her eyes flew open as she took the rest of the steps down two at a time, stumbling when she reached the floor and her knee slammed onto the cold ceramic tile.

Sharp pain shot through her leg, and tears involuntarily pricked at her eyes, blurring her vision despite having her glasses on.

"Mother *fudger!*" she yelped, then pulled herself to her feet.

Why hadn't she just said *fuck*? It wasn't like Evie was in the house to call her out, yet somehow the young girl's possible chastisement niggled its way into Sadie's brain, making her censor herself even in the midst of ridiculous pain.

She limped the rest of the way to the kitchen, sure she'd see the start of a nasty bruise before lunchtime. And there it was, on the fridge, staring back at her in all its taunting glory. The *list.*

Or more precisely, SADIE AND BECCA'S FUDGING FANTASTIC FRIDAY NIGHT DINNER LIST. Because they had to leave the list on the fridge for accountability, which meant only clean language for their Friday night dinner guests.

FIVE FOOLPROOF PATHS FOR FUN (AND A LITTLE TROUBLE) BEFORE THE FINAL FRIDAY

Geez. What a mouthful.

Sadie laughed to herself as she read the title again.

Someone liked their alliteration. Sadie was positive it wasn't her.

She took a deep breath and squared her shoulders, ready to see what trouble the two of them promised to get into before their month was up.

1. Food (try something new).

Okay. This was in Sadie's wheelhouse. She could try something new, try cooking something new. Really, anything food related was up her alley. This one would be easy.

2. Fear (do one thing that scares you).

Um, Sadie was already terrified to read her text exchange with Max from the night before, so she considered that item checked off as well.

3. Find something you lost.

Sadie's brows furrowed. She couldn't remember where this one came from or what it meant. It wasn't like she was going to find the contact lens she'd lost on the beach.

She shrugged and moved on to number 4.

4. French (the kissing kind or the baking kind).

Sadie barked out a laugh. This was definitely Becca's plea for macarons. Her roommate could take care of the kissing kind while Sadie did the latter.

5. Flutter (find something or someone that does this to your heart).

Sadie swallowed. She conjured an image of Max's dimple and felt her heart do exactly as number 5 directed. But then another image popped into her head—the ER doctor who'd taken care of the dog bite on her chin when she was a kid who told her mom he wanted to keep her for observation after hearing a very different kind of flutter during her intake exam.

They fixed you, Sadie, she told herself. *For almost thirty years since, you've been the picture of health.*

She cleared her throat and sniffed away her fear. This was not the type of scary the list was for.

Then it hit her.

"Oh *shit!*" she hissed, not caring if Evie had supersonic hearing and was reprimanding her from a mile away. Because she remembered *everything* now.

Sadie scrambled back up to the loft, to where her phone sat charging on the nightstand. Before she even unlocked it, Max's most recent and unread text popped up in preview on her screen.

Max: Typos aside (which means you're either sleepy or drunk or both)...you want to do me? Just tell me when and where.

Her pulse quickened as she scrolled up through the short but sweet conversation they'd had about dinner—he'd thanked her for talking some sense into him on the porch; about the storm—how Evie wanted to be brave and sleep on her own despite the thunder and lightning after the rain picked up again once they'd gotten home. But Max couldn't bear to leave her door until *he* knew the storm was over. So he'd made a cup of decaf and hunkered down to ride it out— with Sadie on the other end of the line.

Finally, she let herself linger on the last thing she'd texted before dozing off—typos and all.

> *Sadie:* **Bet you didn't knew ur the only other thing that scares me besides my heart. Promised Becca to do a scary thing before we go. Does that mean i should do u?**

She flopped down on the bed, face in her pillow so she could scream.

She'd all but told him everything. Everything she'd meant to tell Becca last night before Never Have I Ever had turned into an alliterative list.

She needed someone to tell her she hadn't completely humiliated herself. She needed someone to tell her what to text back because she had to stop this Max thing before she selfishly took it too far.

After one final scream, Sadie peeled herself off her bed and made a beeline for Becca's door.

She knocked twice. "Please be awake!" she called through the door. "I *really* need your help."

Then she threw the door open.

Becca—wide awake—stared at her like a deer in headlights, blanket clenched under her chin.

"'Sup, Sadie?" she said with a nervous smile.

Sadie's brows furrowed. "*Sup?* You do *not* say *Sup.*"

Becca opened her mouth to say something else, and that's when Sadie caught the slightest flicker of movement from beneath the covers at the *foot* of the bed. Becca's knee jerked, and Sadie heard a distinct grunt that did *not* come from Becca's mouth.

A second later, *Leo's* head popped out from under the blanket where Becca's feet should have been.

"Morning, Sadie," he said with a wink. "You think you could give us another minute or two before Becca helps you with whatever needs helping? I'm trying to help her win her next game of Never Have I Ever."

For a second, Sadie forgot all about *why* she'd barged into Becca's room and instead applauded her roommate for a job *very* well done. Or *almost* very well done.

"Do not rush on my account, kids. I'll just be in the kitchen questioning all of my life choices whenever you two are done."

Leo popped back under the blanket as Sadie backed out of the room.

Oh. My. God, she mouthed to her roommate.

I know, Becca mouthed back.

And then she was out the door, closing it and spinning back toward the stairs.

Sadie's knee throbbed, a bruise already visible, and she had no idea what her next move should be with Max. But she couldn't stop smiling the whole way down the stairs, and into the bathroom. She was still grinning as she brushed her teeth and splashed some water on her face, as she strode through the living room and out the back door until her toes sank into the wet grass and soon after the warm sand, which was quickly drying in the sun.

Becca's happiness buoyed her out of her head and into the moment, this beautiful moment she wouldn't squander no matter what lay ahead.

In the distance, she heard a dog barking. She glanced to her left and saw the goldendoodle, maybe fifty yards off, galloping her way.

Penny! Seriously, that dog had it out for her. But worse was the realization that if Penny was on the loose, it meant Max Beckett wasn't far behind.

Braless *and* shoeless, Sadie began to sprint like it was the zombie apocalypse and she was the last human left on earth. Because until she figured out what to say to him about wanting to do him, she preferred to say nothing at all.

But after only about ninety seconds—which felt more like ninety minutes—her lungs burned, and a painful stitch began to throb in her side. She was pleased to realize, though, that she didn't feel faint or like she couldn't catch her breath. Maybe she'd been worrying for nothing. All the more reason to keep on keeping on, being present in the moment. Except in this particular moment, cupping her breasts as she ran had thrown her center of gravity way off, causing her to pitch forward and *almost* fall more than once in the short span of time.

Not again. Not again. Not a*gain*.

Did she have time to make it back to Leo's tent and zip herself inside? Could a dog chew through a tent to get to her? Her head told her *yes*, so her legs continued to drag her forward the best they could.

When her feet, shins, side, boobs, *and* lungs could no longer take it, Sadie slowed to a power walk and eventually to a stop, hands on her knees as she heaved, the sound of Penny's bark looming closer by the second.

She spun slowly and straightened, ready to face her attacker—with her eyes squeezed shut. Was she terrified beyond all recognition? Of course. But adrenaline wasn't enough to turn Sadie Bloom—a woman who would claim you *could* be allergic to exercise—into an Olympic sprinter, no matter how much her pride—and life—depended on it.

Sadie took off her glasses, folded them into her hand, and opened her eyes. She didn't want to *clearly* see her impending death, but she did want to have some semblance of an idea of how many seconds she had left—and how soon after Max might find her braless, shoeless, just-out-of-bed corpse.

She let out an incredulous laugh. Here she thought her ticker would be the thing to do her in when in reality it was a goldendoodle who was hell bent on taking her out and making sure Sadie was aware of her posthumous humiliation while it happened.

All she could see was the blur of golden curls, and all she could hear was the canine's excited bark as the beast readied to savor the meal she'd been denied almost a week ago.

"PENNY! Dammit, Penny. DAMMIT."

She heard the man's voice before she saw the man himself. But the dog—stopped.

Sadie put on her glasses to find Penny *sitting*, less than ten feet away from her. And jogging slowly, several yards behind, was Max.

Sadie burst into a fit of laughter, yet soon realized tears were leaking out of the corners of her eyes in steady streams.

Oh god. She was crying. No—not crying. Sadie Bloom was standing barefoot and braless in her thicker than thick glasses—and she was *sobbing*.

"Shit," Max said, passing Penny and striding toward Sadie. "Stay, Penny," he added over his shoulder, and the dog plopped down in the sand as if she'd always planned on making that her resting spot. "Jesus. Sadie. Are you okay? Did she bite you? She's never bitten anyone ever, but *fuck*. Tell me what happened. Are you hurt? Can you talk? Should I call 911?"

Sadie let loose a hiccuping sob and managed to shake her head in response.

"No you're not hurt?" Max asked. "Or no you can't talk? What about the 911 question?"

"Not. Hurt," she said through heaving breaths. "Need. A minute. To talk."

Max blew out a breath, his shoulders relaxing, but Sadie couldn't stop the floodgates now that they were opened. She swiped her forearm under her running nose, cursing whatever she might have done in a previous life to deserve such karmic retribution as to *always* run into Max Beckett whenever she was at her worst. With everyone else in her entire life, Sadie was the brave face, the comic relief, the—according to Becca—effortlessly cool.

Not in Glass Lake, Wisconsin. Not when this man and his stupid, earnest, unabashed affection was around.

She felt Max's strong arm wrap around her shoulder before she realized he'd moved closer to her.

"Let's sit down, okay?" he said softly.

Sadie let out a shuddering breath. "But—but what if Penny realizes I'm easy prey and comes at me again?"

Max skimmed a finger across her forehead, tucking a loose piece of hair behind her ear.

"I *know* she's a little rambunctious, but I promise she has never hurt a soul, and she does *not* want to eat you. Plus, I used her emergency recall word, and it worked, so I think— no, I *know*—you're safe. I'll keep you safe."

Sadie nodded and lowered herself to the sand, Max's arm still wrapped around her. She barely knew this guy and certainly shouldn't trust his ability to control what was clearly an uncontrollable beast, but his words felt sincere, and the way he held her made her *feel* like she really was safe, not just from the dog but from anything that tried to pull her from this moment.

Max took a small pack of tissues from the pocket of his shorts and handed it to her.

She let out something between a sniffle and a laugh but accepted his offering. "Do you just carry around emergency tissues in case you find random women bawling their eyes out on the beach?"

He chuckled. "Not random women bawling. Just one particular woman."

She elbowed him gently in the ribs as she blew her nose.

"Ow," he said with a laugh. "Evie's allergies. The pollen count has been pretty high this summer, so I always have some tissues on me just in case. It's super sexy, I know. A man who's always at the ready if you're about to sneeze."

The tears were slowing down, and Sadie's breathing was returning to normal. So she guessed she needed to give Max *some* sort of explanation.

She leaned her head against his shoulder so she didn't have to meet his gaze. Plus, he was wearing sunglasses, and if she caught a glimpse in the reflection of his lenses of what she must look like right now, she'd probably start running again.

Actually, who was she kidding? Sadie was *never* running again.

"Thank you," she said. "For the tissues. It's actually super sweet that you're so prepared for Evie's needs. From what I can tell, you're a great dad, Max." And it *was* also sexy, but she wasn't ready to admit that.

"Why do I sense a *but* coming after that?" he asked. "Does it have something to do with why you want to do me?" he added.

"First of all, *never* speak of my tipsy texting again. And second—" She sighed.

"Here it comes," Max said. "You desperately want to do me, but..."

"But you have enough on your plate without more complication," she told him. "And *I* am complication. And—and I live in Chicago, and you live here. Not that I'm assuming you'd want anything more past the three more weeks I'm going to be here, but—"

"Yikes," Max said. "*Two* buts."

Sadie laughed. "You said *two butts*." She sniffled. "See? Complicated *and* I can't take anything seriously."

He straightened, then leaned away so she was forced to raise her head from his shoulder, which also meant she *had* to look up at him.

His glasses were pushed up onto his head, and his baby blues stared at her with such intent.

"Me having a kid is an issue, isn't it?" he said. "Because the distance thing is not that big of a deal. I travel just as far to take Evie back and forth to her mom's. And you're *great* with Evie, by the way. I'd never even consider bringing a woman into my life who wasn't, which is the reason why I'm a little rusty at this dating thing. *Not* that we're dating. But I like you, Sadie. I've thought about you every day since we met, and I *do* think that if you gave me a chance, we *could* have something that goes beyond the next three weeks. And the dog? Penny? I think we're getting her training down to a science. I mean, her recall word works, and I don't even have to pay Evie when I say it."

Sadie's brows furrowed, and then realization bloomed. "*Dammit* is her recall word?"

Max groaned. "I guess it was my go-to word every time something went *wrong* with her training so that it kind of stuck. Now if she runs off before I can get her leash on—I'm *really* sorry about that, by the way—*Dammit, Penny* seems to work."

Sadie brushed her fingertips over the almost invisible scar on her neck and pressed her lips into a smile.

"Why does that make me like you even more?" she asked, then covered her mouth with her hand.

Max grinned. "So about those two *buts*..."

Sadie sighed. "Fine, Max. I like you, okay? I said it. I like you, and for some reason, despite the ways we keep running into each other, you seem to like me, but yes...there are *buts*." She didn't giggle this time. "Evie is great, like the greatest kid I've ever met next to my niece, but I am not mother or even stepmother material. Trust me. I'm thirty-seven, and my IUD is my best friend. I've *never* been in a serious relationship—by choice, I might add. And yes, despite Penny's amazing recall word and the impending joy I might get if I hear you having to use it in public, *this*...?" She motioned between them. "Would never work. You need steady and committed. What if I can't give you that?"

But why, now, did she want to try?

"What if I fall off the next roof I fix or get pulled into oncoming traffic by a rambunctious puppy before I can yell *Dammit*?" Max gave her his dazzling, one-dimple grin. "I don't know what's going to happen tomorrow or after your time here is done, but I'd be lying if I said I wasn't dying to find out."

Sadie cleared her throat. "And what if I knew I was going to fall off a roof tomorrow. Would you want to know?"

Max furrowed his dark brows, then breathed out a long sigh.

"Right now, Sadie, the only thing I want to know is what it would be like to kiss you."

Sadie sucked in a breath, and something in her shifted. Maybe she hadn't gotten it wrong all these years. Maybe living in the moment—a whole lotta fun and a little bit of trouble—was all anyone could really ask for. Max Beckett would be her little bit of trouble, but somehow she knew he'd also be the kind of FUN that required the word to be written in all caps.

Sadie rose onto her knees and clasped her hands around Max's neck. "I want to know the same thing you do, if that's okay."

He answered her with one soft nod before pulling her into him, brushing his lips against hers. His kisses were tentative and questioning. Careful. But Sadie didn't want *careful*. Careful meant she was fragile and would break, and the Sadie Bloom she'd built herself to be was invincible. Un*break*able. No matter what any doctor said.

So she kissed him a little harder, letting him know that she was strong. That *she* was the one in control. Max took her lead by slipping his tongue past her parted lips, and Sadie hummed a soft sigh against him. He tasted like the perfect summer morning. Like coffee and cinnamon and staying up too late, then wasting the next day away in bed.

Sadie Bloom had kissed her share of men—and even let those kisses lead to something more. But she'd always kept everything on the surface, vowing to live before settling down, as if somehow settling down meant no longer having the all-caps kind of fun.

Maybe it was watching her brother and Alissa struggle as teen parents, losing each other for more than twenty years before finding their way back. It didn't look fun even in lowercase.

Maybe it was her parents' unconventional relationship, two hippies who, while committed to each other, never truly seemed as if they'd settled down.

Or maybe it was a dog bite at ten years old that had turned into a cardiac surgeon closing an undiagnosed hole in her heart that would have been fatal if left untreated. Most fifth graders didn't contemplate life and death or how to outsmart the latter. Sadie thought it was by outrunning anything that might tie her down. So why did she want Max Beckett to tie her to anything he damn well pleased?

She smiled against his lips, the thought eliciting both pleasure and bittersweet longing that made her throat tight and her chest ache as he pulled her into his lap. Was she really collapsing into Max's lap, wrapping her legs around his waist, and wishing for things she certainly didn't want as if they were life-sustaining *needs*?

She was such a hypocrite. She thought Becca was the one with control issues, but Sadie had been controlling the trajectory of her life since age ten. Now she was letting one little scare at a routine checkup send her in the complete opposite direction. And for what? So she could miss out on someone like Max?

She stopped suddenly, frozen in place, his forehead dipped and resting against hers.

"You're spooked," he said, lips still resting on hers and sending tingles from her belly to her toes.

"Uh-uh," she told him.

"You're spooked," he began again. "You're conjuring up all the reasons why we shouldn't do this, but honestly, that sounds like torture. Don't you think? I mean why would we torture ourselves when we could have three more weeks of this?"

He kissed her again, his hands sliding down her back, skimming her butt as they wrapped around her thighs. He was still gentle, still careful, but he also somehow knew that she *wanted* his hands on her like this.

"Ugh," she said with a sigh.

"What?" he asked.

"Nothing. It's just that the universe is kind of a dick."

Max laughed, and she leaned back to look at him. His skin crinkled at the corners of his deep blue eyes, and the sight of that—of being the one to make this man smile all the way to his stupidly pretty eyes—made Sadie ignore all the what-ifs. Here on this beach, in *this* man's lap, Sadie wanted to make him her food (hello, Mr. Yummy); her fear (because he was scary in the most unexpected way); her finding something she'd lost (even though she'd never realized it was missing); her French (yeah, achievement unlocked on that one); and her flutter (the non-life-threatening kind). Max Beckett checked every box on her drunken list, alliteration be damned.

She just had one more *F* to add to the list. "Fuuuuck, you are going to get me in all sorts of trouble," she whispered.

Max laughed again. "That might deserve two donations to the jar."

"Hey," she said. "Are you sure about this? What if the next three weeks are amazing but what comes after is torture?"

He shrugged. "My newly found psychic abilities tell me that it would be worth it."

Sadie sighed. "Fine. But if this crashes and burns, we go our separate ways without protest so that we don't prolong the torture. *And* we don't tell Evie that we're doing whatever it is we're doing. I couldn't bear it if I somehow hurt her."

Max chuckled. "But hurting *me* is fair game?"

Sadie shrugged. "You're the one offering yourself up as tribute."

Yet hurting him was what scared her most.

"I guess I am," he said. " Okay. We leave Evie out of it. I'm in agreement there."

"Wait!" Sadie added, only now realizing who was missing from their second beach run-in. "Where *is* Evie?"

Max sighed. "It seems Delilah has recruited yet another generation of Tom Jones fandom in Evie. Once the morning rush dies down, she sometimes likes to commandeer a table and work on a craft while singing along with Delilah and The Tiger himself. Anyway, she's hanging with D until lunch."

Sadie laughed. "I love that for *so* many reasons."

"Gotta say," he continued, "since I have a little time this morning…I'm curious about what's on your agenda for the rest of the day and if I might be able to—um—assist *taking care of anything you might need.*"

Sadie narrowed her eyes at him. "Like patching another hole in our roof?"

Max shook his head.

Sadie glanced around the still empty stretch of beach, wondering when the paddleboarders and canoers would converge on their quiet moment. But since she and Max seemed equally focused on nothing further than the present… "What did you have in mind?" she asked, the corner of her mouth turning up.

He tucked his hands under her thighs once more and gave her a soft squeeze, then leaned back until he was sprawled on the sand, Sadie still straddling him.

"Whatever you want, Sadie Bloom. You're in control."

Oh, how she wished she were. But the second she lowered herself over him, pressing her lips to his, she knew she could fall in love with this man. And that scared her more than anything else.

Even dogs on a beach.

CHAPTER EIGHTEEN

BECCA

Becca stretched as she let Sadie snooze for five more minutes. Again. Of course, she did her stretching right next to Sadie's bed, sure to really focus on her breathing. Loudly. Right next to Sadie's head, which was buried under her pillow.

"This is *not* snoozing," Sadie said, her voice muffled.

"You're right, Sadie Bloom! Gold star for you!" Becca said, dropping to a squat next to her roommate's head. "I let you snooze while I brushed my teeth and again while I got dressed. Now my shoes are on, I'm all limbered up, and *you*, my friend, are coming running with me."

Sadie lifted her head, her cheek creased with sheet marks, and glared at Becca. Okay, she *tried* to glare at Becca, but instead she was glaring slightly past her line of sight.

"Hey. Four eyes. I'm over here," Becca said with a snort.

Sadie snarled and grabbed her glasses from the nightstand, sure to affix a steady glare this time around. "Aren't you like some Goodie Two-shoes who's not supposed to bully?"

Becca snorted. "No one is supposed to bully. But just once I maybe wanted to tease the popular pretty girl."

Sadie groaned and pushed herself up to sitting. "Am I, like, giving you some weird high school flashback? I don't remember teasing you. In fact, I distinctly recall showing you where your first period biology class was your freshman year when I was a big ol' sophomore."

Becca sighed. "Yes, Sadie. You were very nice to your big brother's teen wife's little sister. Thank you for your guidance. Whatever would I have done without it?"

"Sheesh," Sadie said. "I thought you had this big epiphany that you actually hated running. And *also* for the record...I don't know if I like sarcastic Posh." She shook her head. "Nope. I do not. I also do not remember agreeing to this. Like, ever."

Becca dropped back onto her butt and stretched her legs into a wide V, leaning forward onto her elbows.

"I know," Becca admitted. "I'm doing something that scares me—asking you out on a friend date. Before dawn." Becca forced a smile that felt more like a grimace. "And I don't *hate* running..."

She'd loved it at one point in her life. But Jeff's vision of her had turned it into another cog in the machine of Becca trying to attain a perfection that didn't exist. If she could bring Sadie on board—show her how exhilarating it could be to have one-on-one time with the world before everyone else woke up—then Becca could change the narrative. She could take running back as a thing she loved that made her feel healthy rather than using it as a means to an end.

Sadie's eyes widened behind her thick lenses as she tapped her phone screen and saw the time. "*Five* A.M.? I'm up at *five* A.M. on va*ca*tion? What sort of fresh hell is this? I would like to unsubscribe."

Becca slowly pushed herself up from her stretch and narrowed her eyes at Sadie.

"I promise you that running before dawn—when it feels like the whole world other than you is asleep—it's like nothing you've ever experienced before."

"Yeah!" Sadie agreed, brows raised. "It's like nothing I've experienced before because I'm part of that *whole world other than you* that's sleeping, and I'd like to keep it that way. Can't we sleep in, make some mimosas, and do a leisurely barefoot stroll on the beach?"

Becca sprang to her feet, ripping the covers off the bed before Sadie had a chance to register what was going on.

Sadie yelped, scrabbling for the blanket and sheet, but it was too late. Becca had the lot of it crumpled into a giant ball against her chest. Sadie opened her mouth to protest further, but Becca cut her off.

"I laid out your running clothes on the bed and put the shoes on the floor right at the foot of the bed." She shrugged. "That's what you get for wearing the same size shoe as me.

Come on. It'll be fun. You don't have to be afraid—especially when breakfast at Cool Beans awaits at the end of our trail." Becca batted her lashes. "Pleeeease. I kind of need this."

Sadie pouted, but swung her legs off the side of the bed.

"I can't say no when you're all sincere like that," she said as she pushed herself to standing and then sauntered toward Becca's open bedroom door.

They had a signal now. A really simple one. If the door was closed, *don't* walk in.

Becca still couldn't believe she'd slept with Leo. Even more so, she couldn't understand why after finding their *cute naked houseboy* under the covers and between Becca's legs, Sadie hadn't asked her any more about it. For an entire *week*. What was Becca supposed to do? Bring it up herself?

"Thank you!" she called after her roommate.

Five minutes later, Sadie trudged out of Becca's bedroom looking pretty freaking spectacular in Becca's sage green high-waisted running leggings and matching sports bra.

"I'm not going to wear the tank if that's okay. I'm hot just thinking about going out there, and if I add another layer, I might melt into a puddle before you even get me out the door."

Becca had opted for the pink-and-white camo running set.

"What are you doing?" Sadie asked, and Becca realized she was rubbing her hand softly over her midsection.

"I'm not sure," Becca admitted. "I'm either missing my kids or surprisingly *not* freaking out that my belly feels a little softer since we left Chicago. I think it might be a bit of both. That's another reason for the early run. My kids—*not* any possible loss of muscle tone. The camp lets everyone video chat with their parents today, but they did the time slots by last name, so Grayson and Mackenzie got the early slot at eight o'clock. Gotta get our miles in before then."

"You would run at the butt crack of dawn whether you had a phone call with your kids or not," Sadie said, pulling her hair into a high ponytail with a hair tie she had on her wrist. "And soft midsection or not, B-dubs, you know you're still smokin', right?"

Becca's cheeks warmed. It wasn't that she needed Sadie's approval or even wanted it, for that matter, but something about it rang truer than Leo telling her she was beautiful or that he'd been thinking of her since their unconventional meeting. And it certainly meant more than her ex-husband's appraising—or not so appraising—gaze. Sadie didn't want anything from her, didn't need to boost her ego by showing her off at a party like Jeff used to do. Not that Leo necessarily had to butter her up for her to let him back in her bed because, after the other night, Becca needed *no* coaxing. No sir. No how. That *boy* learned his way around Becca's body in a fraction of the time it had taken her ex, and Leo did so with patience and care and—his *tongue*. Holy wow, that tongue.

"Are you having some sort of moment?" Sadie asked, and

Becca gasped, bringing herself back to *this* moment rather than the one she'd rather be reliving.

"What? No. *You* were having a moment," Becca said.

Smooth.

"I just need to brush my teeth and pop in my contacts. Meet you at the door," Sadie told her, bouncing on her toes. "Maybe it's the shoes, but I think I'm feeling it!"

✵

"I'm *so* not feeling it," Sadie whined after their first mile. She'd kept pace with Becca, which was her more *casual* pace, but still, Sadie was impressive for someone who claimed exercise as one of her top fears. But when she finally slowed to a walk after fifteen minutes, hand pressed to her side, Becca realized her roommate had overdone it at the start.

"Are you limping?" Becca asked, spinning around to face Sadie so that she was now running backward. The morning air was cool and damp, the sky a hazy orange with the sun on the brink of the horizon.

Sadie held up a finger as she caught her breath. "Shins," she finally said. "Feels. Like. Stabbing."

"I told you to stretch," Becca said.

Sadie growled, then winced with her next step and again with the one after that.

They'd made it to town, but Becca's intent was to run *through* Glass Lake's downtown area and to the public promenade on the other side so they could watch the sunrise over the lake.

"Is it really that bad?" Becca asked, trying to mask her disappointment.

Sadie stopped, flexed and unflexed one foot and then the other.

"Title of your sex tape with the naked houseboy?" she asked, brows raised.

Becca's jaw dropped, and Sadie tapped Becca on the shoulder and said, "Tag! You're it!" Then the little faker took off down the street and toward the promenade.

What in the actual hell?

Becca rolled her neck to the left and then to the right, like she was about to throw down. And she was—sprinter style. Maybe Sadie knew what was on the other side of the street, but did she know it was uphill? Because Becca did and had run this path twice already since they'd come to town.

She bounced on her toes and let loose after her challenger, passing her after—she counted—twenty-seven seconds. About twice that much later, the hill kicked in.

By the time the road leveled off, Becca had to grit her teeth to keep going despite the overwhelming urge to stop. She was definitely feeling the effects of taking a few days off. She finally reached the promenade and spun to cheer Sadie as she brought up the rear.

A minute passed, then two, and Becca began to worry. But then there she was, popping over the top of the hill until she finally made it to the gate that lined the wooden walkway along the water. Sadie collapsed against the railing next to Becca, who had done the same, laughing hysterically despite how much it hurt to gulp in each and every breath of air.

Sadie slid down the metal bars, sinking to her knees.

"I think I'm dying," she said amid her own gulps of air. "Nope. I'm sure of it. This is what death feels like." She rubbed her eyes. "And either I just lost a contact, or I can see a white light. Should I go toward the light, Becca? Am I even really talking right now, or have I already left this mortal plane?"

But then Sadie's eyes rolled to the back of her head, and she passed out.

"Oh my god," Becca said, quietly at first. "Are you messing with me, Sadie? Because this is not funny."

When Sadie didn't respond, a switch flipped, and Becca went into doctor mode, carefully laying Sadie down on her back as she checked for breathing and a pulse.

Sadie's pulse was faint but there. If Becca hadn't been a doctor, she might have missed the arrhythmia. But Becca was a doctor, and she felt it plain as day.

Seconds later, Sadie's eyes fluttered open.

"Posh?" she said weakly. "Did I win the race?"

Sadie was able to push herself to sitting and sip from her water bottle. Becca watched her intently, waiting for her roommate's breathing to regulate before pressing her fingers to the patient's wrist again.

The irregular pulse had not subsided.

"You fainted," Becca finally said, her tone cool and collected. She didn't want to upset the patient, but she had to relay the news. "And I felt an arrhythmia. That's a clinical term for an—"

"Irregular heartbeat," Sadie interrupted. "I know."

Becca's chest tightened, a sensation that never happened when she spoke with her patients because Becca was the doctor, the scientist. She knew how to fix the problem or comfort a patient when the unfixable happened.

"*How* do you know?" Becca heard the tremble in her own voice.

Sadie blew out a long, shaky breath. "Because I was born with an ASD that wasn't found until I was ten. They fixed it with a catheter procedure, and I've been heart problem free ever since." A bitterness seeped into Sadie's tone that Becca didn't understand.

ASD. Atrial septal defect. A hole in the heart. She'd delivered a baby once who'd been born with three. It was one of the medical problems that Becca couldn't fix.

"I don't understand," Becca said, Sadie's wrist still in her hand. "If you've been problem free ever since..." Then why wasn't her heart rate returning to normal? Becca knew what the most logical answer was, but for once in her life, she didn't want to be a doctor. She just wanted to be a woman who knew her friend was going to be okay.

"Dr. Park heard the arrhythmia when I came in for my appointment."

"When I signed my papers?" Becca asked, accusation

dripping from her words. "That—that was over two weeks ago! You saw your cardiologist before galavanting off on a month-long vacation, right? Please tell me you got this checked out before we left."

Sadie smiled sheepishly and shrugged. "You ran from your life, and I ran from mine. Though I should probably keep it to a slow jog from here on out."

Becca's eyes stung, and her cheeks filled with heat. "How can you joke about this, Sadie? We need to get you to the hospital. We need to get you back to Chicago. We need…We need…" Tears threatened to spring from her eyes, so Becca sprung from the ground and began to pace, keeping them at bay. "That's it. I'm calling 911. They'll probably have to medevac you to a bigger hospital. I'll call Matthew and Alissa and your parents and tell them where to meet us…" She pulled her phone from the pocket of her running pants and unlocked the screen.

"Wait," Sadie said, pushing herself to her feet. "I'm okay, see?" She posed like she'd just dismounted the balance beam with some sort of flippy, fancy move.

Becca paused, finger hovering over the keypad on her phone. "Don't you dare try and talk a doctor out of seeking medical treatment for her patient."

"Whoa." Sadie held up her hands. "I'm not talking anyone out of anything," she added. "But look. I'm fine." She did a very bad little tap dance, and Becca couldn't help but laugh. "See? If there was anything to worry about, I wouldn't be able to make you laugh like that, would I?"

Sadie continued. "Can we just chalk it up to me overdoing it with the run, and I promise that if I so much as feel light-headed again, you can take me right to the ER? I just want to make it through Friday night dinner as planned before I have to go all doom and gloom and find out if I'm dying or something."

Becca gasped. "How are you not the least bit scared about this? What if the hole reopened? What if it's another one that went undiagnosed? What if—"

Sadie waved her off. "And what if it's not?" She pressed two fingers to her own wrist. "Pulse back to normal," she said. "See for yourself."

Becca took a step toward her and did. Sadie was right. Her pulse was completely normal.

"Fine," Becca relented. "I can't force you to go, but if you feel anything out of the ordinary, you need to promise you'll tell me and that we'll drop whatever we're doing—whether it's Friday dinner or whatever else—and go to the ER."

Sadie held out her hand, and the two women shook.

"It's a deal, Doc."

Then Sadie spun Becca so they were both facing the water, staring out over the lake, where the sun blazed a fiery pink, reflecting off the water and igniting the sky.

"This was why you woke me, wasn't it? Because holy mother fudging shorts!" Sadie whispered.

"I know, right? Also, pretty sure you can swear if you want to. There are no precocious ten-year-olds in sight."

Sadie shook her head. "I'm not risking it. That kid hears

everything, and I'm running out of cash. Guess I'm turning into you."

Becca pouted. "I *swear*. Just not that often. I have young kids in the house, you know."

Sadie placed a hand on Becca's shoulder and squeezed. "I'm not taking my eyes off this ridiculous sunrise, but know that I am rolling them *hard*. Because you're right. There are no precocious ten-year-olds in sight, so we both should be letting loose and saying what is truly in our hearts at this very moment as we are the only two people for miles watching the world wake up. Plus, you almost killed me with that run, so you owe me some Becca Weiland potty mouth."

Becca's mouth fell open. "It's not like you were forthcoming about—oh, I don't know—a major childhood medical emergency."

Sadie shrugged. "You never asked." Then she waggled her brows. "Come on, Posh. Show me that dirty, dirty mouth hiding behind that pristine doctorly image."

Becca growled, then braced her palms on the metal railing in front of her. *Fine.* She could do this—say exactly what was in her heart as she stared at the calm, quiet lake, which looked like an endless sea of pink and orange, like if they broke through the surface, they'd be swimming in liquid fire.

"It's fucking fantastic," she mumbled under her breath.

Sadie slid her hand off Becca's shoulder and down to *her* hand, threading their fingers together. "I'm sorry, but I didn't quite get that. Can you kick that volume up a bit?"

"It's fucking fantastic," Becca said again, this time at a respectable *hey-this-is-the-first-thing-I'm-saying-this-morning* sort of volume.

Sadie squeezed her hand. "Louder."

"It's fucking fantastic?" she repeated, but instead of louder, she turned the statement into a question.

Sadie squeezed harder, then bounced on her toes. "I know you can do better than that. So—on the count of three, we do it together, but we're kicking this shit up to eleven, you got it?"

Becca narrowed her eyes at Sadie. "You just fainted, and since you're refusing to see an ER doctor, you're at least going to follow what *this* doctor has to say. And I say you're not yelling or doing anything else to exert yourself from this moment forward."

Sadie sighed. "Fine, Dr. Weiland," she acquiesced. "But that means you're kicking it up to eleven *yourself*." She raised her brows. A challenge.

Becca bit her bottom lip and grinned. "Challenge accepted."

"Okay," Sadie started. "I can still do the counting, right?"

Becca nodded.

"Here we go," Sadie continued. One...two..."

"Wait! Am I yelling it on three or *after* three?" Becca asked.

Sadie groaned. "If I say I'm counting to three, I have to *say* three. So I'll say the stupid number, and then you'll yell the thing, okay?"

Becca nodded. "Got it. Sorry. I'm just nervous," she admitted.

Sadie smiled and turned to meet Becca's eyes. "I know you are, Bex. And I'm nervous too, about…you know…. But even though you're doing this alone, you're not actually *alone*. Get it?" she asked, no trace of teasing in her tone or expression. "You just have to trust that I'm here for you, Bex, like I know you're here for me. Do you trust me?"

There it was, that sisterly nickname that suddenly made Becca feel safe where she once felt annoyed.

"I do," Becca said. "Trust you, I mean. For some reason when I said *I do*, it felt like we were getting married or something, and I don't want to marry you or *anyone*, for that matter, at least not for the foreseeable future. My kids are enough for me right now, and if someone special comes along—great. But I'm putting my energy into *me* first."

Sadie grinned. "You know, if you married Leo, you could be Becca Beckett."

Becca winced but then squared her shoulders. "I'm not *marrying* Leo. He and I both know what this is." Except if she really did know, she'd be able to form words to define it. But she couldn't. "And besides, if I ever do find myself committing to someone like that again, I'm keeping my name."

Sadie offered her a slow clap. "Congratulations, Becca Weiland. I think you just found something you lost."

Becca's brows furrowed, and then she swallowed a lump in her throat as recognition bloomed.

"Myself." Holy wow. "I'm not going to be lonely," Becca

continued. Because the reality was—she had already been lonely while she was married. So heartbreakingly lonely, it made her want to scream.

It made her want to SCREAM.

"Okay," Becca said with renewed vigor. "On three. One ... two ... three!"

She screamed.

"IT'S FUCKING FANTASTIIIIIIC!"

Becca sang it loud and long, drawing out the final syllable until she ran out of breath and sound.

Sadie grinned and pumped her fist in the air, then offered Becca a round of golf-clap applause, making a show of doing it mildly and without expending undue energy.

Becca laughed. She felt neither lonely nor alone.

A drop of water landed on the back of Becca's hand, and she squinted toward the rising sun, wondering if it had brought with it a morning shower. Then she realized her cheeks were wet.

Oh.

She was crying. In a public place. With someone else to witness.

Her first instinct was to run—fast and far—until she outran whatever it was she was feeling, whatever Sadie was inadvertently witnessing. But the other woman was still holding Becca's hand, squeezing it tight as if she knew the second she let go, Becca would flee.

"It's okay," Sadie assured her. "Wait. No. I take that back."

Becca sniffled as she met Sadie's gaze. "My—public feelings aren't okay?" Of course they weren't okay. That was why Becca wanted to *run*. If she could just freaking untangle her hand from Sadie's, she'd be off like the goddamn Road Runner.

Sadie shook her head. "Your public feelings are *fucking fantastic*, Becca Weiland. And if anyone *ever* tries to tell you otherwise—tries to tell you that how you feel isn't okay because *they* seem to have *all* the answers as to how you *should* feel—please tell them to fucking fuck the fuck off."

Becca snorted, then let out something between a laugh and a sob.

"I think I've been holding all of this in for fifteen years. What happens if I can't stop now that I've started?"

She swiped her forearm under both eyes and then under her running nose.

"Take it from someone who got surprised into feeling *all* of her feelings the other day. On the beach. With a very handsome single dad whose dog once again did *not* eat me for lunch. The waterworks shut off eventually."

"How?" Becca asked, new tears finding new paths down her cheeks.

"They just *do*," Sadie told her with a knowing grin. "Especially when said single dad kisses you like you've never been kissed before, despite your snotty, tearstained face."

Becca gasped. "And you're just telling me this *now*?"

Sadie finally released her grip and threw her hands in the air. "It's not like you were spilling all the tea about Max Junior giving you some under-the-covers lip service!"

"Max *Junior*? Did you really just make an age crack?" Becca asked, eyes wide.

"Baby Max?" Sadie amended with a preemptive wince.

"Oh. My. God. I know I said I wasn't looking to get married, but did you just indirectly call me old? Because I'm younger than you, Ms. Bloom!"

Two weeks ago, Becca would have been mortified. She might have even done something bananas like wax off all her pubic hair because of one or two silvers reminding her that she was on the closer side of forty than thirty.

But now all she could do was laugh—head tilted toward the sky and hands on her belly as she let loose every snort and guffaw that she'd been holding in for as long as she could remember. Because almost two weeks ago, she never could have imagined someone like Leo Beckett—or Baby Max or Max Junior or whatever Sadie wanted to call him—coming into her life and making her feel wanted like she hadn't felt since long before gray hairs started sprouting below her bikini line.

Becca was still a little lost, but every time she stepped out of her comfort zone, she seemed to find another missing part of herself. So why not take another step?

She kicked her shoes onto the promenade and peeled off her socks. Next, she unfastened the fanny pack and let it fall to the ground as well.

"Um, what are you doing?" Sadie asked.

Becca answered by stepping around the other woman and opening a gate that separated the promenade from a long pier.

With each step, Becca removed an article of clothing. First her tank and then—with a little less grace—her compression leggings. She strode farther down the pier in only her sports bra and underwear, but soon both items were strewn on the pier as well. Behind her, she could hear Sadie clapping and cheering her on.

"Get it, girl!" Sadie yelled.

At the pier's edge, Becca sucked in a long breath as she stared into the dark water, banishing thoughts of seaweed and fish and anything else she might come in contact with should she actually follow through with what she was about to do. Because this wasn't a time for thinking. It was time for doing.

So Becca Weiland raised her arms above her naked body, bent her knees ever so slightly, and dove into the water below.

CHAPTER NINETEEN

SADIE

Sadie paced slowly (but really fast and agitatedly in her head) outside the Glass Lake Police Station, listening to her phone ring once, twice, then three times.

"Pick up, Max. Pick *up*. Pick *up*. Pick *up!*"

"Hello?" Max's voice asked groggily as Sadie started saying *Pick up* once more.

"I know it's early, but I didn't know who else to call," Sadie said.

"What happened? Are you okay?" Max sounded alert now, and Sadie's heart squeezed at the concern in his voice. But this wasn't about her or Max or her *and* Max. She still had time to figure that out.

This was about Becca. More important, it was about Becca *not* losing her career or her custody arrangement with her kids because of some silly revelation that got her arrested for indecent exposure.

"Yeah. I'm okay. But please tell me you have a friend at the police station," Sadie said.

It was Sadie's fault. *She'd* promised to be Becca's chaperone the other night, to not let her drink anything other than iced tea or water after she'd gone a bit overboard at the street fest. Shouldn't that promise have extended to staving off acts of public indecency?

"Oh god, Sadie. What did you do?"

Sadie winced, even though Max couldn't see her. "Um, I helped empower Becca into committing a lewd public act, and now she's sitting at a deputy's desk drinking vending machine coffee in handcuffs and wearing nothing but a small, shabby gray blanket like a bath towel."

She heard something that sounded an awful lot like a laugh, but it was muffled and cut off, as if Max was pulling the phone away from his face while simultaneously stifling whatever he was doing.

"Are you—*laughing*?" Sadie asked, anger bubbling up through her words. "My best friend is sitting practically naked in a police station, and you—Max Beckett—are *laughing*?"

Max sighed. "I'm sorry. I wasn't—I mean, I'm putting my shoes on now. I'll be right over. Five minutes tops. Make sure Becca doesn't sign *anything*. She doesn't have to without a lawyer present, and if it's Deputy Dempsey, that overgrown frat boy will try to get her to do so before she even realizes she shouldn't."

Sadie's palms began to sweat. "Does—um—Deputy Dempsey have a tattoo on his bulging biceps of a barcode, under which it says PRICELESS?"

A beat of silence passed before Max responded.

"Yes," he said with a groan. "He's the one with the *bulging biceps*." Did Sadie sense a tinge of jealousy in his tone? "Are you with Becca now?"

"No," Sadie said. "I'm outside, freaking out and calling you!"

"Shit," he hissed. In the distance, Sadie heard an admonishing *"Dad!"*

"Sorry!" Sadie cried. "I didn't mean to wake Evie and get you in trouble. Just—get here as soon as possible, okay? I'm heading back inside."

Sadie ended the call and ran back into the police station to find Deputy Biceps handing the still-handcuffed Becca a pen.

"Don't!" Sadie yelled, running up to the desk and slapping the pen out of Becca's hand before tripping and belly-flopping *onto* the desk, sending manila folders and sheaves of paper—and maybe, was that a paper cup of coffee crushed under her belly—flying every which way.

Becca threw her cuffed hands in the air and glared at the sprawled Sadie.

The two women stared at each other for several long

moments, neither seeming to comprehend the situation they were currently in.

"Way to ruin my sudoku time! Derek bet me I couldn't beat his record, and now I have to start all over if you didn't just spill my coffee all over his puzzle book."

"Sudoku?" Sadie asked, peeling herself off the desk—and then peeling the sopping puzzle book from her belly. "You mean this book?" she added with a sheepish grin.

Becca sighed. "I'm really sorry, Derek. I'm sure my friend's intentions were well meaning, but if you feel the need to throw the book at her too, I won't stop you."

"Oh god," Sadie heard over her shoulder. "What did you do?"

"Um . . . that was way less than five minutes," she said.

"And you should know by now that nothing in Glass Lake is more than—hmmm—four and a half minutes away when a motor vehicle is involved."

Sadie turned slowly—her coffee-stained midsection growing colder by the second—to find Max *and* Evie staring at her, slack-jawed. Evie wore a Baby Yoda nightgown and matching slippers and Max sported a similar Baby Yoda T-shirt and blue plaid pajama bottoms, his feet clad in Adidas slides similar to her own. Evie's curls were a wild bedhead of a mess, and Max's tousled dark waves stood on end in random spots around his head.

Shit, they were cute. And here was Sadie, once more, a freaking disaster. What the actual *eff*, universe?

"D," Max said, moving toward the already standing deputy and pulling him into one of those dude-bro hugs. "I'm sorry," he added as both men pulled apart. "This is sort of my fault. I might have told her you were going to coerce Becca into signing a confession so you could throw the book at her. It was just supposed to be a little prank. I didn't realize—"

"She'd throw her whole body into defending her friend?" Derek asked, rubbing his palm over his closely cropped sandy hair. "Also might have cost me an extra hour or two of paperwork, and I'm supposed to bring snacks to the twins' soccer game this afternoon. You going to explain that to my wife?"

"Wait, wait, wait, wait, *wait!*" Sadie said, holding up her hands as if she were directing traffic. "The overgrown frat boy has twins...and a *wife?*"

Becca groaned and started to stand, but her blanket seemed to threaten staying on the chair if Becca moved, so she gripped the top where it was tucked together like a towel and simply resituated herself in her seat.

"Yes. Twin girls," Becca said. "I saw the picture on his desk and asked about his family, then told him I was a twin mom too, that I'm going to FaceTime with my kiddoes in—ooh!—like ten minutes, and we started swapping stories and playing sudoku, and everything was great until you came barreling back in and gave poor Derek extra work to do this afternoon."

"Overgrown frat boy?" Deputy Derek said, crossing his arms and raising a brow at Max.

Max shrugged. "We *were* in a fraternity together. And you have always been buff as hell."

Derek chuckled. "You can lift with me anytime, Maximus."

Maximus? So not only did Max absolutely know someone at the police station, but they were, like, *besties?*

Max laughed. "Yeah. No. I can't. You are in another league, my friend. Anyway, sorry about the mess. I'll help clean it up. And you're not really throwing the book at Becca, are you?"

Derek glanced back at Becca, who waved at him in her handcuffs.

"One of my newbies caught her naked on the pier and already wrote up the citation, so I can't do anything now that it's in the system, but it's only listed as a miscellaneous municipal ordinance violation. As long as she doesn't incur any other misdemeanors in future, it'll be expunged from her record within five years. We just needed to finish the rest of the paperwork before I let her and your friend go."

"But…but…" Sadie started. "Why is she still in handcuffs?"

This time the deputy offered his own embarrassed grin. "I forgot to take them off until she reached for my pen. If you hadn't dived onto the table, she'd be uncuffed by now."

Sadie's cheeks flamed. "I was *so* worried, and to *you*…" She pointed furiously at Max. "This was just some opportunity for a practical joke?"

"Dad?" Evie accused, elbowing her father in the hip. "I think you're in trouble."

"Come on," Derek said to Becca and then turned his attention to Evie. "Let's let Dr. Weiland get her clothes back on, and then we can find a quiet place for her to do that video chat with her kids while these two"—he motioned back to Max and Sadie—"clean up the mess on what used to be my very organized desk."

Becca grinned. "Do you want to meet Mackenzie and Grayson, Evie?"

"Can I, Dad?" she asked Max.

"Of course, Peanut. Go have fun," he said, bending down to kiss her on top of the head.

Sadie would have thought the gesture cute if she hadn't still been so furious with *Maximus.*

"Do—um—*I* get to meet the twins too?" Derek asked, and Sadie couldn't believe she thought for a second that the big pussycat of a deputy was an overgrown frat boy.

"Of course!" Becca said. "They will *love* you, especially when they find out you're a twin daddy too!"

Derek freed Becca from her handcuffs, then led her and Evie away from the desk, Becca's belongings in a tote bag slung over his elbow, above which that bulging biceps *bulged,* and Sadie couldn't help but stare.

"So…" Max started, and Sadie spun slowly to face him, her teeth gritted and jaw tight.

"So…" she mimicked, crossing her arms.

Max shoved his hands in the pockets of his pajama pants, rocking back and forth on his heels. "On a scale of one to ten," he continued. "How badly did I mess up?"

Ugh. Screw that earnestness in his tone and the worry in his blue eyes. It wasn't fair, him using his inherent sweetness as a weapon against her.

"Just stop it, okay?" she pleaded, the crack in her armor already threatening to expose her growing feelings for this man.

"Stop what?" he asked, the corner of his mouth quirking into a hopeful grin with that *stupid* dimple.

"*That*," she said, irritated as she waved him off. "That dimple and that sincerity. I don't know what to do with either of them."

Max shrugged and took a step closer. Sadie glanced around the small office space, which was practically empty save for two other people—a uniformed woman and a man dressed in civilian clothes—who busied themselves at their desks when Sadie looked their way.

She groaned and grabbed Max by the wrist. "Outside," she told him.

She wasn't going to let him sweet-talk his way out of this in front of an audience.

Max followed obediently, and Sadie tried to ignore the pulse in his wrist beating against her thumb. Other than their make-out session on the beach—and what a session it had been—they'd yet to reconnect, physically speaking.

Which meant that now, when Sadie was supposed to be furious, she was also maybe, possibly, a little bit turned on.

Nope. Nope. Nope. *Maximus* was going to get a piece of Sadie's mind before he got a piece of her ass.

When they were finally outside in the very spot where Sadie had desperately called and asked for his help, she dropped his hand and opened her mouth to let him have it, but he beat her to the punch.

"I'm an asshole," he admitted. "Plain and simple. You were worried about your friend, and I made things worse instead of making them better. I selfishly gave myself a laugh at your expense, and that was a shitty thing to do. I was caught off guard being woken from a deep sleep—which is not an excuse or attempt at laying blame on you for doing so because I can't even tell you how happy I am that you called *me* in an emergency—and I didn't realize how worried you really were because I thought you would have already realized Derek was a teddy bear. Plus, I missed you and didn't know how to tell you that, so I resorted to behaving like the overgrown frat boy I told you Derek was." He drew in a long breath and then blew it out.

Sadie's mouth was still hanging open when he'd finished, and for a few beats, she just stood there, staring at him.

"What was that last part?" she finally asked.

"That I acted like an overgrown frat boy?" he asked with a nervous smile.

She shook her head. "Before that."

His brows drew together. "Oh, the part where I thought you would have already known Derek was a teddy bear?"

Sadie groaned, her hands balling into fists. Did he not realize what he said? Or maybe he didn't mean it? Or maybe he really was an overgrown frat boy disguised as a good guy, still messing with her.

"Oh!" he said, recognition blooming in his expression. He took a hesitant step closer to her, and when she didn't protest, another, until he was close enough to skim his fingers along her temple, to hook his finger under her chin to tilt her head up so her mouth was a breath from his. "I missed you," he said softly. "I know on the outside I look like I have all my shit together, but inside I'm still that clueless teenager who doesn't know how to tell the girl he likes her, so he pulls her pigtails or plays a not-so-harmless prank to save face and is a total shit for doing so."

She shook her head, swallowing the lump in her throat. "You are so much more than a clueless teenager," she said, pressing her lips into a tight smile. "I'm still pissed, but that was one hell of an apology," she added, then stood on her toes to press her lips to his.

If this thing was going to go any further with them, she needed to stop running from her possible future. She'd call her cardiologist as soon as the office opened and figure out the next steps.

"Also," she continued, lips still against his, "I missed you too." She wrapped her arms around his waist and pulled him close as they kissed and nipped and tasted, right there in the middle of town for all the early risers to see.

"You know you're cleaning that desk all by yourself while I put my feet up and watch, don't you?" Sadie asked, smiling against him.

"Oh, one hundred percent," Max replied, smiling right back. "But can we do this for a few more minutes? If Derek is FaceTiming with Becca and her kids, they'll be gone for a while. That guy is a rock star with his own kids and everyone else's, so he will for sure make that call run longer than expected."

She answered him by sliding her hands up his torso and then hooking them around his neck.

Max Beckett truly was unlike any other man she'd met. She felt safe in his arms. She trusted his words. She—*felt* things when she was near him, things she couldn't articulate because she had no frame of reference. But when she kissed him, her chest grew tight, and her stomach plummeted as if she were on a continuous roller coaster drop. Everything about him excited and terrified her all at once.

A throat cleared, and Sadie and Max jumped apart to find Derek standing in the open doorway.

"Right," Max said. "The desk. My fault, my job. Guess I better get to it." Despite their one-person audience, Max still leaned down to kiss Sadie once more on the cheek before giving her a wink and a smile on his way back into the building.

Sadie spun around to follow him, but Derek held up a finger, stepping all the way outside as the door closed behind Max.

"Can we talk a second?" he asked.

"Of course," Sadie said. "Especially if it means Max gets a head start on that desk and I don't let my guilt get the best of me, thereby helping him clean the mess for which *he* is responsible."

Derek smiled as he approached, but with a sense of uneasiness she hadn't noted when they were inside the station.

"Max is a good friend," Derek began.

"Oh," Sadie said, drawing the word out. "This is the 'What are your intentions with my friend?' speech, right? Are you sure we shouldn't do it in one of those interrogation rooms with a two-way mirror?" She gasped. "No, really. Can we do it there? I've always wanted to see if you really *can't* see through the mirror."

Derek cleared his throat again, then nodded toward a park bench on the sidewalk in front of the station.

"Okay," Sadie said. "No interrogation room."

Derek strolled over to the bench but stopped beside it, waiting for Sadie to sit first.

"This is still Wisconsin," she said. "Right? Because I feel like I've stepped into, like, an upside-down version of a Jane Austen novel."

"My lady," Derek said with a small bow before sitting beside her, and despite how ridiculous the big, burly deputy looked—especially with that barcode tattoo—Sadie found herself blushing and demurring as the *gentleman* took his seat.

Derek sighed. "Max has been through a lot."

Sadie nodded. "I know. I mean, I don't *know*, but I know."

"Right," he said. "The divorce but also his own parents and the whole Leo thing."

Sadie pivoted so she was almost sideways on the bench. "Okay, what *is* the whole Leo thing? Shelby and Delilah have hinted at it, but they said it's Max's story to tell, and he hasn't told, so I really don't know what I'm up against."

Derek gave her shoulder a gentle squeeze with his giant hand. "Have you told him *your* whole story?" he asked.

"What? How would I?" she stammered. "I mean we've only known each other a couple of weeks." Did Becca tell Derek what happened at the promenade? Was it selfish of Sadie to keep her health history to herself until she knew if her future was maybe, possibly, uncertain?

"Look," Derek said. "You seem like good people. You destroyed my desk all in the name of saving your friend from signing herself into the big house. By the way, you know her ex was a lawyer, right? She knows a thing or two about the law."

Sadie rolled her eyes. "You know Becca for, what, twenty minutes, and you know *her* whole story, but I'm at fault for using caution with Max after only knowing him for twelve days?"

She wouldn't admit that it felt longer, with both Max *and* Becca. The woman who felt like a judgmental distant cousin and the man who kept seeing Sadie at her most vulnerable? She suddenly couldn't imagine a day going by where she didn't think of one or both of them, where she didn't want to use her body as a human shield to keep Becca out of jail or use her body in *other* ways to feel closer to Max. This trip had somehow opened a gate Sadie hadn't even realized she'd closed.

"I see a kindred spirit in Becca," Derek said. "She looks like a tough cookie on the outside, but she loves to love . . . like I do."

Sadie shook her head and laughed. "Your wife is one lucky woman." Derek opened his mouth to reply, but Sadie interrupted, "Wait! I know what you're going to say, that *you're* the lucky one, blah blah blah . . ."

Derek laughed. "It's not about luck, Sadie. It's about trust and honesty and letting the right one in. Max doesn't trust easily, but I can see he trusts you. I just don't want to see that blow up in his face is all." He shrugged. "I said my piece. The rest is up to you."

He stood, bowed once more, and then tipped an invisible hat.

Sadie laughed, but her heart squeezed tight in her chest. If she had told Max, "Hey, so I was born with this congenital heart defect and funny thing . . . it might still be defective," would he have run the other way and let her be? Was she actually the asshole? Sadie couldn't change what happened tomorrow any more than she could turn off her feelings for the man she never intended to meet. But how could she ask a man with a wounded heart to put his trust in hers when it might be broken beyond repair?

CHAPTER TWENTY

BECCA

So Ethan is all recovered, Gabi is going stir crazy know-ing they're supposed to be on vacation, and Mom and Gigi want to open the bakery alone tomorrow. Together. *Just the two of them,*" Alissa said, her eyes wide as she stared back at Becca from the phone screen.

"Okaaaay," Becca said slowly, her arms tired as she held the phone up in front of her face. "Why do I feel like you're about to ask me for a huge favor?" she added.

Alissa gave her a nervous smile. "Well, since it technically *was* their rental, and you had so much fun during that Friday night dinner thing you did last week with the salon owner and her wife, I was hoping we could all crash the party?" She winced. "Matt said he'll be on toddler duty—Elliott's pull-ing himself up and cruising around the furniture—so I can have some wine. You have wine, right? I *really* need some wine. We have the Pack and Play, and Elliott's a really good sleeper. I know the place only sleeps two, technically, but we can make do with couches or sleeping bags or whatever. Gabi and Ethan just really need this."

Becca raised her brows. "Gabi and *Ethan* need this?"

Alissa groaned, then blew a red corkscrew curl out of her face. "Okay, fine. *I* need this. *I* need to talk to adults about more than just whether or not they want almond milk, coconut milk, or oat milk in their coffee. And as much as I like to discuss whether or not there are seeds in the raspberry rugelach—there *are*, by the way—I'm finding that shoptalk is not filling my bucket of much-needed adult social interaction with wine. Did I mention wine? WILL THERE BE WINE?"

Alissa closed one eye, then brought her other one closer to the screen. Much closer. *Too* much closer, so that all Becca could see were her sister's auburn lashes.

"Have you—fallen into your phone?" Becca asked.

"Um," Alissa said, creating a more respectable distance between herself and her camera. "Are you naked?"

Becca's jaw dropped. Then she scoffed.

Alissa gasped. "Scoffing! You scoffed! That's *my* tell, which means if any of me rubbed off on you, *you're* about to tell a lie, so don't even try it, missy!"

Becca closed her mouth, then opened it again, thinking of what to say when she finally landed on, "Oh, fuck it. I just got out of the shower after my early-morning run—and run-in with the police—and what can I say? I like walking around naked now. When I'm alone, of course."

Alissa shook her head, blinking rapidly. "I'm sorry. You're going to have to slow down and speak a little louder for those of us in the cheap seats because the only part of what you just said that made sense was the part about your morning run. Everything else is simply—ohmigod. You said *fuck*. I cannot remember the last time I heard you swear! Where is my baby sister and what have you done with her, you evil alien clone?"

Becca laughed, then—instead of speaking up—dropped her voice to a whisper. "I got arrested for skinny-dipping off a public pier."

Alissa stared at her, stunned. After a beat she said, "I don't care if you want us to crash your little Shabbat gathering or not. We're coming, and I want some of whatever's in that water up there."

Becca sighed. She hadn't even mentioned Leo yet. What would Alissa say if she did? *By the way, I'm sleeping with a guy in his twenties, and it's the best sex I've ever had?* Wait. This was her sister. She could tell her anything.

"Also, Liss?"

Alissa tilted the phone so Becca could see her sister's hand on her heart.

"Bex, I honestly don't think I can take another big shock right now. I'm a frizzy-haired, sleep-deprived, too-tired-for-sex-but-I-miss-it, forty-one-year-old woman who is the happiest she's ever been but also a teeny, tiny bit envious of the two weeks you've had since I saw you last. I want to hear it all, but Matt is almost done packing us up, and then we're going to hit the road." She smiled nervously.

Becca wasn't disappointed about keeping Leo a secret. In fact, hearing Alissa call her *Bex* made her realize the real reason for Becca's recent shift—the catalyst for her even coming on this trip.

Sadie.

"If you promise to bring your chocolate babka...No! *Two* chocolate babkas, then I'll consider inviting you and Matthew to our little Shabbat gathering. Elliott, of course, is always on the guest list. Max's daughter, Evie, will have *so* much fun with him!"

Becca threw her hand over her mouth, but it was too late.

Alissa narrowed her eyes at her sister. "Um...who's *Max*? The only people I've heard you talk about are Shelby, Delilah, and now apparently some deputy who is your new bestie. But I'd have remembered mention of a Max. And there has been zero mention of said name."

Becca lowered her hand slowly to reveal her nervous smile. "He's just another local Sadie and I met. It's a really small town. The kind where everyone knows everyone."

"Oh," Alissa said, nodding. "You mean like the entirety of the Jewish community. I was playing Jewish geography with this woman at the bakery who always buys a box of black-and-whites on Fridays when her son and daughter-in-law come for dinner. We finally got to talking. One thing led to another, and bam! Wouldn't you know it? Her *other* son felt me up over my shirt at summer camp in middle school. With my permission, of course."

Becca gasped, and Alissa waved her off.

"I didn't *tell* her that! I just remarked that I knew which cabin he was in and that he looked like he had very capable hands. *Kidding* again," Alissa added as Becca launched into another gasp. "My point is that everyone knows everyone in small towns and in the greater Jewish community, so what is this Max's last name because maybe I know him? If he's Jewish, that is. Though sometimes a non-Jew or two slip into the algorithm." She shrugged. "I don't make the rules. I just play the game."

Becca could see the color drain from her own face in the thumbnail video on her phone screen. First, she didn't want to stick her nose into Sadie's business by telling Alissa that there might be something brewing between Sadie and Max. Second, the Jewish geography thing wasn't hyperbole. If anyone could trace a connection down to Max and Leo Beckett within six degrees or less, it was Alissa.

"You know you sound just like Mom, don't you? You're turning into your mother. How does that feel?"

Alissa waved her off again. "I'm done running from my fate. If I'm going to turn into Mom, it might as well be sooner rather than later. Also, you're stalling, and don't think for a second that if you do so long enough, my addled toddler mom brain will get you off the hook. I may not remember where my reading glasses are, but I sure as shit will remember to hound my newly single baby sister about any utterance of a strange man's name."

Becca laughed. "You're maddening. Do you know that? And also, your glasses are on your head."

A smile of recognition bloomed on Alissa's face as she reached up and patted the readers atop her pile of auburn curls. "You just gave me twenty minutes of my life back, baby sis! Now *spill*."

"Beckett," Becca said with a groan. "His name is Max Beckett, and he's nothing more to me than a guy who lives on the other side of the lake and is a local contractor in town."

Alissa waggled her brows. "A contractor, huh? Sounds like he's good with his hands."

"I'm ending this call," Becca said.

"Wait! Wait! Wait! Sorry! Okay. He's *just* a guy who lives on the other side of the lake . . . and is good with his hands." Alissa bit back a grin.

"Hanging up . . ." Becca said, raising her hand high so her sister could see her index finger lowering toward the screen to sever the connection.

"Okay, fine! I don't know the name off the top of my head, so there's probably no connection, but if there is one, I'll find it before we get there by sundown!"

Her sister barely got in the last word before Becca did, in fact, end the call.

Suddenly, spending some alone time in her room—while

legally disrobed—didn't seem so appealing when only the second of their dinner parties had just doubled in size.

Becca threw on her robe and scrambled out of her room just as Sadie was scrambling up the stairs.

"They're *all* coming!" Becca and Sadie said at the same time.

"I just got off the phone with my brother," Sadie said.

Becca nodded. "Just hung up on my sister."

Sadie raised her brows. "Impressed, but I don't have time to give you props. We have six hours to get this place in shape. And also, we need more food."

"And wine," Becca added. "Alissa said that Matt would be on toddler duty, but I feel like maybe we should get rid of the coffee table in the living room. Maybe carry it up to the loft? Then they can set up the Pack and Play." Becca scratched the back of her head. "Are we going to need another table for dinner?"

"And chairs? I'll call Max. He seems the type to have a folding table and chairs. Oh! I just had the best idea. Maybe we can set up *outside*! Eat on the beach!"

It *did* sound amazing. Especially the thought of Leo across the table from Becca. Or next to her. Or—

"Um... Full disclosure... I might have accidentally mentioned Max to my sister, and now she's going to spend the rest of the day and ride up here playing Six Degrees to Max Beckett," Becca admitted.

Sadie laughed. "I'm the one who's been single and dating

practically since your sister met me. She's not going to have much interest in Max once she meets his baby brother and sees how he looks at her sister."

Becca's stomach tightened. "Can we *not* use the word *baby* in any sort of Leo description? I know you think I'm all that and a bag of chips—"

"You mean hot as fuck," Sadie interrupted.

"Whatever. Can we—I mean—how about let's not infantilize the man I'm sleeping with, okay? I'm having a hard enough time reconciling the whole situation with my over-analytical brain. So if Leo can just be Leo and Max just Max and no one is referred to as a baby, that would be great."

Sadie spun Becca back toward her room and pushed her through the door. "You need to get dressed *now*."

"Are we going somewhere?" Becca asked.

"Yes!" Sadie said, still pushing her. "To town for all of the supplies. And do you think you can keep your clothes on so we don't have to take any detours to the police station? I mean, I don't want to keep you from having another much-needed epiphany, but you could end up behind bars next time. Or worse."

Becca dug her heels into the carpet, ready to whirl on her roommate and remind her that she was besties with the town deputy and could likely skinny-dip anytime she wished, except Sadie—momentum still pushing her forward—face-planted into Becca's back with unexpected force.

Sadie shrieked, and Becca spun to find Sadie cupping her hands around her nose.

"I think your bony shoulder just broke my nose!" Sadie cried.

Becca rolled her eyes. "My shoulders are *not* bony, and you didn't break…" She gently pulled on Sadie's wrists, urging her to lower her hands. But when Sadie complied, Becca saw that the skin above her lip was smeared with blood.

"Oh shit," Becca said.

Sadie's eyes pooled with tears, and Becca grabbed her friend by the wrist, pulled her into the bathroom, and sat her down on the toilet, all the while shielding her view of the mirror.

"It's that bad that you won't let me see?" Sadie said with a sniffle and then a whimper. "Ow. That hurts."

Becca grabbed a washcloth from the linens under the sink and shook her head. "I know it's easier for hotels and renters and whoever to use white linens since they can be bleached, but when it comes to nose bleeds?" She shrugged, ran the cloth under the cold faucet, and then gently dabbed at the skin beneath Sadie's nose, being careful not to come in contact with the injury—*yet*. "Looks like the initial blood spill is leveling off, so it might not be that bad."

"Blood *spill*?" Sadie said, her eyes wide. "Oh my god. Of *course* this would happen right before I see Max. You know how you're always talking about me being effortlessly cool?"

Becca nodded. "Since the day I met you." She dabbed at the base of Sadie's right nostril, and she didn't flinch. But the second she tried the left, nudging the cartilage a little harder than she'd intended, Sadie hissed in a breath. "Sorry," Becca said, her tone clipped and clinical as she went into doctor mode.

"Yeah, well, it *is* your fault," Sadie said with a pout.

Becca raised a brow. "Says the woman who was using excessive force to make me get dressed."

Sadie opened her mouth to protest, then instinctively threw her hands over her face again.

"I can't believe I did this," she whined—albeit a muffled whine. "I'm *not* effortlessly cool, Becca. It actually takes a *lot* of effort, and for some reason, my best effort doesn't even work in this town because Max has only ever seen me covered in sand, sweat, mud, a police deputy's desk full of *wet* paperwork, and/or tears. And now what? Am I gonna have, like, two black eyes and a swollen nose?"

Becca bit back a laugh. She was almost certain Sadie had only given her nose a nasty bruise. She seemed to be breathing fine out of both nostrils, but a quick look with a penlight—and a short but likely painful examination—would hopefully confirm Becca's hunch.

"You really like him," Becca said, a statement rather than a question as she once again lowered Sadie's hands, this time to her lap.

Sadie sighed. "I don't know. I have zero frame of reference. I've never worried so much about looking like a disaster in front of a guy before, but then again, I've never *been* this much of a disaster in front of any other guy before."

Becca opened a drawer under the bathroom counter and

withdrew a small, zipped-up red pouch. The white letters printed across it spelled out: F-I-R-S-T A-I-D.

"How many first-aid kits do you *have*?" Sadie asked. "You're more prepared than a Boy Scout. Oh, hey, you know who's young enough to be a Boy Scout?" Sadie snorted, then winced, and then winced even harder when the wincing seemed to be causing the pain.

"Um, first? Thank you, universe, for a little karma there. And second, you're making this much harder on yourself than it needs to be. Let's just get this part over with because once we're done, you'll get to ice that pretty little schnoz of yours."

Becca unzipped the pouch and pulled out her penlight. "I'm just going to take a look inside."

"Wh-what are you looking for?" Sadie asked.

"Your breathing sounds really good, and the bleeding didn't last long, so I just want to double-check and make sure there isn't any blockage because if there is…"

"Blockage? What do you mean, *blockage*? Will there be, like, a bone protruding into my nasal cavity? Oh my *god*. I just wanted to get to the store and start planning the night. Now *everyone* is coming, and I'm going to have *blockage*? And how do you even know how to examine me? How many babies have you delivered while also breaking the mother's nose?"

Becca huffed out a breath and shook her head. "I'm going to pretend you didn't say that and also give you a friendly reminder that I spent time in almost *all* parts of the hospital during my med school rotation. I've actually examined more than one broken nose. Now stop laying blame and start by *raising your head so I can look up your nose!*"

Sadie jutted out her chin indignantly and raised her head.

Becca shone the light in what she knew was the "good" nostril, and then moved to the other.

"Visual examination looks promising," she said. "But I have to do a physical examination as well."

Sadie sucked in a sharp breath and lowered her head. "Like, you're going to touch it?"

Becca nodded. "We can go to an ER if you want. They can numb you so you won't experience any pain during the exam. Oh wait, if we do that, I'll also have them give you an echocardiogram so we can rule out any possible heart issues you're running from. Or we can get this over with, hopefully confirm that nothing is broken, get you a nice bag of peas to rest on your face, and figure out what we can do for a houseful of guests arriving in less than six hours. But it's your call."

Sadie worried her bottom lip between her teeth as Becca kept her poker face, not reacting to the already-visible swelling at the bridge of Sadie's nose and under her left eye.

"You'll do your best not to hurt me?" Sadie asked hopefully.

"You really don't want to go to the ER." Becca groaned. "Fine. I'll do my best to be quick, yet thorough."

Sadie huffed out a laugh. "That's what she said."

Becca forced a smile, and Sadie blew out a breath.

"Okay," she said. "I trust you."

Becca switched from a squat to her knees, leaning back on her heels for purchase. She cradled Sadie's head in her hands as if the two were about to kiss, but instead Becca pressed her thumbs softly to Sadie's cheeks, just under each eye.

Sadie breathed in, then held the air in her lungs.

"Okay so far?" Becca asked.

Sadie squeezed her eyes shut and nodded.

"You're doing great, Sadie. But I need you to relax your face. I know it's scary, but I'm right here with you. You can do this."

Sadie finally exhaled, her shoulders relaxing. She didn't open her eyes, but she was no longer squeezing them shut. Instead she simply looked like someone randomly sleeping on a toilet. After a minor bar brawl.

Becca pressed her thumbs higher, just under each of Sadie's eyes. The right side felt fine, but the skin on the left felt puffy to the touch.

"I'm going to move closer to your nose now, okay? I'll tell you everything I'm doing before I do it so there won't be any surprises."

Sadie nodded again, her whole body going rigid.

"Just breathe, honey," Becca told her. "I promise we're almost done."

Again, Sadie let out her breath, relaxing into Becca's hands.

She rubbed her thumb in soft circles right along the bridge of Sadie's nose but just to the right. With each circle's completion, she pressed a little harder against the bone, grateful when nothing moved or cracked.

A tear leaked out of the corner of Sadie's eye.

"I'm not crying," Sadie said, despite her physiology belying her words. "My eyes just leak automatically whenever I experience pain."

Becca smiled. "So the definition of crying?"

Sadie opened her right eye to glare at Becca. "Just so you know, I wasn't a crier before this trip. This is somehow your influence."

"Excuse me for actually caring about you and helping unlock your vulnerable side," Becca said. "That's what you get for making me like you."

"You like me," Sadie teased, then winced. "Ouch. Are we almost done?" Sadie asked. "Because you said you'd be quick, and I—um—hurt and would really like to get to the part where I slap a bag of frozen peas on my face. Please and thank you, Dr. Weiland."

"Right," Becca replied, realizing she was still cradling the other woman's neck in her hands. "I did promise brevity." Plus, it felt like Sadie was cutting her off at the pass. Later, once they were past this nose thing and the larger-than-expected dinner party thing and the how-do-I-tell-my-sister-about-my-young-lover thing. "Here we go," she said coolly, then slid her right thumb over the left side of Sadie's nose bridge.

Another tear slid down Sadie's cheek as a teeth-gritting "Fudge!" escaped her lips.

"Impressive," Becca said. "In the throes of pain and still

censoring yourself for a little girl who isn't even here. If I didn't know better, I'd say you've fallen as much for Evie as you have for Max."

"I haven't *fallen*—I mean, Evie is sweet, and the swear jar thing is cute. I'm just playing along. It doesn't *mean* anything. I'm the fun aunt, remember?" She winced as Becca pressed against a tender spot, but she didn't cry out or leak any more tears.

In the midst of her teasing, Becca managed to complete the physical exam, confirming that the injury was confined to the left side.

"All done, by the way. You did great, Sadie. So you want the good news or the bad news first?" Becca asked.

"Do you mean there are worse consequences than suffering through a dinner party with a broken nose?"

Becca sighed. "The good news is your nose is *not* broken. It's just a contusion. Everything inside looks good. Bleeding is minimal after the initial gush. You're a little banged up, and the wound is going to be pretty tender for at least the next week or two, but for the most part, the worst is over."

"Okay," Sadie said, finally opening both of her eyes to meet Becca's gaze. "Then what's the bad news?"

She guessed now was as good a time as any to let Sadie see what she saw. It wasn't like she could remove all the mirrors in the house without Sadie noticing.

"You're pretty swollen already. And based on the redness here..." She shone the penlight on the bridge of Sadie's nose as if she were holding a laser pointer. "And here." She waved the light back and forth underneath Sadie's left eye. "You're going to have quite a shiner by dinner."

Sadie groaned—a much calmer reaction than Becca had been expecting.

"Why would this day be any different than the others since we arrived in this seemingly parallel universe?" Sadie asked. "I mean, I have no game here. I can't stop feeling my feelings or winding up in either the messiest or more precarious situations—or both. And now I'm going to look like the newest member of *Fight Club*—not that I'm allowed to talk about *Fight Club*."

Becca collapsed onto her butt and blew out a breath.

"So you're not mad at my bony shoulder or at me for hurting you during the exam?" She knew the injury was an accident, but Becca hated that she was still indirectly responsible for hurting someone else.

For hurting Sadie.

Sadie waved her off. "It was *my* fault," she admitted begrudgingly. "And—you're a really good doctor, Becca. I don't know what you're like in the delivery room, but you're pretty great when it comes to triage."

Becca raised a brow.

"What?" Sadie asked. "I've watched an episode or a hundred of *Grey's Anatomy*. Just because I don't want to go to the hospital doesn't mean I held back from watching McDreamy and McSteamy do their thing. I could probably treat *you* the next time *you* get hurt."

Becca laughed. "No, you couldn't."

"No," Sadie admitted. "I couldn't. So—thank you. You're really good at what you do." She brushed her hands off on her thighs, then shooed Becca's feet out of her way. "Time to check out this shiner and see how mortified I need to be for everyone and their mother—or sister and brother and Beckett loverboys in our case—to see me in my current and likely grotesque state."

This time Becca snorted. No matter what Sadie thought of herself behind closed doors, she absolutely had the kind of *game* Becca never did and never could.

"You know, even with a swollen nose and soon-to-be-black eye," Becca said as Sadie stood—mouth agape—staring at herself in the mirror. "You, Sadie Bloom, will always be hot AF."

CHAPTER TWENTY-ONE

SADIE

O kay, let's go down our list," Sadie began, staring at her phone screen. "Sourdough."

"Check," Becca replied after a quick riffle through the shopping cart.

"Rustic wheat."

"Check."

"Plain old white bread for the toddler and possibly Evie, though I'm guessing she's more adventurous than our nephew."

Becca sighed. "As much as it pains me to say...check."

"And finally, just in case, gluten free."

"All carbs are present and accounted for," Becca confirmed. "And can I just say that you're a genius with choosing grilled cheese for tonight's menu? I mean, I doubted you at first, but now that I see this grocery cart and all the possibilities, it's like an entire restaurant's worth of options."

Sadie grinned—even though her bruised face wanted to protest—and took stock of the myriad ingredients and fixings she'd grabbed on a whim as they combed the aisles of the store.

Jalapeños and tortilla chips because she knew her brother loved Mexican food. For him, she'd make a sandwich with a kick—and a surprising crunch.

Camembert and pear for something a little more upscale. "This is for you," Sadie said to Becca as she pulled the wheel of soft cheese off the shelf and placed it on the cart.

"Oh my god. How did you know that I *love* Camembert? I barely ever eat it, though," Becca had said, her cheeks flushing as she did. "That changes tonight," she'd added with a surety Sadie hadn't seen in the woman prior to this trip—one that she really liked seeing now.

Sadie understood wanting to be healthy and keeping up your appearance all in the name of confidence and feeling good about yourself. But she knew now that, for Becca, that was only half the story. She'd cultivated this image of who she thought she should be and only now was starting to find comfort in her own skin. It felt good knowing that she'd maybe played a small part in her friend getting to this point in her emotional recovery.

That was what they were both doing, wasn't it? Sadie had thought she was simply putting life on hold for four weeks to soak up some lake house sun and maybe drive her boss's sister a little bananas—just for fun, of course. Instead she'd found an unexpected friend in someone she hadn't expected to like, let alone trust.

But here they were—Dr. Becca Weiland literally letting her hair down and Sadie dropping her breezy facade and lowering her walls so close to the ground that she was as metaphorically naked as Becca had *actually* been naked on the public pier. Add to that Sadie's bruised nose and Becca proudly wearing her shower flip-flips in public, and they certainly made quite the pair.

"Okay," Sadie said after they'd made sure all grilled cheese ingredients were accounted for. "It's time for the wine."

"*And* iced tea," Becca added. "We need to pace ourselves."

Sadie laughed as they pushed the cart through the small local market and over to the even smaller liquor section. "You can take the girl away from responsibility, but you can't take responsibility away from the girl."

Becca shrugged, her dark locks bouncing against her shoulders. "I am who I am, even if I'm finding a better version of me. Plus, as long as there is *zero* schnapps, I think I'm in the clear."

Sadie held up her pinky finger. "I solemnly swear that while I may be up to no good tonight, there will be *zero* schnapps involved in my nefarious adventures."

Becca wrapped her pinky around Sadie's and laughed. "*Nefarious* might be a little outside my comfort zone for a grilled cheese dinner party, but... ditto to what you just said."

"Sadie?"

"Becca?"

The two women, pinkies still entwined, turned their heads in the direction of the two voices—the two *male* voices—and saw Max and Leo each standing with bottles of wine in their hands. Together.

Sadie flipped the clip-on shades up from her glasses—since her contacts had to come out as soon as her left eye started swelling—more in awe of what she was seeing than aware of what she was showing, both her bruised eye and nose as well as the fact that she actually owned clip-on sun shades for her ridiculous glasses.

"Jesus, Sadie," Max said, setting his bottle back down on the shelf. "What the hell happened?"

Oops.

"Oh, you know—pissed off my roommate, and she let me have it," Sadie jested, retreating behind her humorous deflection rather than just admitting to Max that once again she'd turned something as simple as walking into a disaster and had almost broken her own nose.

"Really?" Becca replied, crossing her arms. "That's what you're leading with?"

Sadie realized, though, that it was more than just how seemingly accident-prone this town made her. They hadn't actually told Max and Leo about the additions to the dinner party, and now that they were faced with that reality, she was feeling some feelings she didn't expect to be feeling.

Like excitement.

But also fear.

"Okay, fine. Would you believe me if I told you that I was rushing Becca to get dressed and she stopped suddenly while I was behind her, so I accidentally face-planted into her bony shoulder, nearly—but not *actually*—breaking my nose?"

Max stared at her for a second, the worry in his blue eyes softening and a smile turning up his lips. "After this day started with you waking me before dawn to rescue Becca from jail and then body-slamming Deputy Derek's desk? Yeah, that tracks."

Sadie laughed as he stepped toward her, slipping his hand behind her neck, his fingers threading through her hair.

"Can I kiss it and make it all better?" he asked. "If I promise to be careful?"

"Right here in the market?" she asked. Out of the corner of her eye—the good one—she saw Becca and Leo moving farther away.

"Right here in the market," Max said, his deep voice soft and sexy.

Sadie bit her lip and nodded, feeling like a giddy teenager yet knowing—despite her aching face—that this moment would end so much better than any kiss from her teen years had.

"Does it hurt?" he asked, gingerly lifting her glasses off her bruised nose and pushing them up onto her head.

"It did. I mean it does. But surprisingly not right now," she admitted, her voice barely above a whisper. Because even though it was the truth, Sadie was pretty sure she couldn't feel any pain at the moment.

He brushed his lips gently onto her cheek, just below her black eye, then placed a featherlight kiss onto the bridge of her nose.

Sadie hissed in a breath between her teeth.

"Shit," Max said. "I'm sorry."

"No," Sadie told him as he stepped back. "It's okay. I'd rather you kiss me when it hurts than have you not kiss me at all."

She lowered her glasses again—wincing slightly—so she could see the beautiful man in front of her.

Max's shoulders relaxed. "Sadie Bloom, are you admitting that you *like* me?"

He was so handsome in nothing but a T-shirt and cargo shorts, even if it was a Milwaukee Brewers T.

"I think we've already established that I have some very confusing feelings when it comes to you, Max Beckett."

He laughed, and Sadie couldn't help but notice the lines at the corners of his eyes as he did, how they were evidence of a lifetime of smiles, one of which, right now, was all thanks to her.

"So do I have to wait for dinner to hear the full story of your nearly nose-breaking face-planting, or do I get the inside scoop on account of those very confusing feelings you have and because I got to see you first?"

"Dinner!" she cried, realization setting in. "Right. So I should probably tell you that my brother, Becca's sister, their one-year-old son, and twenty-four-year-old daughter and boyfriend are crashing the party tonight. I was so focused on having enough food and getting the place ready in time that I completely neglected the fact that you meeting my family tonight might be a *little* too soon for— for whatever is going on with us here." She motioned back and forth between them, then buried her face in her hands. "You can totally bail," she said through her fingers. "Like, this is definitely too much too soon, especially for me, so I don't blame you if you and Evie want to bow out for the night. How about this? I'll count to five, like we're playing hide-and-go-seek or something, and if after that I look up and you're gone, no hard feelings, okay? I'll just text you tomorrow or Sunday after everyone has left. Did I mention that they're all sleeping over? I probably should have led with that. *Anyway,* this is your out. So—yeah. Here we go. One...two...three...four...and...five."

She kept her face covered for an extra second or two, then finally dropped her hands to her sides to find Max Beckett still there, a bottle of wine in each hand.

"Do your brother and sister-in-law like red or white? Maybe I'll just get both?" he said.

Sadie's throat tightened, and her eyes pricked with tears. *Seriously,* she was ready to rename this place from Glass Lake to Sob Lake because this place and this man and this unexpected kindred spirit she'd found in Becca were all too much. And yet here she was, standing her ground, when two weeks ago her first instinct would have been to run.

She swallowed, thankfully keeping the tears at bay. "You want to meet my family? With Evie?"

He sighed. "I don't know if you've noticed, but that little ten-year-old of mine is actually the mature one in our family. She's the one who told *me* that I need to put myself back out there and find happiness outside of my life with her and Penny."

"Wow," Sadie said. "Maybe I should hire her to be *my* life coach too. Where is that little sage?"

Max laughed. "Living her best life at Cool Beans, learning how to froth milk and lip-sync to Tom Jones."

Sadie nodded at the bottles of wine in Max's hands. "Both, then," she said. "Alissa—Becca's sister—just recently stopped breastfeeding and I'm guessing will be hitting the booze hard tonight while my brother is on toddler duty. You really want to do this?" she asked, realizing she wasn't posing the question for Max alone.

"Are you sure *you* want to do this?" he countered, settling the bottles into the shopping basket that had been resting by his feet. "I can cover my eyes and count to five if you want to make your decision without any judgment on my part."

Sadie sighed and stepped toward him, pressing her palms to his chest.

"No," she admitted. "I'm *not* sure. I don't know how to *be* sure. But I want you and Evie there tonight. I strangely find myself wanting you there whenever you're not. So if you can deal with that level of surety—or *un*surety—then I guess it's *Meet the Blooms* night. Or at least some of the Blooms. No parents," she said with a nervous laugh. "Because I am *definitely* not ready for that."

Max bent down and kissed the top of her head. "*Meet the Blooms*, it is."

☼

"Did Leo say anything about why he and Max were shopping together?" Sadie asked as she and Becca brought the last of grocery bags into the kitchen. "I kind of forgot to ask, and the two of you took off for a little while, so I figured you maybe got the scoop."

"Yeah," Becca said, setting her bags on the island. "I bet you forget a lot when you get all googly-eyed like you do when Max is around."

Sadie pulled a grape out of one of her bags and pegged it at Becca, hitting her square in the nose.

Becca yelped and then laughed. "Real mature, Bloom."

"I do *not* get googly-eyed," Sadie insisted. "And you didn't answer my question. When you and Baby Max disappeared . . ." Sadie raised her brows, and Becca shot daggers at her with her glare. "Did you happen to ask him if he and Max had buried the hatchet?"

Becca's cheeks went crimson.

"Oh. My. God," Sadie said. "You had *sex* at the market?"

"Shhh!" Becca said, looking around their empty kitchen. "And no. Not *at* the market. But maybe in the back seat of his car in the parking lot of the market?" She bit back a smile.

"Oh. My. *God*," Sadie said again. "Who *are* you? And what if you got arrested again?"

Becca threw her hands in the air. "I know, right? I mean, I *don't* know. It's like there's something in the air here—other than humidity, that is." She ran her fingers through her unusually wavy hair. "But for the first time since—well—*ever*, I'm not thinking about the consequences or worrying about the future. I'm just having fun."

Sadie could relate. She'd fashioned her whole life out of not worrying about the future and just having fun.

"I feel like we've swapped lives or something," Sadie said. "Because I can't stop thinking about how everything I've done since the moment we got here is going to affect *my* future." And Max's and Evie's. It felt weird to worry about someone else other than herself. It wasn't as if she'd lived a selfish life. Just a protected one. Now she felt like she had the happiness and well-being of other people in her hands. "I don't know if I like it," she admitted.

Becca sighed. "I don't blame you. It's exhausting. Like, I don't know if I've ever been more worn out than when I was trying to be the perfect doctor, the perfect wife, and the perfect mother. I'm not going to say that women can't have it all, but when it comes to life in general, something often has to give. This is just make believe." She waved her hands around the room. "But it's the welcome reprieve I didn't know I needed. We have to go back to reality eventually, right?"

Sadie started separating their refrigerator items from the dry goods so she could store everything appropriately. She wasn't sure what even was reality anymore—now or two weeks from now.

"Leo is on the same page as you, right?" Sadie asked. "The whole *just having fun* deal?"

Becca opened the bakery bag of sourdough and pulled out the end piece, nibbling at it as she spoke. "I don't see why he wouldn't be. I mean, he knows my life is in Chicago, that my job and my kids are there. I can't imagine he'd want any part of that, especially when he's young enough to start his own family with someone his *own* age."

Sadie sighed and grabbed herself a piece of bread as well.

"So you haven't talked to him," she said to Becca, a statement rather than a question.

Becca shrugged. "What's there to talk about? There isn't a future for us, so why dwell on it? I mean he obviously feels the same way."

Sadie looked down at the crumbs on the island, then up at Becca's hands as they frantically tore at the heel of bread between her fingers.

"Is that why you're wasting a delicious, crusty piece of bread by turning it into confetti?"

Becca pegged a piece of her doughy confetti at Sadie, but it landed somewhere on the island, short of its destination.

"You weren't going to use this one for a sandwich anyway. If I've learned anything about you as both a pastry chef and a burgeoning gourmet cook—because yes, these badass grilled cheeses are going to be gourmet as hell—you would not forgo presentation for practicality. Ergo, there is no way in hell

Sadie Bloom would use mismatched pieces of bread for one of her sandwich creations."

Sadie sighed with a smile. "I guess I can't argue with you there."

The weather had cooled since the last storm, and they'd taken to leaving the inside door to the screened-in porch open when they were home, which was why both their heads turned when they heard a splash in the distant waters outside.

"Now that things are—you *know*—it's creepy if we pause for a quick drink on the porch, right?" Sadie asked.

Becca scooped her bready mess into her palm and dumped it into the trash. Then she grabbed an opened bottle of sparkling rosé from the fridge and quickly filled a glass.

"It's creepy for *you*," she said to Sadie. "Not for me."

Becca brushed past her and out onto the porch without another word.

"Don't get any ideas, Doc!" Sadie called after her. "It may not be illegal on the private side of the beach, but this dinner party is *not* a one-woman job. I'm fine working on prep alone, but when it's time to start grilling, I'm going to need a sous-grilled-cheese-chef!"

Becca didn't answer, which meant she was likely enjoying the show—or joining the cast.

Sadie couldn't help but laugh, despite the pain it brought to her tender wound.

When she finally got all the groceries unpacked, the perishables in the fridge and the packages of bread lined up on the counter, she decided it was time for icing the face round two. She grabbed the bag of peas she'd thrown back into the freezer that morning and emptied what was left of the opened wine into her own glass before stretching out on the couch, glasses propped on her head and frozen peas plopped on her face—save for her mouth, of course, because everyone knows that's where a good, crisp, summer rosé belongs.

Soon, every one of her muscles relaxed. Warmth spread through her from her belly all the way up to her neck and all the way down to her toes. She felt like she could drift off, and why not? They'd shopped in record time and chosen a meal that could be cooked almost on demand. A little disco nap could hardly hurt. In fact, it would leave her refreshed and ready to take on the evening with renewed vigor.

So she let her breathing slow, let her eyes flutter shut, and let the delightful combination of wine and frozen peas numb her pain and lull her into a blissful sleep.

☼

"Shit! Shit! Shit! Shit! Shit!" Sadie heard from far off at first, but it sounded like it was getting closer. "Sadie! Wake *up*! Wake up! Wake up! *Wake up!*"

She felt hands on her shoulders now, and something wet and heavy sliding off her face. Was she bleeding? Excessively drooling?

"I'm up," she said groggily, pushing herself up onto her elbows, the soft bag of peas hitting the floor with a *thunk*. "Okay," she said with a chuckle. "That makes more sense."

"We overslept!" Becca said, squatting on the floor next to the couch. Her hair looked damp and her tank was wrinkled—as well as inside out and *backward*.

Everything started to click into place. The wine, the peas, the power nap she'd decided to take only a few minutes ago. Unless it had been slightly *more* than a few minutes ago.

"What happened to your hair?" she asked Becca. "And your clothes. Are the waves breaking *inside* the porch?"

Becca winced. "I met Leo outside, and we went for a quick swim. Then—um—we decided to dry off in his tent, and…well…one thing led to another, and we decided to take a quick nap. I figured if we overslept, you'd come looking for me eventually to help with dinner. It was just supposed to be a power nap. I didn't think *you* would be taking a nap too!"

Sadie bolted upright, knocking her nose against Becca's forehead and then swearing enough to fill an entire jar and then some as stars clouded her already blurry vision since her glasses were somewhere buried in the pillows of the couch.

"Shit!" Becca yelled. "Dammit! Are you okay?"

Sadie swiped her forearm under her nose, and it came away smeared with blood.

"Did I just break it?" Sadie cried.

Becca shook her head. "I mean, I don't think so. It's a fresh wound, so you probably just loosened up some of the blood from earlier that might have been trapped behind some clotting."

"That's so gross," Sadie said, now pressing her arm to her

nostrils, her desire *not* to bleed all over herself and the furniture outweighing the pain of even touching her nose.

She scrambled to her feet, swaying for a second before righting herself and then racing toward the downstairs bathroom.

"What time is it?" she called back to Becca.

"Five fifteen!" Becca called back, though Sadie could hear her padding across the floor after her—until she heard a yelp and then a *splat*.

Shit.

Sadie was barely over the threshold of the bathroom door when she came to a halt, pivoted, and saw Becca on her ass where she had very clearly been on her feet just seconds ago.

"What the fudge?" Sadie said aloud. "Are *you* okay?"

"*Yes*," Becca said, waving her off. "I'm fine. I just tripped over my flip-flop." She pushed herself up to her feet, took one step forward, and collapsed like she'd suddenly gone boneless.

"That is *not* fine!" Sadie said. "Don't move!" She rushed into the bathroom, stuck a tissue up each nostril, washed her hands and arms, and then ran back to Becca, lowering herself to the floor beside her. "Which foot is it?" she asked. "Though I'm guessing it's the one you're squeezing with both hands."

"I rolled my ankle," Becca said. "I don't think it's broken, though."

Sadie pulled Becca's hands away and hissed in a breath.

"Fuuuuck," Sadie said, not caring about Evie hearing from a mile away. "Why is it that swollen already, then?"

Becca shooed Sadie away and proceeded to give her ankle a physical examination.

"I didn't hear a crack," she said coolly. "There is swelling, but nothing looks misshapen...no numbness, just excruciating pain...and pain is concentrated on the soft area rather than directly over the bone. Any ER doctor worth their salt would diagnose this as a sprain."

Sadie stared at her for a long moment.

"No tears?" she finally asked. "No freaking out that we have guests arriving in just under an hour, and you might not be able to walk? Let me help you up so we can determine if you're going to be couch bound tonight or not." Sadie reached for Becca's arm, ready to support the other woman's weight as she tried standing again, but Becca shook her head, her jaw tight.

"The diagnosis is sprain. I should elevate and ice it, but we need to get dinner ready first." She looked down at her inside-out-and-backward tank, then up at Sadie, who definitely looked worse for wear as well. "We need to get *ourselves* ready, or we are going to have a *lot* of explaining to do to our guests."

Sadie sighed. "Okay, but can't you just let me *help* you?"

Becca shook her head again. "*I'm* the doctor. I'm the one who should be helping *you*." She swung her legs behind her so she was up on her knees. Sadie quickly stood as Becca then pressed down on the floor, rising up on her good side before gently setting her sprained side down on the floor.

She sucked in a breath, and Sadie readied herself to catch her falling roommate, but Becca didn't collapse.

Sadie narrowed her eyes. "You know, I get defaulting to clinical mode when you're actually on duty, but I saw you take care of Leo. I saw you take care of *me*. Why don't you afford yourself that same warmth and care? Why don't you let someone *else* take care of *you*?"

Instead of answering, once Becca seemed to find her footing, she raised her hands to Sadie's face and examined *her* instead.

"Still not broken," she assessed. "But you look like hell."

Sadie would have snorted if her nose hadn't been swollen and packed with tissue, so instead, the sound came out like a cough.

"You're one to talk," Sadie said. "You look freshly fucked, but all the color has drained from your cheeks, which also makes you look like you might throw up. It hurts more than you're letting on, doesn't it?" She didn't wait for Becca to answer because, for some reason, she didn't think Becca would confirm her suspicion. "Go get cleaned up, and I will too. I'll set up the island as a sort of grilled cheese station where everyone will pick their fixings, and I'll turn their pile of ingredients into an ooey, gooey masterpiece. We'll do everything on the fly, each sandwich made to order like it's my own little food truck."

Her chest squeezed, and Sadie wondered if she wasn't

getting enough air into her lungs now that breathing through her nose was temporarily not an option. But it wasn't her lungs that felt tight. It was something deeper, a place she couldn't quite name. So she shook it off, then shooed Becca toward the stairs.

"Can you make it?" Sadie asked. "Because we *can* call this whole thing off. There's no rule that says we have to make this work."

Did a part of Sadie *want* Becca to put the kibosh on the whole thing, saving them both from mixing their fantasy with the real world?

"No," Becca said. "I guarantee you Alissa has been looking forward to this since we spoke this morning. She needs a night of socializing with adults. Of her wineglass not going empty. Plus, I feel like our moms working the bakery together tomorrow is a kind of social experiment I don't want to disrupt." She laughed, then winced, then laughed some more. "I'm not sure what the universe is trying to tell us by beating us down at a *pretty* critical moment today, but we have nowhere to go but up now, right?"

"Famous last words," Sadie said with a laugh. "I'll be ready in ten as long as the old schnoz is no longer a gusher."

"I just need a quick rinse in the shower," Becca said. "Here goes nothing!" She pivoted slowly, lifted her foot with the ankle swollen twice the size of its counterpart, and took a step forward. She pressed her lips together as she put weight on it, but she was able to take another step forward after the initial first.

Sadie waited and watched, making sure Becca didn't fall as she hobbled toward the stairs.

"You're so stubborn!" Sadie called after her.

"And you're clumsy as hell!" Becca called back, *almost* covering the strain in her voice.

"Only here," Sadie mumbled as she spun around toward the bathroom and trudged back to her destination.

Was everything that had happened today—starting with Becca's arrest—some sort of sign from the universe that they just weren't understanding?

Sadie didn't usually believe in signs. That was her brother. Matthew was all about signs and magic and knowing from the moment he saw Alissa Adler in the hallway during freshman year of high school that he would one day marry her. Sure, he probably hadn't planned on them getting pregnant their senior year or married and divorced before they turned twenty-five. But after an almost two-decade detour, they were back where they were supposed to be—living their unconventional happily ever after, emphasis on the *happily*.

Sadie Bloom had put off the idea of happily ever after, thinking she'd get to it eventually. Now she wondered how long ever after meant and if it was even fair to ask Max to be a part of something so uncertain. *Maybe* all that seemed like bad luck today was simply a sign that everything in Sadie's life was about to change. For the better? God, she hoped.

Sadie turned on the shower and stepped inside.

She let the water wash away the pain.

She let it wash away the worry that her future looked anything like her past.

If the only way to finally move forward was to be clumsy as hell, then Sadie was ready for all the bumps and bruises along the way.

CHAPTER TWENTY-TWO

MAX

"How do I look?" Max asked, realizing it would have been better to ask the question *before* he was about to knock on the rental's door. It wasn't like he could run home and change, not now that Delilah and Shelby had parked behind his truck and were strolling up the driveway. He hooked a finger under his collar and rolled his neck. "The tie is too much, right?"

Evie sighed. "I wasn't going to say anything, but since you're asking…can you come down to my level?"

Max lowered himself to a squat.

"You don't need to try so hard," Evie told him, loosening his tie and then unthreading it from under the collar of his lightweight denim button-down. "Next I'm just gonna…" She unbuttoned the top two buttons of his shirt, then did the same to his sleeves, deftly rolling each one to just above his elbows. "Okay. Stand up," she said, and when he did, she untucked the shirt from his slim-fitting khakis—which he never should have bought, by the way. He was almost forty. Was he allowed to wear pants whose cuffs were barely larger than the circumference of his ankle?

"*Bra*-vo," Shelby called with a slow clap as the two women met them on the front porch. "*Now* he looks like a DILF."

"What's a DILF?" Evie asked.

"Here," Delilah said, pulling a dollar from her waist pouch. "Just take this for when you're old enough to know." Then she looked Max up and down, nodding her approval. "Though Shelby *is* right. If you were my type, you'd definitely be a DILF, but since you're not and the only man for me is one who shakes his pelvis up onstage, I'm going to leave you to Sadie. What's with the formal attire anyway?"

Max sighed. "I haven't met another woman's family since I was barely old enough to drink. I don't know the protocol. I'm rusty as hell and basically doing everything wrong."

Delilah sighed and cupped him on his cheek. "You're adorable, not rusty. But yeah, this is a big step, considering you only met a couple of weeks ago, isn't it?"

"He's her lobster," Evie said.

Both Delilah and Shelby laughed.

"I'm her what?" Max asked.

"You know. From that old show that Mom watches. *Friends*? Sometimes we watch it together, and there's this episode when you realize that Ross and Rachel are meant to be, and Phoebe calls him her lobster."

"Because they supposedly hold claws in the tank," Delilah replied with a chuckle.

Shelby sighed. "I love that episode. *So* romantic."

"*Wait*," Max said, making the time-out symbol with his hands. "Mom lets you watch *Friends*? But there's like—I mean, the show has some grown-up themes in it like—"

"Sex?" Evie said, hands on her hips. "*Please*, Dad. They taught us all about that last spring at school. Plus, Mom said I can ask her questions whenever I want and that she'll answer them to the best of her ability. Like, at school they taught us about sperm and eggs and how a baby gets made when one meets the other...But they didn't exactly tell us *how* the sperm *gets* to the egg." She shrugged. "So I asked Mom."

Max's mouth went dry, and his palms grew clammy. How had he missed his little girl becoming not so little anymore? The divorce had robbed him of more than just time. It robbed him of experience. Not that *he* was exactly ready to have the birds and the bees talk with her, but now that the opportunity had come and gone without his knowledge, he mourned the conversation they would never have.

Okay, maybe he didn't exactly mourn this one, but the point was that he'd missed parts of Evie's life already, and he would miss more in the years to come.

He cared about Sadie more than he'd expected, and he wanted to see this thing with them move forward, but she was right to point out his responsibility as a father. Evie came first, always. But Sadie already got that. He was sure that if she felt the same, they'd figure out the next steps when the time came. Tonight he just had to worry about impressing her family... and keeping his daughter from growing up too fast.

"So..." he said hesitantly. "You know what *sex* is, but you don't know what a DILF is?" He shook his head. "I can't believe I just said *DILF* to my daughter."

"I mean, I could look it up on your laptop when we get home..." Evie mused.

"No!" Max cried. "Peanut, please do *not* do that. I was just trying to gauge how much growing up you'd already done without me. I am *not* trying to rush you any further." He scrubbed a hand across his jaw, then dropped back to a squat in front of her. "You know you can ask *me* anything you want too, right? And I'll also answer you to the best of my ability." He swallowed the lump in his throat. "I might not be there every day, but I am *always* here." He pressed his hand over her heart. "And you are always right *here*." He picked up her hand and placed it over his.

Evie nodded, her eyes glassy, and Max wanted to kiss her cheeks and make even the possibility of tears vanish into mist. Maybe he couldn't fix what had already been broken, like his marriage, but he could swear—the good kind that didn't require a dollar in a jar—to only make choices that kept him from breaking his daughter's heart again.

"Can I ask you a question, Dad?"

"Of course, Peanut." He cupped her cheek in his palm.

The corner of Evie's mouth quirked up, and he saw the dimple that the two of them shared. "What's a DILF?"

He barked out a laugh. "If I give you ten bucks to add to the jar, do you promise not to ask me for another ten years?"

She pursed her lips and considered. "How about I give you ten *months*?" she asked.

He pulled his phone out of his pocket and removed a ten-dollar bill from the clip on the back of the case. "Deal," he said, handing it over.

"Damn," Shelby said. "We haven't even knocked on the door, and girlfriend already has eleven bucks!"

Delilah nudged Shelby with her elbow. "You mean twelve?"

"Aw, crap. I'm always doing..." Shelby groaned, pulled two singles from her pocket—because everyone knew to have plenty of singles when Evie Beckett was around—and handed them to the increasingly wealthy young girl.

"Can we go in now?" Delilah whined. "I'm getting hangry."

Shelby pressed a hand to Delilah's lower back. "My poor girl was short staffed today and never got a chance to pause for lunch."

Max sighed as he looked at the three women surrounding him. For a boy who'd grown up in a splintered family, only to follow in the same footsteps as his parents, he couldn't help but smile when he was reminded of the family he'd found, even if they weren't all related by blood.

You have a brother too, a voice whispered in the back of his mind. *Or are you still blaming him for the things you've lost?*

"Half brother," Max grumbled to himself.

"What's that?" Shelby asked.

"Huh? Oh, nothing," he replied, not realizing he'd spoken out loud.

His inner monologue relied too much on logic while the man himself often made decisions based on matters of the heart. Maybe someday the two would find a way to meet in the middle.

He raised a hand to knock, but the door swung open before he had the chance.

Speak of the devil—or Leo Beckett himself. It seemed Max had a habit of conjuring that brother his mind wouldn't shut up about, both today at the market and now here at the door.

"You know, you are getting *so* much better at revealing your disappointment the moment you see me," Leo quipped. "I mean, there was barely a millisecond before I knew you regretted all your life choices that led you to this door."

Max sighed and picked up the two narrow gift bags of wine at his feet. "Would you prefer I greet you the way I'd planned on greeting Sadie?"

"Come right in, everybody," Leo said, swinging the door wide so the entire group could enter and no such greeting could occur.

"Uncle Leo!" Evie launched herself into her uncle's arms.

"Small Fry!" Leo replied, catching her and twirling her once before setting her back on her feet.

"Guess what? I made thirteen bucks just on the porch."

Leo raised his brows as Shelby and Delilah brushed past, then he narrowed his gaze at his brother.

"It's not what you think," Max explained, though he didn't know why he was justifying himself to Leo. "Most of it was a bribe."

Leo crossed his arms and gave Max a knowing grin. "Remind me to take parenting tips from you if I ever have kids of my own."

Evie gave her uncle one more hug and then followed Shelby and Delilah into the house.

Leo, however, stood there grinning from ear to ear as he stared at Max. "Nice outfit, by the way."

It was only then that Max saw it—Leo's short-sleeved denim shirt, cuffed and rolled tight against his biceps. Instead of khaki pants, he wore khaki board shorts, and where Max had opted for slip-on canvas loafers, Leo kept it casual in a pair of leather flip-flops. And that dimple—the damned telltale. If anyone doubted the two were related, all they had to do was match their dimples—and apparently their attire. Though Max suddenly felt a little less DILF and a little more just plain *dad* when he caught a glimpse of what he must have looked like a little over a decade ago.

"Can we *not* do this tonight?" Max asked.

"Do what, exactly?" Leo replied, answering Max's question with his own.

"The button pushing. The baiting. The—*all* of it," he said. "It's getting exhausting."

Sadie had been right. They were both grown men behaving like children, and for what? Where had it gotten them after all this time?

Leo blew out a breath. Now his crossed arms looked less like a gesture of disdain and more like—protection.

"I thought this was what you wanted," Leo said flatly. "I mean, if we're not button pushing and baiting, then what are we? Because this was never what I wanted, Max." He shrugged. "I just wanted a brother who maybe wanted one too."

He dropped his arms and walked away, not waiting for Max to answer.

"You really are an asshole," he said softly to himself, and glanced around the great room to see if anyone—if *Evie*—had noticed. But for once, he was in the clear, probably because he'd spoken the truth.

The house was abuzz before him, which meant he and his tiny entourage had been the last to arrive. Max suddenly felt lost in a place he'd lived almost all his life, in a house he'd been in countless times before Sadie Bloom blew into town. But for some reason, tonight everything felt new and unexplained.

His daughter growing up.

His brother extending an olive branch when Max knew it should be him.

A woman who constantly reminded him of the man he wanted to be—and who might soon have the power to shatter his heart.

"Penny for your thoughts?" he heard a woman's voice ask. "Or do you only carry singles in case you come across a strip club—or the ten-year-old swear police?"

He blinked, waking himself from his haze, realizing Sadie was standing only a few feet away.

She closed the distance between them, then lifted her sunglasses up onto her forehead.

"Jesus," he said. "Why do you look worse than when I saw you a few hours ago?" Her mouth fell open, and he held up a finger. "Nope. Wait. Let me try that again: Sadie Bloom, you are the most beautiful woman in the room—always—but why the hell does your injury look worse than before?"

He wanted to reach for her, but the skin on the side of her nose and beneath her left eye looked puffy with mottled purple bruising where earlier there'd been only a hint of red.

"Hey," she said. "I was able to get my contacts in, so I consider that a win. But yeah. One face-plant today didn't seem to be enough, so I decided to try it again against Becca's forehead. In case you're wondering, the forehead won."

He skimmed a damp lock of hair off her forehead and behind her ear. "I'm afraid to leave you alone anymore," he said softly, pressing a soft kiss to her temple. "You obviously need me to keep you safe."

She laughed, then pressed her fingers to her cheek as her smile turned into a grimace. "I didn't have a single injury in over twenty years. Not even a paper cut. But I come to Bumblefuck, Wisconsin—otherwise known as Glass Lake—and get the shit kicked out of me right and left as soon as I meet this strange man named *Max*."

Max's eyes darted around the room, and Sadie grabbed his hand.

"Evie's outside with my brother, sister-in-law, and their toddler, showing them the beach. No way they can hear me with waves coming in."

He let out a breath just as his chest grew tight. "Do you really think I'm somehow the reason you keep getting the"— he changed his voice to a stage whisper—"*shit* kicked out of you?"

She dropped his hand and slid both of her palms up his torso, stopping to rest them on his chest.

"I think you're the reason for a lot of change that seems to be taking place in my life. Unexpectedly, I might add. But I'm not afraid of it," she told him, rising onto her toes and planting a kiss on his lips. "I am scared of you knowing all of me, though. Even though I want you to."

Despite the wine bags dangling from one hand, he wrapped his arms around her and squeezed her tight.

"I want to know all of you, Sadie. And for the record, I'm scared as hell about how I feel when I kiss you," he admitted, then nipped lightly at her bottom lip.

"Oh, thank god," she said. "I am too. I just thought it would help to put on a brave face when my actual face looks like a palette of watercolors gone wrong."

Shit.

Max was falling for this woman. Two weeks in and he was more certain of it than he'd been after two years with Evie's mom. But how could he have known? He thought what they had was love until she told him it wasn't. Even if he'd figured it out on his own, he didn't regret his past, getting his heart broken. Not when it meant Evie coming into his life. But now he had a second chance at happiness outside of him and his daughter. He had a second chance at happiness *for* him and his daughter.

A throat cleared, and Sadie unclasped her hands from behind Max's neck.

"Sorry to break up the party, but isn't it customary to introduce yourself before you devour my sister's face?"

Max stepped back to find a man his same height and build—with Sadie's same sandy hair save for some silver at the temples—staring him down.

"Matt, *no*," a woman chided as she blew an auburn corkscrew out of her face.

An adorably chubby toddler—with his own head of red curls—she held in her arms also said something that sounded like, "Matt, no!" Though coming from a toddler just learning to talk, it could have been anything from *apple* to *asshole* and everything in between.

"You must be Max," the woman said, extending a hand as she bounced the toddler against her hip. "I'm Alissa, Becca's sister. And this wannabe tough guy is Matt."

Matt cleared his throat again.

Alissa groaned. "Sorry. This wannabe tough guy is *Matthew* until he decides that you're good enough for his sister, in which case he will let you call him Matt." She leaned closer to Max and whispered in his ear, "But please keep calling him Matt all night long just to drive him crazy."

Sadie hooked her arm through her brother's.

"We talked about this, Matty," she said. "And you promised to behave."

"Yeah but…" he started. "Gabi almost married Ethan without me getting to give him the third degree. Now they're *living* together, and I just have to deal with that? At the very least, ya gotta let me have this one, Sadie. Let me be the overprotective, overbearing big brother I was meant to be all those years when you were trying to get my attention, and I was too dumb—or too caught up in being a dad—to notice."

I just wanted a brother who maybe wanted one too … Overprotective, overbearing big brother I was meant to be … Shit. Was it really that simple? Something inside Max shifted. He grabbed Matthew's hand and gave it a firm shake. "It's great meeting you, *Matt*, but I gotta go do something." He dropped the other guy's hand and gave him the two bags of wine.

"I'll grab the folding tables and chairs in a few," he said to Sadie, then mouthed *Sorry* before he made a beeline through the living room and out the back door.

Leo was exactly where Max thought he would be, sitting on the sand, watching the small waves break on the shore.

Max picked up a rock and skipped it across the water.

"Where's Becca?" he asked.

Leo kept his eyes on the lake, and Max was grateful for the gesture.

"We decided to pretend there was nothing going on between us so she wouldn't have to explain anything to her sister. Makes sense, right? It's not like this is anything serious. I mean, she's a doctor, and I'm—me."

Max's chest ached. "I never asked you why," he said.

Leo stood and brushed the sand off his shorts, finally turning to face Max.

There was no smile, no taunt in his eyes. He looked open and vulnerable, like he'd been waiting his entire life for Max to utter that one word. *Why?*

Max cleared his throat. "Why you insisted on sharing a room with me and keeping me up all night playing *Floor Is Lava*. Why you took off on your bike without your helmet and got into that wreck when you were six. Why Derek had to cuff you in the middle of a brawl outside the pub. Why are you always hurting yourself—on my account?"

Because on some level, hadn't Max always known Leo had been vying for *his* attention?

Leo huffed out a bitter laugh. "You're only asking because you already know," Leo said, reading Max's thoughts. "But I'll let you off the hook for that last one. The bar fight had nothing to do with you and everything to do with me giving a girl a ring and her telling me I'm not good enough. So . . . rest easy, okay? That one's not on you."

Shit.

Shit. Shit. Shit. Shit. Shit.

"I'm—sorry," Max finally uttered. "I was a dumb kid who already felt like he'd lost. My family got torn apart so you could have yours." God, he really was a dick. After going through a divorce of his own, he should have been able to see his own childhood better. To see his parents as people who were just trying to figure life out just like he was now. To see

Leo as the innocent bystander who simply got caught in the middle of Max's resentment. "I wanted to punish my father for leaving, Leo. But I didn't know how. So I punished you instead. Somewhere along the way I knew I was wrong, but I didn't know how to stop." He let out a bitter laugh. "And then you grew up and started giving me hell right back, which I so fucking deserved, and here we are."

Sadie was right. Holy hell, she was fucking *right*. Something shifted the minute she showed up on that beach. Somehow, letting Sadie into his life had made it easier to see the other person who'd been vying for a spot in Max's world pretty much since the day he was born.

Leo ran a hand through his dark hair, then squinted up at the setting sun.

"No shit," he said. "I've had you figured out since I was about Evie's age. Why do you think I keep giving an asshole like you chance after chance to figure yourself out?"

Max picked up another stone, skipping it out into the deep.

"I really am a huge asshole," he admitted.

Leo picked up a stone as well and tossed it out into the water, his skipping even farther than his brother's. "The hugest," he said, and Max could see the corner of his mouth turn up, the telltale dimple forming in his cheek.

"What do we do now?" Max asked, grabbing another stone. "Like, hug or something?"

"Um, no." This time Leo laughed. "I don't know if you've noticed, old man, but I'm *not* Evie's age anymore. I've got my own shit to work through before I'm ready to get all emotional with my big bro."

"Can you at least tell me *why* the tent?" Max asked. "Especially in the middle of the storm when you know I wouldn't have turned you away."

Leo grinned. "I *like* the beach. And if I need more stable shelter, I can just use my own house."

Max froze mid-throw. "Your *own* house? What the...? Wait, do you mean...?"

"I'm not just a random houseboy," Leo continued, saving Max from his stammering. "I had some money put away and invested in vacation rentals. Ted and Andrea took me on as partner, and I took over the mortgage for the property next door to Becca and Sadie. But I'd appreciate it if you didn't say anything because I kind of like Becca thinking I don't have anywhere else to go in a storm."

Max laughed and shook his head. "You've got it pretty bad for her, don't you?"

"We're not having this conversation right now."

"Okay...but I have to admit I'm really impressed with what you've made of yourself. I kind of think we should hug."

Leo's expression hardened. "Not. *Yet*," he said, a muscle ticking in his jaw. But Max still saw the ghost of a grin.

Max smiled, his shoulders relaxing. "Fair enough," he told him. "We've got time. And I'm not going anywhere."

They stayed there like that for several minutes more, two brothers standing side by side, skipping stones in silence.

CHAPTER TWENTY-THREE

BECCA

Somehow, they pulled it off. Sure, they had to drag an extra chair outside so Becca could elevate her swollen ankle and keep it on ice. But she'd made it through the assembly line that was Sadie's kitchen island grilled cheese station, watching in awe as her roommate—no, her *friend*—created art out of bread and dairy. Delicious art of which no evidence remained, now that everyone reclined in their chairs, hands on their bellies after an upscale diner-style feast.

"Did Becca ever tell you all how I *broke* my ankle, and Matt had to carry me to the ER on his back?" Alissa asked the table.

"Um—*no!*" Shelby said, slapping the top of the table. "But it sounds romantic as hell, so count us all in."

Becca laughed as her sister regaled the group with what was, in fact, a romantic-as-hell story.

The Shabbat candles flickered in the soft breeze, and

everything felt right with the world, as if they were in a bubble of perfect that could not be popped.

"Sades," Matthew said, popping the last of his apple cider doughnut in his mouth. "Why don't you sell these at the bakery?" Then he looked at Alissa. "Why don't you sell these at the bakery?"

"Um..." Alissa said. "Because..." Then she scrunched up her nose. "I think Elliott has a dirty diaper." She turned her attention to the high chair on the grass next to her. "Do you have a dirty diaper, little man?" She blew raspberries on his neck, and Becca's nephew shrieked with delight as her sister scooped up her baby and piloted him inside.

"That was weird, right?" Matt asked.

"Very weird," Delilah agreed. "And I barely know her."

"Bex?" Matt asked. "Do *you* know what's up with your sister?"

"What?" Becca replied. "I mean, no. I don't know."

Becca couldn't focus on what it was *now* that made her offbeat sibling seem—well—off *beat*. Instead she was feeling a sudden pang of loss, realizing she hadn't seen her kids—not in the flesh—in two whole weeks. It would have been the same if she were at home since they didn't return from camp until tomorrow, but something about being removed from the familiar made her feel even farther away from them.

She wanted to feel close to *someone*.

Leo had somehow ended up seated next to her, but he seemed a million miles away. She knew it was her doing, keeping things discreet, but that didn't mean she had to like it. Without thinking, she reached her hand toward him, her fingertips brushing against his, but before they could truly make any sort of connection, Alissa came jogging out from the porch, Elliott only halfway re-dressed in her arms.

"Jeff!" she whisper-shouted, and even though the whole table heard, the only one who knew this one name was something worthy of dramatic action was Becca.

She snatched her hand back from Leo and shot up from her chair, swearing as she put unexpected weight on her injured foot.

"Here?" Becca asked, realizing all eyes at the table were on her and Alissa.

"*Here!*" Alissa confirmed. "In the great room. I'm guessing I know who told him where you were."

Becca gritted her teeth. "*Mom,*" she said, jaw tight. "I was trying to protect his image for his children by not telling her everything. She must think he's still God's gift to daughters and that I actually *want* him back." She added, "Excuse me, everyone. I—uh—have to go deal with something."

She couldn't bear to make eye contact with Leo, so instead she kept her gaze on her sister as she backed away from the table and limped toward the house.

"What are you doing here?" she asked when she'd finally made it to the front door.

"You're hurt," Jeff said, genuine concern in his eyes.

"No shit," she replied, sarcasm and venom dripping from her tone.

"…And you swear now," Jeff added.

"Yep!" She spread her hands out in front of her as if to say *ta-da!* "I say whatever the fuck I want *whenever* the fuck I want, and your opinion doesn't matter anymore."

Okay, so the wine had flowed freely at dinner, and *maybe* Becca's filter had already called it a night. But she'd never let loose on him. He put himself on a goddamn dating app when they were married, and Becca had resolved—and *dissolved*—their marriage with civil discourse and mostly communicating through their lawyers. Now, it seemed, all she'd left unsaid was going to burst forth like Mount Vesuvius.

"Okay," Jeff admitted. "I suppose I deserve that."

"And another thing," Becca started, pointing at him with her index finger and taking a step forward. But pain won out over her adrenaline, and her knee buckled.

Jeff caught her before she hit the floor. And then he freaking scooped her into his arms like he was Edward Cullen carrying Bella Swan over the threshold after their wedding. But Jeff Weiland was *not* a sparkly vampire, and Becca certainly was no damsel in distress.

"Put me *down*," she growled.

"I'm going to," he told her, his voice strained as he carried her toward the couch. "Just. Need. To get you. Off. That. *Foot*." He heaved a breath and dropped her over the side of the couch.

Becca placed a pillow under her foot, as if she'd always intended to wind up exactly where she was. Then she leaned back and crossed her arms.

"Let's have it," she said.

Jeff's brows furrowed.

"Come *on*. I heard you huffing and puffing. You obviously want to comment on the weight I've gained."

Jeff scrubbed a hand over his jaw. "I was huffing and puffing because I don't normally carry *any* full-sized humans around the house, no matter what they weigh. And before I noticed you were limping, I was about to tell you that you looked amazing. I've *always* thought you were beautiful."

Despite the compliment and how it made her cheeks heat, she wasn't going to give him an inch.

"Funny how finding my husband on a dating app makes me feel like he's not that into me anymore." She swallowed. "Sorry. I meant *ex*-husband."

Jeff rounded the couch and sat down next to her. His brown hair was longer and more unkempt than she'd seen it in the past. And his jaw—usually clean-shaven—was covered in stubble.

"Becca," he started, her name a plea on his lips. "You can always run off a little vacation weight, right?"

And, there it was. "What are you doing here?" she asked, her voice breaking on that last word as all of her unresolved feelings had bubbled to the surface. This man made her believe that love came with conditions. As long as she was pretty enough, fit enough, laughed enough but not too much . . . and certainly not too loud, he would deem her perfect. He used her to boost his own ego, but she used him too, to fill her bucket of self-worth when she and she alone was the only one who had the power to do that.

"I miss you," he told her matter-of-factly. "I miss our family."

She let out a bitter laugh. "I thought I did too, you know? If I hadn't found you on that app, I would have stayed in a marriage I didn't even know was eating me alive. You freed me by divorcing me, Jeff. The only thing I miss is what I thought marriage was supposed to be. But I certainly don't miss us."

He placed a hand over hers and gave it a squeeze. "Technically, babe, *you* divorced *me*."

She exhaled shakily. "I can't do this, okay? I can't. You need to lea—"

His lips were on hers before she could finish her sentence, and for a second his familiar scent and taste and the feel of being where she always thought she wanted to be took over. She let herself be enveloped by the memory of what could have been but actually never was as she sank into the kiss.

But the sensation lasted for only a few seconds before it all felt—wrong.

She pushed him off her and straightened herself against the back of the couch.

"Let me see your phone," she said coolly.

"What? Bex, I don't understand."

"Your. *Phone*," she said again, holding out her palm.

He sighed and handed it over.

She typed in the passcode he'd had more than a year ago and laughed when it worked, the first piece of evidence that she was on the right track.

She scrolled through his apps until she found a folder with

not one, not two, but *three* dating apps in it. She opened the first and glanced at his profile.

> Father of two, divorced, no drama with my ex. Just got out of my first relationship since my divorce and am still a little raw. Go easy on me, ladies. Or ... maybe don't.;)

Becca didn't need any more proof than this, but just to drive the matter home, she gave a cursory glance at his profiles on the other two apps, finding exact duplicates of the first.

"You really are something, aren't you?" she said, tossing his phone back at him. "It's all about the thrill of the chase to you, isn't it? It's why marriage bored you. It's why no relationship you'll have after marriage will last. And it's why you're back here telling me you *miss* me less than a month after legally signing me *out* of your life. I'm not a game, Jeff. I'm not some fucking prize to be won. And I'm *not* going back to mediocre sex now that I know what it's like to climax. Like *really* climax. With a man who took the time—which wasn't *long*, by the way—to get to know my body and ways to touch me that seriously make me feel like I'm either having an out-of-body experience or about to break into a million pieces."

She balled her hands into fists, hating that she was sitting down for the rant of her life. "And another thing. I miss our family too. Like—shit. It hurts my heart every time I think of how this will change things for Mackenzie and Grayson, how their lives will sometimes be harder than I wanted them to be or more painful than I wanted them to be, but if we had stayed together? If I'd allowed myself to settle for loveless complacency instead of true happiness, what kind of example would I have been setting for my children? So—thank you, Jeff. Thank you for being an asshole and for forcing me to see that *I* matter. That my *happiness* matters. And that I'm going to be one hell of a kickass mom now because I'm no longer leaving myself out of the equation." She exhaled a shaky breath. "And also, don't you ever fucking call me Bex again."

A riot of applause erupted over Becca's shoulder, and she craned her neck to see that everyone who'd been outside was now *in*side, standing in the dining room, watching it all unfold.

"You're—seeing someone?" Jeff asked, incredulous. Because of course that was all he'd gotten out of her tirade.

"You're seeing someone?" Alissa called from the dining room.

Becca swung her feet off the couch and pushed herself to standing, letting all of her weight fall on her good foot.

"*That* guy!" she said triumphantly, pointing at Leo. "I might have already known long division by the day he was born, but he knows my body in ways you *never* will, Jeffrey."

Max cupped his hands over Evie's ears. "Jesus, this is amazing, but can we keep it PG-13, folks?"

Leo grinned his beautiful half-dimpled grin. Then she motioned subtly with her head for him to come to her, and two seconds later, he was at her side.

She wasn't sure what to do next—until Leo Beckett scooped her into his arms.

"Oh. My. God," Becca said. This wasn't *Twilight*. This was *An Officer and a Gentleman*, her mother's favorite movie, which she made Becca watch when she was in middle school. She wouldn't admit it back then—because what middle school kid gave their mom the satisfaction—but it had been one of the most romantic movie endings she'd ever seen. And now she was *living* it.

Leo was Richard Gere in his Navy whites, and Becca was Debra Winger being whisked out of the factory where she worked.

"Where to?" he whispered in her ear.

"Your tent," she whispered back.

And then Dr. Becca Weiland, the woman who always took care of everyone else, was whisked out of the house and to a sexy young man's tent on the beach, a chorus of applause trailing after them, and her ex-husband likely off to find someone new to catch and eventually release.

✵

"I loved your doughnuts, Aunt Sadie," Gabi announced, once they were all perched on Adirondack chairs around the campfire. "But you cannot have a bonfire without s'mores."

Becca and Sadie's niece had already plated graham crackers and chocolate squares for everyone—save for the toddler and the ten-year-old, who were both passed out in the living room—and was distributing them around the circle while jumbo marshmallows were skewered and wood beneath the fire popped and crackled.

"You ever going to marry my daughter?" Matthew asked, glaring at Ethan.

"You ever going to marry Gabi's mom?" Ethan retorted, and both Becca and Alissa snorted.

"I keep asking," Matthew lamented.

"So do I," Ethan admitted. "What is it with these Bloom girls, anyway?"

Matthew sighed, then held his marshmallow over the fire. "Son, I've been trying to figure them out for over twenty-five years."

Gabi stopped short, directly across from her father and her eternal fiancé.

"Dad...did you just call Ethan 'son'?"

"I heard it!" Ethan exclaimed. Then he put his arm around Matthew's shoulder and added, *"Dad."*

"Shit," Matthew grumbled.

"He so just lost the upper hand," Alissa whispered in her sister's ear. "Also, speaking of upper hand—that boy is *so* into you."

She nodded toward Becca's other side, where Leo had her injured foot propped on a pillow on his lap. He kept a hand protectively covering the bag of frozen peas that had become Becca and Sadie's first-aid best friend.

"He's *so* not a boy," Becca whispered back.

Alissa chuckled. "Oh, honey. They're *all* just boys parading as men. But that's why we love them. They keep us young."

Becca coughed. "Love? I don't—it's way too early…"

"Your chocolate and grahams, ladies," Gabi said, handing each of the two sisters a plate and saving Becca from having to examine her feelings any further. Then Gabi leaned down and kissed Becca on the cheek. "Also, way to go, Aunt Bex!" she whispered.

Becca lovingly shooed her niece away and then took stock of the scene before her. Max on the other side of Leo, the two brothers deep in conversation about something involving tile backsplashes and rental homes. Sadie on Max's other side, her chair pulled close so her head rested on his shoulder. Across the way, Shelby and Delilah lovingly arguing over whether or not a Tom Jones cover had merit when *some* people thought the songs should only be sung by The Tiger himself. And finally, Gabi took her spot next to Ethan, where they relentlessly teased Matthew for his slip of the tongue, one she knew he'd never live down.

It felt like family, so much so that Becca's heart hurt at the thought of leaving all of this in two short weeks.

"Should we play a game?" Alissa asked.

Becca groaned, but Alissa elbowed her in the arm.

"Remember how I told you I *needed* this. That means I'm going to live. It. Up."

"Even if it means acting like a middle schooler?" Becca asked.

"*Especially* if it means acting like a middle schooler," Alissa confirmed. "I'll start with you. Truth or Dare, baby sis?"

Suddenly all eyes were on Becca.

"Fine," she said. "Dare."

Alissa gasped. "Seriously? You *always* choose truth."

"When?" Becca asked. "Like thirty years ago?"

She couldn't risk her sister putting her on the spot in front of Leo about—well—anything.

"Come on. What's your dare?" Becca taunted. "Just keep in mind I'm an injured woman."

Alissa pursed her lips and narrowed her eyes. "*Fine,*" she said, mimicking her sister. "Climb onto Leo's lap and dip-kiss him. And before you protest, your feet don't even have to touch the ground. In fact, you're already halfway there."

Becca's cheeks burned.

"Um...what's *dip*-kissing?" Delilah asked.

"It's the bane of my mother's existence," Gabi said. "She's the only hater of that Times Square V-J Day kiss with the sailor and the nurse."

"I am *not* a hater. I just don't see how kissing like that is comfortable for either party involved. How do you truly enjoy the kiss when either you're using your core to keep yourself stable or you're using all of your strength to keep someone from hitting the ground? It just adds a level of physics to kissing that isn't necessary."

Gabi held up her hands. "I rest my case. But also now, whenever she sees any sort of photo on social media or a magazine cover where two people are dip-kissing, it will be followed by at least a five-to-seven-minute PowerPoint presentation on physics and kissing."

"Prove her wrong, Leo!" Shelby called from across the circle.

"Dip your girl and dip her *good*," Delilah added.

Becca couldn't help but laugh. She turned to face Leo, who patted his lap.

"Challenge accepted," he said.

So Becca pushed herself off her chair, balancing for a moment on her good foot before sliding onto Leo's lap.

He hooked his arm around her waist, then slid the other under her thigh.

Then he *stood*, hooking her leg over his hip to keep her ankle safe, and her other foot slid to the ground.

Becca clasped her fingers around his neck...and then he leaned in, dipping her and kissing her all at the same time. She felt the kiss from her lips, to her belly, and all the way to her toes. She never once thought about keeping herself from falling, and she was pretty sure—as Leo kissed her harder, his tongue slipping past her lips—that he wasn't thinking about physics either.

In fact, Becca was certain there wasn't a coherent thought in her brain at all as long as his lips kept doing what they were doing, kept kissing how they were kissing.

He stood with ease—no huffing and puffing like Jeff had when he'd carried her to the couch—and lowered her gently back onto his lap. Then he leaned past her and shot Alissa a self-satisfied grin.

"What*ever*," Alissa said. "It's not like it was a controlled study."

Becca snorted, then quickly covered her mouth, but Leo pulled her hand away.

"I love your laugh," he said. "I love everything about you, Doc."

"Um—thanks?" she replied. Because why not take a perfect moment and make it totally awkward as hell?

CHAPTER TWENTY-FOUR

SADIE

"Truth!" Sadie cried, holding her wineglass up in the air and falling back onto Max's lap.

Despite the two men coming to some sort of a cease-fire, Max clearly didn't want to be outdone by his little brother. So as soon as Becca had settled into Leo's lap, Max had offered his up to Sadie. And duh—she sure as hell wasn't going to say no to that.

"What *is* this?" Alissa asked. "Some backward parallel universe where you are Becca and Becca is you?"

"Is that your question?" she asked Alissa drily.

Alissa gasped. "No. Of course it's not my question. My question is…My *question* is…" Alissa groaned. "I was all ready to have *her* dip Max. I wasn't prepared for a truth. Does anyone else have a question?"

"Oh!" Delilah said, raising her hand. "I do! I do!"

"Take it away," Alissa told her, handing her the floor.

"Tell us about your dog hang-up," Delilah said. "Why does Penny freak you out? I mean, other than the fact that she says hello by knocking you on your back. It is the way with her."

Sadie felt sick. She wanted to tell Max everything but not with an audience. Especially not an audience that contained her brother and Alissa, who also didn't know about recent medical developments.

Matthew looked at Delilah and then at Sadie. "You had an incident with a dog? I didn't know that was still a trigger for you. I'm sorry, Sades."

"A trigger for what?" Gabi asked. "Why don't I know this story?"

"You weren't born yet," Alissa said.

"Hey," Max whispered. "You don't have to talk about this."

Sadie unclasped his hands from her waist and crawled off his chair and back onto hers.

Sadie needed to stop avoiding what might be the truth, and Max deserved to know what he was getting himself into before she hurt him.

"It's okay," she finally said. Then she looked up at her brother across the way, his face glowing in the firelight with such love. "Because you don't know the real reason why it got to me. Only Becca does. So I guess it's time to rip the bandage off."

She swallowed and blew out a breath, then shook out her arms.

"I was born with a hole in my heart. It's called ASD, or atrial septal defect. So I'm kind of defective." She let out a nervous laugh. No one else joined her. "Wow. Okay. Tough crowd. Long story short is no one caught it, not until the neighbor's dog took a chunk out of my chin and a routine exam at the ER found an arrhythmia. I had a simple-ish procedure where they didn't have to do open heart surgery, and the hole was closed. The end." She cleared her throat. "Or so I thought."

She sat forward, planting her feet on the ground, and Max's palm pressed reassuringly against her back. Becca encouraged her with a smile, but she could see the worry in her brother's eyes as if he knew what was coming but wouldn't believe it until he heard it.

"At my annual visit to my gynecologist, she—um—heard an arrhythmia and, because of my history, wants me to follow up with my cardiologist. She thinks that either there could be another defect that was never caught in previous exams, or the original could have reopened."

"And you haven't followed up yet?"

Max's hoarse voice came from behind her, and his hand slid from the small of her back.

Before she could face him, Matthew was out of his seat and striding toward her. He wrapped her into the biggest, tightest, big brother hug and just held her.

"I'm scared, Matty," she whispered. "I know it's the worst excuse for behaving like a kid about this, but I'm so scared to find out."

He kissed her forehead, then took a step back to look her in the eye. "It could be nothing...or it could be something. You don't have to face this alone. But you do have to face it."

She nodded and swiped at the tears leaking from the corners of her eyes. Then she whispered in his ear, "Does Max look angry? I wanted to tell him, just not like this."

Her brother sighed. "He sort of excused himself and took off toward the beach."

Sadie spun toward the lake and could barely make out his shadow, he'd already made it so far from the firelight.

"Shit," she said.

Her brother nodded toward the water. "Go. I'm guessing his intentions with you are on the up-and-up."

She scanned the circle of friends and family who were all doing the same thing, shooing her toward the beach. So despite her promise never to engage in the activity again, Sadie Bloom ran after a man and, hopefully, toward her future.

"You know, a girl in my potential condition probably shouldn't be running," she called out to him, slowing to a jog as she approached him.

Nothing. Not even a pity laugh. Okay, so humorous deflection was not the way to go.

She stood beside him now. "Max, please let me explain."

But he wouldn't face her. He just stared out at the moonlit water, tossing rocks into the darkness of the lake.

"Max?" She took a step closer. "Max..." She reached for his elbow, and he finally stilled. "I could be fine, you know."

"You think this is about whether or not you'll be okay?"

He shook his head, then pivoted to face her. "Wait, that came out wrong. Jesus, Sadie. Of course I care about whether or not you'll be okay. But it just hit me that I am way more in this than you are, which I know is too much too soon, but fuck it. I'm falling in love with you. And I know you're not in the same place I am, but what happens now? You just leave, chalk this up as a summer fling, and I never know if you're okay?"

Sadie was definitely feeling an arrhythmia right now, but there was nothing medical about it.

"I'm sorry," she began. "I know I'm supposed to be groveling for not being entirely honest with you, but can you say that thing you said again?"

He crossed his arms, his face glowing in the moonlight. His beautiful, dimpled, loving face. But she needed to hear him say it again.

"I love you, okay? I'm not angry that you didn't tell me, just—I don't know—I guess it hurt to know that this really was just a fling for you."

She cupped his cheeks in her palms.

"You sweet, amazing, clueless man." His eyes widened. "I didn't tell you because you have Evie and Penny and a whole life already. How could I tell you that I was falling in love with you and then spring this on you? Derek was worried that I'd hurt you and for good reason. I did. I was selfish, and I'm sorry, Max. I really am."

She'd tried, though, hadn't she? Tried to push him away before things got this far.

He wrapped his hands around her wrists and lowered them to his chest.

"Sadie, do you think you don't deserve love if you might be sick?"

She felt his heart hammering against his chest, and it made hers ache.

"I thought I had all the time in the world, so I kept putting it off... taking life seriously. Then I meet the most amazing man right when life throws me for a loop, and what? I'm supposed to ask him to jump aboard when he's got his own wounds to heal? I deserve love, sure. But you deserve something with a guaranteed shelf life."

He slid his fingers through her hair and clasped his hands behind her neck.

"Give me the chance to decide." He kissed her forehead. "Let me choose whether or not I want to hop aboard before you assume that I don't." He kissed her cheek. "Because it could be nothing, right?"

She swallowed the knot in her throat. "Or it could be something."

He kissed her other cheek. "And did I hear you say something about falling in love with me? The waves hitting the shore kind of drowned that out."

She laughed even as tears streamed down her cheeks. "I love you, ya DILF."

Max shook his head with that one dimpled grin. "I'm going to write a sternly worded email to Delilah and Shelby for that one."

He kissed her lips, and god, yes, Sadie deserved this. She just wanted to know she had years left to make this man feel twice as loved as she felt right now.

"Is there room?" Max asked, his forehead resting against hers.

"Where?"

"On that loop-de-loop ride you mentioned before."

A hiccupping sob escaped her lips before she whispered, "Yes."

"Then I'm hopping on board, Sadie Bloom. Wherever it takes us from here."

CHAPTER TWENTY-FIVE

BECCA

Let me look at you two again!" Becca said, releasing Mackenzie and Grayson from her embrace, kissing their chubby cheeks, and then hugging them again. "I missed you *so* much!"

"Are you really going back on vacation?" Mackenzie asked.

"Right after we got home?" Grayson added, as if she needed him to push the dagger farther into her heart.

The thing was, even after a night under the stars in Leo's extra-large sleeping bag, Becca somehow knew her quick trip home to see the kids would be nothing of the sort. She'd had an amazing two weeks with a wonderful friend and a beautiful man. But this was easier than dragging it out and saying good-bye. This was best for both of them.

"No," Becca said with a grin. "I'm not going anywhere.

Not when I can be with you little rug rats!" She chased them around the house on her aching but *better* ankle, tickling one twin and then enlisting her captive to help capture the other.

That night, when she tucked them both into bed, Grayson put his hands on her cheeks.

"I know you're happy to see me and Kensie," he said, using his sister's nickname. "But you look *really* happy, Mom."

"Yeah!" Mackenzie called from her bed, where she'd already been kissed and tucked in. "I like how happy you look. It makes *me* feel happy too."

When she'd finally turned out the light and pulled their door closed behind her, she sighed. Even after being away from her for *two* whole weeks, they saw her. Like *truly* saw her.

Later, when Becca crawled into bed, she pulled out her phone and brought up Leo's number, laughing when she was reminded of how she'd named his contact.

Naked House MAN

She'd already been enough of a coward to leave with the promise of returning, so she wouldn't do it in a text. Instead she hit the green phone icon and listened, heart racing, as the phone rang.

He picked up after the second ring.

"So this is how it ends, huh?" he said, zero hint of surprise in his voice.

"You knew?" she asked.

He let out a sad-sounding laugh. "I'm no match for your kids," he admitted. "I knew I never had a chance once you got in the van."

Becca laughed too. "How can you talk about my minivan and my kids and still sound like you wish I hadn't left?"

"Because I wish you hadn't left."

Her throat tightened, and her heart ached. "I *just* got divorced. I have *no* idea what I want from the rest of my life. But I know I never would have gotten to where I am right now without knowing you."

She heard him sigh. "Is this where we burst into song about how we're better for knowing each other, but this is where *our* story ends?"

"It is *not* fair that you're only just revealing now that you know *Wicked*—or any musical theater, for that matter."

"See how much you're missing by not spending the last two weeks of your trip with me?"

He was right. She *did* miss him even though she'd woken that very morning naked and in his arms.

"I'm sorry," she said softly.

"I'm not," Leo replied. "I'll never be sorry I met you, and if you're ever up my way again..."

He didn't finish the thought, and Becca was grateful that he wasn't asking her for a promise she didn't know if she could keep.

"Hey, Becca?"

"Yeah, Leo?"

"Happy Birthday."

SADIE

"What do you mean I'm *fired*?" Sadie asked as Alissa folded up the Pack and Play, and Matthew chased Elliott around the room. "I *own* a quarter of the bakery."

Alissa shrugged as she went on a scavenger hunt for toddler socks, picking up one, then two, then three, four, and five. How were there so many?

"You're not dying. You beat this once before, and you'll beat it again. I'll buy you out," Alissa told her, finally turning to face the inquisition. "Do you know why I never put your doughnuts on the menu?"

Sadie crossed her arms. This ought to be good. "I'm listening."

"Because you don't belong in a North Shore bakery waiting on all the bubbes and yentas who fight over who gets to bring the babka to mahjong that week. You belong in a vacation town diner making fancy grilled cheese and your secret doughnut recipes. I *love* working with you, Sadie, and I love waiting on all my favorite bubbes and yentas, but you have been living *my* life when it's high time you started living yours. And that means calling your cardiologist the second I walk out that door, taking care of this silly heart thing, and then following that silly heart wherever it takes you."

Alissa kissed Sadie on the cheek and then left her standing there with her mouth hanging open as her soon-to-be former business partner stuffed the handful of socks into a diaper bag and dragged the Pack and Play out the front door.

In the distance she heard a dog barking on the beach.

She grabbed her cell phone and brought up her doctor's number, hesitating only for a second before she hit the green button to initiate the call.

"Hi, yeah, this is Sadie Bloom. I need an appointment with Dr. Russell. Oh really? First thing Monday morning? That's—um—perfect. Thank you. I'll be there."

She ended the call and glanced out toward the beach, where Max, Evie, and Penny chased a Frisbee along the shore.

Time to see what life threw at her next, a crazy twisting loop? A terrifying drop? Or maybe a slow ascent to something bigger and better than she'd been able to imagine. It all scared the hell out of her, but she wasn't on the ride alone.

EPILOGUE

Twelve Months Later...

Sadie Beckett rubbed a hand over her belly. They'd only found out that morning, and even though there were superstitions about revealing the pregnancy too soon, there was one person she couldn't wait to tell.

She took one last look at the empty booths, the red leather stools at the counter, and the backward white letters of the painted sign on the window that read SADIE'S.

"What do you think?" Max asked, setting the large mason jar filled with various-sized bills next to the old-fashioned cash register. The word *Swear* was written and crossed out on the glass, replaced with the word *Tips*.

"If I donate my collection to the diner, does it mean the restaurant is part mine?" Evie had asked before skipping out the door to go grab Shelby from the salon and Delilah from the coffee shop.

"We're *family*," Sadie had told her, pulling her in for a hug. "Sadie's isn't mine. It's *ours*."

Family came in all shapes and sizes. Some family members were blood, and some were found. Either way, it was the people with whom you wanted to share your highest highs— but also your lowest lows. Sadie traced her fingers over the long scar on her chest beneath her shirt, the one Max kissed every morning when she woke up and every night before she went to bed. No matter what life threw at her, she never had to put on a brave face or go it alone. She understood that now.

"You ready?" Max asked, rounding the counter and joining her at the door.

"She's going to make it, right?" Sadie asked, backing up to his chest and wrapping his arms around her.

"She'll make it," Max assured her.

He spun her to face him, then dropped his head to place a kiss on her not-yet-swollen middle.

Sadie's heart fluttered—the good kind.

"You think Baby Beckett's excited for opening day?" he asked, straightening to his full height.

Sadie clasped her arms around his neck.

Baby Beckett. Hot, happy tears pricked the corners of her eyes. "Definitely," she replied.

"And you?" he added.

"I'm excited for *all* of it," Sadie told him. "Today, tomorrow, and everything that comes after."

"Happy opening day and everything that comes after, Mrs. Beckett," Max said.

"Why, thank you, Mr. Beckett."

He kissed her all the way to the door, reaching over her shoulder to unlock it. She spun and flipped the CLOSED sign to OPEN, and Sadie welcomed her future in a bumblefuck town called Glass Lake.

※

Becca still had an hour before the diner closed, but she couldn't seem to put the van in drive now that she'd stopped outside the house she wasn't even sure he still owned.

This was crazy. With Sadie's surgery, she and Max eloping, and then diving headfirst into the diner, there hadn't been much reason to come back. But now it was opening day, and despite performing two back-to-back C-sections, Becca had made it in time to congratulate her best friend on this amazing milestone.

But she was stuck, the van idling outside a strange house, wondering if the person who lived inside had thought about her even once in the past year the way she'd thought about him.

"Fuck it," she said, putting the van in park and throwing open the door.

She said the F-word a lot these days. Not because she was an angry person but because she wasn't the Becca she was a year ago, and she no longer limited herself to what she thought others expected of her.

Except tonight she was maybe a little angry...at herself.

For giving him up, for thinking they were all wrong when nothing before or after had ever felt as right. Becca still didn't know if they had a future, but she did know that right now, today—hell, the whole past year—she missed the possibility of what they could have been.

She marched up the driveway and straight to the front door, reminding herself if she didn't face down this fear quickly, she'd miss the tail end of Sadie's opening.

So she rang the doorbell.

Nothing.

She raised her hand to knock, and a small spider dropped down from a web in the doorframe.

Becca yelped. Then she laughed. If she could face the possibility of rejection, she could certainly handle a tiny spider.

Because she still had Sadie, a woman who was at first nothing more than a begrudging roommate, then a friend, and now the second sister she never knew she needed.

But Sadie Bloom wasn't the only person Becca had come to see today.

She waited for the spider to ascend its web again, her thumb tracing the newly healed tattoo on the inside of her wrist—an arrow in the shape of a heart. But Becca hadn't truly followed hers. Not yet. Not until today.

The spider disappeared into the corner of the doorframe, and she finally knocked.

Again, zilch.

She rang the bell and knocked at the same time as if that were some magic combination that would conjure him.

But it didn't.

Then—as she peered through the front window like a peeping Tom—she saw it, beyond the bay window in the back. A tent.

She kicked off her wedges and strode around to the back of the house, then onto the sand, moving slowly at first, then faster as she approached the tent, where it perched just shy of the water.

Soon she was running, the lake breeze whipping at her hair and her long, flowy skirt. She was out of breath when she finally dropped to her knees in the sand, and then she heard his voice.

"I know," he said with a laugh. "I love you too. I promise we'll be there soon."

A lump rose in Becca's throat. She shouldn't be surprised that he had moved on—found happiness with the right person. But she felt like she'd been punched in the gut, and the air felt harder to breathe.

Without thinking, she pressed her palm to the tent, leaning on it for purchase.

"Hello?" the voice said from inside. "Is someone out there?"

"Sorry!" Becca said in an exaggerated, high-pitched voice. "Wrong number!"

Wrong number?

She tried scrambling to her feet but tripped on her skirt and pitched forward right as Leo Beckett unzipped the door, and Becca fell inside.

"That was Sadie on the phone," he said matter-of-factly. "She's waiting for us."

Becca pushed herself up on her elbows and then scurried to her knees so they were eye to eye. "Waiting for *us*?" she asked, brows furrowed.

He nodded. "I waited for you, and now they're waiting for us. It's opening day, you know."

She swallowed and dared to let herself hope.

"How long have you been waiting for me?" she asked. "Because I still don't know—I mean what if we're not—?"

Leo cut her off, wrapping an arm around her waist and with the other cradling her head. "I've been waiting until I could tell you this in person," he said. "Happy Birthday, Doc." And then he dip-kissed her right there in the tent like it was the most natural thing to do.

Thirty-seven.

Best. Birthday. Ever.

ACKNOWLEDGMENTS

Thank you, my wonderful readers, for your Bloom Girls love and for your patience in waiting for Becca's story. Surprise! You get Sadie's too! But because I would not be me if I didn't weave a little romance in here and there, I also bring you Leo and Max. This book is for siblings of all types, whether we grow up with them in the same home or meet them along the way. One of my favorite story tropes is the found family, so I thank you for picking up this little tale of ex-sisters-in-law who find family in true friendship; estranged brothers who find common ground; and new friends who make a vacation rental feel like home.

This book wouldn't have made it into your hands without a keen editing eye, so thank you, Madeleine Colavita, for always seeing the big picture and knowing how to best get from "Once upon a time…" to "happily ever after."

Thank you, Emily, for championing everything I do. I'm

so grateful for the years we've worked together and those still to come!

Speaking of found family, while I have no sisters by birth, I'm so lucky to have four by choice! Megan, Lea, Jen, and Chanel, I cannot wait until we can find each other in real life again. It's been too long!

Thank you, Mom, for giving me my own display shelf in your new house! Thanks, Dad, for buying but not reading. Haha! And always, *always* to the family who supports me always being on some sort of deadline, S and C...in case I haven't already told you today...I love you 3000 x infinity.

ABOUT THE AUTHOR

A corporate trainer by day and a writer by night, **Amy Pine** can't seem to escape the world of fiction, and she wouldn't have it any other way. When she's not on deadline (or sometimes when she still is), you'll find her binge-watching her favorite K-dramas and dishing about them on her podcast. She hails from the far-off galaxy of the Chicago suburbs.

You can learn more at:

AJPine.com
Instagram @AJ_Pine
Facebook.com/AJPineAuthor